# MARCO POLO,
# IF YOU CAN

Novels by William F. Buckley, Jr.

# MARCO POLO, IF YOU CAN

## WILLIAM F. BUCKLEY, JR.

DOUBLEDAY & COMPANY, INC.
GARDEN CITY, NEW YORK    1982

FOR HUGH KENNER

This is a work of fiction. Some of the figures who appear, how-
ever, do so under their own name.

Library of Congress Cataloging in Publication Data
Buckley, William F. (William Frank), 1925–
    Marco Polo, if you can.
    I. Title.
PS3552.U344M3      813'.54
AACR2
ISBN: 0-385-15232-9
Library of Congress Catalog Card Number 81-43245

[When] Khrushchev came here in 1959, he had it in mind to seek what we would now call détente, so as to devote more Soviet resources to Soviet consumption. I often wondered why, in the midst of these efforts by President Eisenhower and Khrushchev to come to some understanding, the U-2 incident was allowed to take place. No one will ever know whether it was accidental or intentional.

> [Senator] J. William Fulbright
> Interview, *The Saturday Review*
> January 11, 1975

# CHAPTER 1

After the first day Blackford Oakes wondered why the court, as everyone persisted in calling it, went on and on, in such tedious detail. Not that he was physically uncomfortable. During the preceding seventeen days he had even dreamed, during the acuter moments of workaday distress, of the comforts of a straight-backed chair, while the ritual removal of the manacles made him feel like the man on the flying trapeze. One thing that greatly and uncommonly bothered him was the density of the cigarette smoke. On the other hand, he reflected, why should he have supposed that just because you're not allowed to smoke in courtrooms in America, you wouldn't be allowed to smoke in courtrooms in Moscow? That old cultural chauvinism—his face broke into just a trace of a smile causing the prosecutor, who was going on at great length about the atrocities of the United States and its paid agents, to stop in mid-declamation and wave to the generals sitting on the raised platform, behind a long desk serving all three, who for reasons Blackford had given up trying to penetrate were always leafing through heavy manuals while the prosecutor spoke, as though they were in hot pursuit of any violation of judicial punctilio.

"*See*, Comrade Generals, *the smirk* on the face of the defendant? The smirk of fascism!"

The prosecutor wore civilian clothes, a double-breasted, ill-fitting, broad-lapeled brownish suit that looked as if it had been washed in clam chowder. Thus Prosecutor Gorchakov—the names of the court officials, neatly typed, had been given to him by his defense attorney, who during the past five days had sat in the chair next to Blackford, smoking cigarettes end to back, taking notes without ceasing. Blackford wished he had even a rudimentary knowledge of Russian: he had not even been trained to identify Cyrillic characters. What *could* Dr. Valerian Ryleyev be writing? Letters? A pornographic novel, maybe? Whatever. At least it gave him an excuse, which Blackford didn't have, for avoiding hour after hour of looking at the face of Prosecutor Gorchakov, heavy with a kind of saggy, bluish fat as though Nature, early on, had reached out and given his whole face a black eye—and how gladly Blackford would have changed places with Nature to make *that* happen.

But, come to think of it, there weren't many people Blackford Oakes wouldn't right now gladly change places with. He permitted himself to close his eyes. In order to avoid a tirade like yesterday's—when his request for a handkerchief had indignantly been ruled in contempt of court—he contracted his features, so that the prosecutor could plausibly pass off the closed eyes as a sign of mortification as the prisoner took in, through his earphones, the recitation of his crimes in the jerky English of the three female translators who relieved each other at intervals of twenty minutes exactly. Blackford had visual access to the great old clock just under the picture of Lenin, behind the judges: how he wished he might have his wristwatch back. But the absence of a watch was as nothing compared to the absence of any reading material; nothing—he had even asked for a copy of *Das Kapital*, but the jailer thought this calculated insolence, reporting it to the major, who took the trouble of coming down from his upstairs office to tell Blackford he would not get his dinner that night, the black bread, cheese, and lukewarm soup. The soup. Ugh. Boiled, Oakes had from the beginning supposed, from the carcass of a seditious fish, the species sentenced to genocide by Prosecutor Josef Gorchakov during his early career, when he was just practicing. But then, No-Reading was itself an improvement on those three nightmarish days which he struggled, with strain, to forget; that odd surrealistic admixture of physical pain, a drugged consciousness, the insistent questioning, the bright light: what was it—he had allowed himself, briefly, to wonder—that caused his whole body to contract in spasms of pain? Electricity perhaps, but applied where? He couldn't remember. He had taken to bellowing out nursery rhymes during the questioning, for some reason favoring especially the two or three French ditties he suddenly recalled from the old nurse with whom he had frequently been left in Scarsdale, in the preschool years when Blackford's father would go off endlessly with his mother to compete in the air shows. *"Savez-vous planter les choux?/À la mode de chez nous?"* he would sing out, again and again. *"Sur le pont, d'Avignon/L'on y danse, l'on y danse . . ."*

The chief interrogator, the ghastly Yakubovich, knew better than to take this as calculated anything, let alone calculated insolence. He was too experienced in his profession: prisoners, under torture, were capable of anything, from cursing to screaming to praying to—singing nursery rhymes. Blackford suddenly stopped his rumination. The prosecutor was going now into the background of the prisoner.

"As you know, Comrade Generals, it does not at the moment suit the convenience of the state to divulge the true name of the prisoner. Accordingly the valiant guardians of the socialist motherland, who never rest in their struggle against imperialism abroad and counterrevolution at home, have requested that the prisoner's name be kept secret, in order to confound his masters and give us the time we need to penetrate the whole of the plot against socialist independence and unity. The court docket refers to him merely as the American Defendant McKINLEY. Now, Comrade Generals, although he is only thirty-four years old, McKINLEY has engaged in a squalid career of espionage and other forms of hateful work against the Soviet state . . . for most of the past nine years."

Gorchakov, without giving details, stressed that McKINLEY had worked for the CIA "in England and France, Hungary and Germany and Sweden. . . ." Gorchakov gave examples of the hideous behavior of the reactionary elements in each of these countries. Oakes wondered at the prolixity of it all: on and on it went, no expletive without an intensifier, no accusation without the finger pointed at him—as though the generals could forget where he was situated, there being no one in the prisoner's box save Blackford; and, behind him in the little courtroom, only a half-dozen uniformed KGB guards, one or two officers and three civilian officials. But the court stenographer, to judge from her concentration and the rapidity of her finger movements, was not missing a word. This was very far from a "show trial"—Blackford had reflected on this every day. On the other hand, it was also far from the summary justice the military courts of the So-viet Union are constitutionally permitted to mete out in extraordinary situations involving the national security. Clearly a record was being built. To what end one never knew, but such are the habits of cautious totalitarians. Blackford wished he could summon the powers of concentration to think it all through.

Why was he so weary? What—since the torture stopped—was it that drained him of his strength? He managed, in the small, chairless cell, to do his calisthenics every morning, but during the day mostly he dozed, hoping the endless days would pass; hoping that today Washington would make its move; wishing, above all earthly things, for reading matter; wishing that, while at school, he had devoted himself more assiduously—as Sally always reproached him for not having done—to committing a body of poetry to memory. His training in mechanical engineering gave him problems to hypothesize and wrestle with; with these he would begin to occupy himself, but then he would run out of mental strength. Was it the diet? He wondered what he weighed under his normal 170? Perhaps, if ever he got home, he could remember it all and write a book: *The Lubyanka Reducing Formula*—Guaranteed to Work in Just 17 Days, or you get to shoot the author; he'd be rich, and maybe Sally would marry him. If he was rich and also promised to leave the Agency. Having been kicked out of it only three years ago, why hadn't he left it behind, once and for all?

He recalled the physical principle of hysteresis, describing the lag between bodies that theoretically should move in synchronization. Three cars stop behind a red light, light goes green, three cars resume motion? No. The first does. Then the second. Then the third. . . . If there is a fifth, the light has probably turned red again. If he had maintained his secular momentum, gone on the green, where would he be now? *Right now?* Again he closed his eyes.

"Sally darling, would you bring me my slippers?"

"Get your own goddam slippers, pretty boy. You forget I'm not some Third World flunky of the kind you've been used to bossing about. I am an assistant professor of English literature at Georgetown University, and just as Jane Austen would have done in our day, I believe in women's rights."

Blacky would have picked up her slender body, stretched her out on the couch, and joyously and lasciviously consumed her. . . . *"Guilty, this man McKINLEY, of every crime against socialist idealism, rapine, plunder, and, of course, espionage."* How did that goddam Gorchakov know that Blackford was just plundering Sally? Thought control, that's what is. . . .

Why oh why didn't they get on with it? There was the goddam airplane, a huge picture of it anyway, right there in the courtroom; big arrows pointing to the tail section where the camera had been. And the incriminating materials in his seat pad: military identification cards, U.S. and international driver's licenses, Selective Service card, social security card, PX ration card, medical certificate, two flying licenses, American dollars, French francs, Turkish lira, Chinese yuan, Italian lira, German marks, Soviet rubles, two gold watches, gold coins, seven gold rings, pistol with silencer, morphine, flares, a large silk American flag poster in fourteen languages reading, "I am an American and do not speak your language. I need food, shelter and assistance. I will not harm you. I bear no malice toward your people. If you help me, you will be rewarded." And, to top it off, a needle dipped in curare. Why was it going to take five days in court—seven? twenty?—to prove that McKINLEY had landed in the Soviet Union when his airplane suffered a flameout, that his aircraft had been equipped with a camera, substantially destroyed along with the exposed film? Any idiot could deduce beyond a reason-

able doubt after fifteen minutes—let alone fifteen times fifteen
times fifteen minutes (How long would that be? He concen-
trated: fifty-six hours, a good, round, seven-day trial. At this rate
it would go the full seven days. Gorchakov hadn't even begun to
denounce the airplane.)—anyone who couldn't figure out that
old McKINLEY was up to no good in the skies over the Soviet
Union shouldn't ought to be . . . a great big Soviet general, cer-
tainly not in Khruschev's army. *L'on y danse, l'on y danse, tout
en rond.*

Blackford tried to remember what it was the defense attorney
Dr. Valerian Ryleyev would find extenuating to say about him.
Good old Ryleyev. A distinguished career. He had defended the
people at Nuremberg. Wonder what he said about Hermann
Goering? Loved animals? He had also defended Beria's chief
aides. (All were executed.) When Ryleyev told Blackford about
his distinguished former clients at the first of the three confer-
ences they had had, no one of them lasting more than an hour,
Blackford had asked, with sudden solemnity, if he might have, to
study, an English translation of the defense offered by Ryleyev
on behalf of Goering; or von Ribbentrop, for that matter; but
Ryleyev said the documents had not been translated, and went
on to counsel Blackford to behave demurely in the courtroom,
to show contrition, to apologize for his role in U.S. imperialism,
to stress that he was, after all, merely the agent of his superiors.
Blackford said he understood . . . was that what the lawyers
called the "Nuremberg Defense"? Dr. Ryleyev looked hard at
Blackford, but the boyish face was one of unimpeachable sincer-
ity and innocence, and Dr. Ryleyev mumbled something to the
effect that no, the Nuremberg Defense was a little different, but
McKINLEY should leave legal theories to the defense attorney
to cope with, and Blackford said very well, he would do exactly
as he was told. Ryleyev then said that the probability was that
the prosecutor would ask for fifteen years, with a strong possi-
bility that he would ask for death. Blackford's heartbeat quick-
ened. But he was not hearing anything unexpected; he had heard
it all before, heard it at length at the final briefing at Atsugi, and
before that in Washington. After all, he had volunteered for the
mission. For Michael.

Dumb bastard. Blackford, not Michael. Michael was dumb too, in a way. He really *did* love his neighbor as himself, and his only neighbor that afternoon in Berlin, in that garage, was Blackford. Somebody once said it was no use being asked to love your neighbor as yourself if you don't love yourself at all. Right? So that Michael must have loved himself; and even so he did it. . . .

A whole hour had passed without Blackford's listening to what the translator had intoned into his ears—mostly this and that about the airplane and its paraphernalia. But now his attention was arrested by Gorchakov's frenzied motions. The prosecutor had suddenly concluded his case, disturbing Blackford's intuitive sense of Soviet judicial rhythm by the startling brevity of his peroration. Prosecutor Gorchakov had wheeled about, turning his back on the generals, and faced McKINLEY, inches separating their noses.

"Comrade Generals, for such enemies of the people, the penalty—the only acceptable penalty—is death."

Blackford had read that during the famous show trials in the thirties, the customary closing was "Death to the mad dogs!" Did Gorchakov's milder exhortation suggest that he was playing favorites? Or maybe he was a little . . . queer on McKINLEY. All the girls went after him, but some boys did too. Wonder what Marxism-Leninism says about homosexuality? Oakes, why don't you grow up, for godsake; do you realize that all that stuff in Washington *might just not work?* You've been exactly twenty-two days out of any contact whatsoever with any representative of the United States Government. Not one living human being on the other side knows for sure where you are, unless we've got a mole in the KGB here you don't know about. Rufus *et al.* anticipated a *public* trial. So already we were wrong on *that* count. It could be we will be wrong on counts two, three and four!

Count four was the one designated to get him home to Mother.

But if we don't get to count four, old McKINLEY will be made to kneel down in the cellar of the Lubyanka and then they'll fire a bullet through his head. Talk about hysteresis! There was a silence in the courtroom. The generals and the officials seemed to be blowing smoke at double the normal intensity. Might they be smoking two cigarettes at a time? But the hour had come now for Dr. Valerian Ryleyev.

The thin, angular, stooped figure, self-consciously academic in the precision of his gestures, dressed in undertaker black, splotches of white hair over each ear, rose, so to speak, in stages. He turned first to the court. "Comrade Generals." Then to the prosecutor: "My distinguished colleague, Josef Antonovich." Then to Blackford. "Defendant McKINLEY."

In pained tones, Dr. Ryleyev went over the evidence. Indeed, he could not doubt that McKINLEY was flying the airplane; he could not doubt that the purpose of the airplane was illegally to photograph Soviet defense installations; he could not question that McKINLEY was not entitled to any of the immunities that attached to uniformed prisoners of war; he did not doubt that the legal code of the Soviet Union, most specifically Article 2, authorized the death penalty for acts of espionage against the state; he did not doubt that the penal code of the Soviet Union was a measured and noble mirror of the demands of a society destined by history to be the precursor of international socialism. What then could he find to say, Comrade Generals, on behalf of McKINLEY? Why, said Dr. Ryleyev, after a long pause, the Soviet Constitution stipulates that every defendant—no matter how heinous his crime, no matter how obvious his guilt—should be represented by a defense attorney to plead his case. Dr. Ryleyev was, accordingly, enacting his responsibilities under the Soviet Constitution, and herewith requested that the penalty proposed by the prosecutor be commuted from death to thirty years of hard labor.

He sat down. He did not look at Blackford. Blackford looked up at the judges. One after another they snuffed out their cigarettes, stood, and walked out into their chambers.

A guard brought in a tray with tea, which he passed about, first to the prosecutor, then to the defense attorney, then to the prisoner. The English-speaking major advised McKINLEY that he was at liberty to walk about the courtroom, and, under guard, to use the toilet facilities.

"Do you have anything to read?" Blackford asked the English-speaking officer.

He opened his briefcase, and gave Blackford a copy of *Time* magazine. It was three weeks old. Blackford sat down slowly with it, as though fingering the Shroud of Turin.

But, after a half hour, he couldn't read on. His circumstances dominated his thoughts. . . .

"You know, Blacky, they'll stay out maybe three, four hours, maybe more. Two of 'em will play chess, the third will read a book or play solitaire. The verdict, and the penalty, were decided well before the trial started. There isn't anything that happened in the trial that'll change that. Unless the Kremlin changed its strategy, for whatever reason, during the trial. If that happened, word will get through to the generals, don't worry. But don't let yourself think that because they're out there for a while, they're thinking it over. . . ."

It was almost exactly four hours.

The clerk called for silence. The principals and the small group of witnesses took their seats.

The presiding general rose.

"The Military Division of the Soviet Supreme Court has reached a verdict in the matter of McKINLEY." Blackford, standing, now listened carefully to the translator.

"We find him guilty as charged on all counts.

"We sentence him to be shot at dawn tomorrow morning, April 30, 1960."

Valerian Ryleyev rose, coughed twice, and said, "Comrade Generals, I beg leave of the court to appeal the sentence."

"Permission granted. Unless the Supreme Court commutes the sentence by May 6, the sentence will automatically be carried out."

Ryleyev whispered to Blackford, *"Thank the court! Thank the court!* Quickly, quickly."

"I thank the court," said Blackford.

The presiding general gaveled the proceedings to a close. Two guards approached Blackford and manacled him. Following the major, they walked past the half-dozen rows of chairs to the door, down a single flight of stairs, into the waiting car. Ryleyev, standing on the sidewalk, leaned down before closing the door.

"I shall bring along a draft of the appeal in the next day or two."

The car sped off in the light, post-seasonal snow. Inside, the car was well heated. The driver had kept it snug, the heater on, throughout the chill afternoon. It was a short drive to 2 Dzherzhinsky Street, where the building stood, firm as Soviet authority, vessel of the people's justice.

—it was handed over to him. Blackford had reached for his own pen, signed the paper, and felt an antic impulse to look up solemnly and ask the Director whether he would like it if Blackford made him a gift of the pen as a souvenir?

But given the gravity of his offense—Blackford, giving way to sentimentality, had failed to warn the Agency about the shipment of an important piece of cargo to the Soviet Union, in order to save the life of a Russian scientist—Blackford kept reminding himself that the Agency's decision to permit him to resign, rather than be dismissed, must have been a significant concession. He did not know the stern-faced Director with the trim white mustache and endlessly lit pipe in hand, having had only one or two meetings with him during the six and one half years he had worked for the Agency since being recruited as a graduating senior at Yale. Under the circumstances he was not able to calculate confidently what the motives of the Director might be in treating with relative calm Blackford's delinquency and suggesting that Blackford resign, though to be sure in such tones as made the alternative to resignation very clear. True, the Director had, without extraordinary ceremony, made a commendatory remark or two about Blackford's work over the years. And (Blackford felt morally sure about this, though in the world of intelligence he recognized that nothing was safely taken absolutely for granted) the Director made a point of declaring that he did not doubt Blackford's loyalty to the anti-Communist enterprise. But, after all, Dulles knew that a dissatisfied ex-agent is not as desirable an ex-agent as a less-than-dissatisfied ex-agent. That last, really, was the category he found himself in. Blackford could not dispute the justice of his severance: the Director had done what he had to do. Assuming he were in other relevant respects normal, Blackford could not now go out into the world with a festering resentment that might make him bait for an enemy, foreign or domestic.

The Director, who would spend hours and weeks pondering ambiguities, was the least ambiguous man in town about when an appointment with a subordinate was over. Blackford having handed over his resignation, the Director rose. Had there been any hesitation in extending his hand? That was one of the questions Blackford now pondered.

# CHAPTER 2

After the session with CIA Director Allen Dulles that afternoon in October 1957, Blackford Oakes returned to the little apartment house, climbed the stairs, turned the key to his living room on the right, sank down into the deep armchair and looked out at the falling light streaming obliquely into the room, filtered by the red and orange leaves of the oak and maple trees in Mrs. Carstairs's courtyard. He sat without moving or turning on the light, meditating on the ten minutes just spent with the man who, at 4:20 exactly, had ceased to be his employer.

When you resign from the Agency (Blackford learned), you don't resign as of a given day, but as of a given time. He smiled as he thought that it was—at least in his case—a perquisite of resignation that he was spared the trouble of drafting the instrument itself. It had been neatly typed up, and sat on Mr. Dulles's immaculate desk. At the appropriate moment—the Director having looked at his watch and noted the hour with his fountain pen

So what? It could not now affect him. All clerical problems—back pay, that sort of thing—took care of themselves automatically. His back pay would come: cash, in an envelope, delivered by an older man whose name he did not know, the precise time of whose materialization at 40 Woodward Street Blackford never knew, but who managed to confront him every month or so with sums of money, the annual total of which always came out about right. During protracted stays abroad, the equivalent of the old paymaster would somehow turn up. Blackford had thought that the Director might ask what Blackford intended to do, and he was prepared to reply that such information was only available on a Need-to-Know basis. But that would have been not only cheeky, but—really—provocative. In any event, it was all unnecessary because the Director, having shaken hands, touched a button; instantly the door was opened by a secretary, and Blackford turned and walked out.

What *does* one do when one is dropped from the Central Intelligence Agency—at age thirty-one? His mind was lightly probing the question when the knock on the door came: Michael. His knock was distinctive—somehow it conveyed both diffidence and affability. Quickly Blackford leaped up to flick on the switch that would light up the four lamps in the comfortable, book-lined room: he was not given to letting people know that he had been interrupted in introspection.

"Am I disturbing you?" Michael smiled toothily through his five o'clock shadow, providing a vivid contrast in black and white. At five-nine he was shorter than Blackford by three inches, but his body, never for very long in repose, made it hard to guess Michael's exact size. He spoke not only with his hands, but with his shoulders and hips. His hair was dark and plentiful. Slung over his shoulder was a towel. "I was going to shave"—Michael Bolgiano and Blackford shared a bathroom—"unless you're in a hurry. . . ."

Blackford was always delighted by Michael's presence. They had shared the top floor of Mrs. Carstairs's four-apartment building for three years. Michael also worked for the Agency, and tended to disappear, like Blackford, for weeks and months at a time. Neither knew anything of the work of the other, though there had been moments when both yearned to speak about an assignment. Social contact between deep-cover agents was discouraged. But Blackford was relieved of the most formal construction of this prohibition when his occupation became known to the enemy after his first operation. And Michael—whatever he did—wasn't under any social interdict, so that in the course of several years they had frequently dined together and, more than once, caroused together. A year ago it happened that their vacations coincided. Sally was out of town lecturing at a summer seminar in Oklahoma. Michael never permitted his ephemeral female friendships to interfere with his relatively dogged pursuit of outdoor pleasure, and Blackford suggested that Michael join him in an improvised barnstorming tour in the new-model Cessna-310 Blackford's father (who had the Washington-Maryland franchise) made available to him whenever he wished it. It had been a splendid holiday. They flew as far west as Laramie, south to Mexico City, north to New Orleans, and back—landing at midnight, just before the airport discouraged all except emergency landings. Michael said it was positively the best fortnight of his entire life, notwithstanding Blackford's penchant for idiot acrobatics, and Blackford said it was amazing what fun you could have with an eighty-five-thousand-dollar airplane and no traffic cops.

"And nobody to shadow," Michael had added.

"And nobody to shadow you," Blackford said. They were fraternity brothers.

"Go ahead," Blackford said, gesturing expansively toward the bathroom. Then, impulsively—he didn't want to see Sally tonight—"Free for dinner?"

"Sure," Michael's dark eyes lit up. Any comradely suggestion, social or adventurous, from Blackford—or from anyone else, Blackford supposed—aroused sheer pleasure in Michael Bolgiano. Forty-five minutes later, Blackford found himself at the corner table at La Noisette, looking vaguely at a menu with which both were thoroughly familiar.

They drank white wine, and then red; and, with the coffee, slivowitz. Michael, as usual, was the happiest man in town. His distinctiveness was that little things made him happiest. Blackford could not imagine Michael elated because he was about to marry the most wonderful woman in the world, or because his aunt had left him a million dollars, or because the United States had just won a war, or Adlai Stevenson lost an election: he was made happy by things like a good ham sandwich, an exciting movie, an engrossing book, warm air ("balmy!"; "really sensual!")—or cold air ("exhilarating!"; "makes you kinda tingle, doesn't it, Black?"). So it had been, all evening long. Blackford didn't know what it was—almost surely not the booze: he had long since learned to seal hermetically his professional thoughts from the reach of any gab-inducing liquor. But, presumably because giving the matter instant reflection he could find nothing unprofessional in saying it, he blurted it out.

"I'm no longer with the Agency."

Michael put down his glass. Just as all of Michael could light up, all of Michael—shoulders included—could shrivel with concern.

"What . . . happened?"

The slight delay in the verbal exchange between intelligence operatives was the inflection that stood for: "—to the extent you are permitted to speak about it."

"I was canned."

Michael's surprise turned his face into yet another fully orchestrated mode. Nobody could be more surpised than Michael when Michael was surprised. The idea that someone of Oakes's manifest abilities, sophistication, quickness of mind, demonstrated ingenuity, could cease to be useful to the Agency was quite simply unthinkable. He waited for Blackford to relieve him—

"It was my fault. All you need to know is, I didn't do something I should have done. And it wasn't unintentional. That's really all there is to it. I am officially unemployed."

Clearly, what mattered most to Michael was the awful prospect that Blackford would move away from Washington.

"What do you want to do?"

"Right now? Make love to Sally. I mean, *with* Sally." (Sally, feminist forever, had instructed him in the correct use of the preposition.) "What do I want to do tomorrow? Screw with Sally."

"What do you want to do when you *aren't* screwing Sally? I mean, other than think about screwing 'with' Sally."

"Well, I'd like to screw Khrushchev and help bust up that act, but that isn't easy to do on a free enterprise basis. So—I guess I'll do what I'm trained to do. Build something, or help build it. Did I ever tell you I once built—or rebuilt—a chapel? Every bit of it, stained glass and all. It was . . . an experience."

And so it happened that, at eleven the following morning, Blackford Oakes found himself in the Hill Building, standing before the receptionist of the firm of Ambrose & Gaither, Architects. The receptionist smiled at the trim young man with the rusty blond hair and casual manner; dressed in a khaki suit, white shirt, and blue striped regimental tie, he was carrying, moreover, no briefcase; just the morning paper, folded in his hand.

"I'm here to see Mr. Bolgiano."

Manifestly disappointed that the engaging stranger would not be lingering for a while in the waiting room, the receptionist pointed down the hallway. "Third cubicle on the left," she said. "His name is on the glass."

Blackford had never met Michael's family, but Mr. Bolgiano was transparently aware that he was greeting his son's best friend, and solicitously asked him to sit in the little chair by the side of the desk, on which was piled neatly the bookkeeping paraphernalia of Ambrose & Gaither, Architects. Blackford was surprised at how old the bookkeeper looked. Not entirely surprised by his heavy accent, however, because Michael had been born in Italy, arriving in America with his mother at age twelve, at the outbreak of the war. His father joined them several years later.

Mr. Bolgiano fussed over Blackford, fetched him a cup of tea, and told him that, based exclusively on what he had learned from Michael, an appointment had been made with Mr. Gaither himself, who had instructed the bookkeeper to bring in his son's friend any time, Mr. Gaither's schedule being flexible all morning long.

"That's awfully nice of you, Mr. Bolgiano. What did you tell him about my . . . professional background?"

"I told him you been mostly in-a Europe, like Michael says, okay?"

Blackford nodded. He had a résumé in his pocket and after a little conviviality with Mr. Bolgiano, to whom Blackford expressed his admiration of and fondness for Michael, he was led to Gaither's secretary. She spoke softly into the intercom, and motioned pleasantly to the walnut door on which, in discreet and stylish lettering in inch-high brass, was posted simply, "Mr. Gaither."

There was a startling resemblance, Blackford thought, to the Director himself. Tweedy, glasses, gray hair, a small, whitish mustache, even the pipe. But Mr. Gaither's face was so freckled, the flesh tones appeared as little cosmetic afterthoughts. Mr. Gaither took a long look at Blackford, asked him to sit down, made small talk about the remarkable success the Soviet scientists had achieved with their Sputnik satellite, an obligatory reference to the Braves having won the World Series, and then asked Blackford whether he had brought with him a curriculum vitae.

"Yes sir. A sort of abbreviated one." He handed him the piece of paper on which he had typed that morning:

> Blackford OAKES. Born Toledo, Ohio, December 7, 1925. Schooling: Scarsdale, N.Y., HS. Greyburn Academy, England (one term). Yale, B.A., 1951, mechanical engineering.
>
> Government service. World War II, army fighter pilot.
>
> Consultant, Greenhouse Foundation, research on development of structural techniques in British architecture.
>
> Consultant to U.S. mission in Germany, in charge of reconstruction of St. Anselm's Chapel.
>
> References on request.

"What kind of references, Mr. Oakes?"

"Well, sir, beginning with Yale, there are some professors there. Then foundation executives . . . the army people I worked with in Germany."

"What was your most recent job?"

"Actually, after I finished the chapel I took a lot of time off. I've been all over Europe. My mother lives in London."

Gaither stared at him. "You don't by any chance know my nephew, Nelson Gaither? He was Yale 1950. Works for the CIA."

"No sir," Blackford said. He caught a trace of a smile in Gaither's face, but did not return it.

"You come very highly recommended by Mr. Bolgiano's son in the State Department, and if you will give me those names and addresses I'll send out some routine letters. Right now, we need a competent draftsman with your background. We're competing for the congressional contract to build the memorial to FDR. The competition is hot, but we *want* it. We've hired three draftsmen who are competent in mechanical engineering and who might have a few ideas. Can't give you any contract, no guarantee. If you work out and we get the commission, you stay. Otherwise, you can just add one more consultantship to your résumé. Pay, three hundred dollars. All right?"

"I'd like to think about it for a day or two if I can. Without losing the option of accepting?"

"Very well." Gaither's mood suddenly changed, and he leaned back in his chair. "Out of curiosity, do you have any ideas that spring to mind for a memorial for FDR?"

"Well," Blackford said pensively, "obviously I haven't thought much about it. Marble, I guess. Some kind of modern design— simple; like FDR's grave, which he designed himself. Then maybe with some memorable quotations from his speeches?"

"Such as?"

Blackford thought for a while. "Well, there's the one about balancing the budget." He bowed his head in concentration. "Then there's the one about . . . er, our boys will never fight in foreign wars. Er . . . there's the Four Freedoms and the future of Poland . . ."

"Thank you, Oakes."

Blackford raised his head and smiled. "I'd be glad to do a little more research, sir, if you like."

"Don't bother. Practice up on your draftmanship." Mr. Gaither rose and extended his hand.

"Thanks very much, Mr. Gaither. I'll call in in a couple of days."

After Blackford had left, Gaither buzzed his secretary. "Get me Amanda on the line."

"Amanda? What kind of thing gets you fired from the CIA?"

"Dad, what an odd question. Well, at one end if you steal an atom secret and give it to the Russians—that'll do it every time."

"I'm in a hurry, Amanda."

"You mean: nondramatic firings? Well, a guy can be passed over for promotion. Or maybe he was on a project that terminated, and there wasn't anything for him to tackle. Could have had a fight with his boss."

"I don't suppose you could find out anything about the background of an ex-CIA agent if I asked?"

"No, Dad. That's one of the other things you get fired for doing."

"Thanks, darling. See you." He put down the telephone and turned his mind to means by which to perpetuate the memory of FDR on earth. It would help balance *his* budget.

# CHAPTER 3

"Hans? This Hans Steiner?"

"Yes, Steiner here."

"This is Bill Ottley."

"Who?"

"OTTLEY! O-ldest T-ime T-ested L-iving E-xample of Y-urinary bliss. I haven't pissed in twenty hours. Put that in your book of records, Fritz. I mean Hans. Did they ever call you Fritz? I mean, as a boy? I always think of Germans as Fritz. Now Hans, got something here, my bosses at BBDO–BBD ayand Ooooh. B-iggest B-astards D-oing O-ll the Lawd's work! We got something real hot here. Gotta have photographs. Deadline. Space reserved: *Life, Look, Ladies' Home Journal, Cosmo,* you name it, Fritz. Hans. Can I come over? *Special* rates for special work."

"When do you wish to come, Mr. Ottley?"

"*Mr. Ottley!* Fritz, I must've told you *one hundred times* you call me BILL. Or you can call me Sunshine—lots of people do.

Why not? The sun's gotta shine on people who only have to piss once a day—right, Fritz? Hans? *When?* Like, ten minutes ago. I've got nine-ten. Can I come—two assistants—right now?"

"I was doing other work . . . Bill."

"Other work! There's no such thing as other work when O-T-T-L-E-Y calls, there's only *this work!*"

"I suppose I could put off the other."

"What other?"

"I am photographing a seventeenth-century engraving for a Christmas card company."

"*Christmas* card? Shee-yit, Fritz, Christmas is four months away. December twenty-fifth, remember? When do they cele-brate Christmas in Germany? You people invented the Christmas tree, didn't you?"

"The Christmas tree originated in Germany, that is correct."

"Well now, don't let me down. Remember, we've been doing business four—five?—years, and when Bee Bee Dee and Oh-oh-oh want something, they want it fast, and from the best. You are the best—right, Fritz?"

"I'm glad you like my work . . . Bill."

"Come on, no modesty. You're the best. You don't have much of a plant, but what do we need much of a plant for—we're not promoting the Sistine Chapel. Hmmm. Wonder who has that ac-count? Know anybody at the Vatican, Fritz? You people didn't bomb the Vatican back then, did you, Fritz? Now level with me, because *nobody* fools O-T-T-L-E-Y."

"No, we—I mean, they—didn't bomb the Vatican."

"Well, then, I'll think about that one, but meanwhile, is it go-go-go?"

"What do you wish photographed, Bill?"

"Spaghetti. With our new sauce—get this, Fritz—Salsa del Sarto. Class? Bee Bee Dee and Oh-oh-oh specializes in class. Our clients are class. Be there by ten? Don't *say* anything. Just unlock that door, and get ready to see your old friend Sunshine. And you don't have to tell me where the men's room is: won't need it. Well, maybe the girls. We'll use your stove. Seeya, Fritz!"

Ottley leaned back in the chair of Steiner's little studio. The in-tricate ligature of the camera had been carefully composed to bring it down at exactly the desired angle. Steiner had spent two hours arranging the lights. The two women had cooked the spaghetti and poured the new sauce, and Steiner had studied it.

"It's gotta look *hot*, Fritz. It's got to look—*succulent*. It's got to show the yellow cheese streaks running through the ketchup. It's gotta look the way it is, only better."

"We'll have to use some artificial substances, Bill."

"So? I care? President Eisenhower cares? Nikita Khrushchev cares? Go ahead and pull out the stuff, ya got it all in those cabinets, Fritz baby. My job is to stay here till I can go to the office with a negative."

Steiner busied himself with his considerable inventory of powders, paints, plastics, rubbers, designing a spaghetti sauce that would impersonate Salsa del Sarto and survive the heat of the lights and the attrition of the engraving. He puttered about, opening drawers, spreading his artifacts out on the table. The cooks, their work done, were on standby. They sat at the far end of the studio eating sandwiches they had brought with them and watching "Our Miss Brooks" on television.

"How you like this business of Khrushchev coming over to see Ike?"

"I have read about it," Hans said, bending over the table.

"*Obviously* you've read about it, everybody's *read* about it. First seven months of the year old Khrushchev rants and raves about all the missiles he's got to blow us up with—and then Ike invites him over. Big deal. They're going to take him cross-country. See America. I guess the idea is, see America before he blows it up. What do you think, Hans?"

"I don't follow politics."

"Come on. You're a German."

"I am a citizen of the United States."

"Well, yeah. But you came over what, 1951?"

"1947."

"Land of opportunity, eh? Well, you're doing all right, I guess. Why don't you expand? That's *American*, expand. BBDO was once a small outfit, biggest in the old Yoo Ess of Aye now. What you need is somebody to give you a little advice. Begin by moving to Manhattan. It's a pain, let's face it Hans, to come all

the way over to Fulton Street in Brooklyn to get a little spa-
ghetti photographed. Bet some of your customers have to stop
between Manhattan and Brooklyn to take a piss, not old O-T-T-
L-E-Y, the original dehydrated man."

"Thank you, but I am content here."

"How much you make, like last year? How much did you
make in 1958?"

Steiner was handling tweezers, arranging the rubber-spaghetti
strands. Ottley could barely hear him.

"How much? Oh, enough to pay the bills, and a little more, a
little for the old age, not much."

"What about your family?"

"I don't have family."

"Oh come on, Hans. I mean, life isn't only work. After hours
is another life, ho ho ho. Don't you have a little somebody to
look after you? When you get . . . cold . . . in bed?"

"My landlord keeps the apartment upstairs well heated."

"Now I'm not talking about *that* kind of heat, Fritz baby.
How old are you? Maybe sixty? Well, one of my bosses was
sixty last week, and guess what, he married—for the fourth time.
Maybe number four will bring him an account, wouldn't be sur-
prised. But you should've been there. I was invited, yup. Not to
the wedding, that was just for the brass, and family, I guess. But
to the reception. You were married, weren't you? Must've asked
you that before, but I forgot."

"My wife and I were separated."

"Kids?"

"My only daughter was raised by my wife."

"When did you see them, I mean, last?"

"In 1945."

"Do they write you often? What's your daughter do?"

"I don't know. They live in East Germany. They don't write
to me."

"You know where they are?"

"No." Steiner walked back to the cabinet, ran his fingers down
the little trays, searching for, and finally finding, the elusive
shade of red putty. "I have only a sister who sends me Christmas
cards, and maybe a postcard sometimes."

"Whajudoo for old Hitler? I mean, I don't mean it was your fault, but you must've been in the action somehow. Let's see, war began 1939, you'd have been what, thirty-eight, forty?"

"I worked as a photographer in Bremen, at the boatworks."

"Boatworks, you call 'em! That's where they made most of those submarines, right?"

"No, that was—yes, I suppose so. But I was in the photograph division of a naval architect who worked on destroyers, not submarines."

Ottley yawned. "Some life. What made you decide to come over here?"

"My wife went to East Germany, but I don't like politics, so I came here. I read in the paper there were jobs here for commercial photographers."

"So you just arrived in Brooklyn and went to work?"

"The immigration people were very helpful, very nice, and a few friends from before the war helped me."

"How come you know English so well?"

Hans straightened up and stretched, to relieve the long strain of leaning over the table. His hair was gray, his eyeglasses rimless, his face featureless. One knew he had eyes, nose and a mouth, because people do, but they asked for no attention. Ottley could understand why he hadn't kept his wife, or attracted a substitute. Efficient old drudge, though, you had to hand it to him. He looked about the utilitarian studio—everything tidy, but not aggravatingly so. Nothing was conspicuous at 252 Fulton Street.

"Ever do anything except commercial photography?"

"Occasionally I take portraits. Mostly for my neighbors." Steiner leaned over a large sink and plucked a negative from a clip. "That's the cleaning woman's daughter in her First Communion dress, yesterday. Felipa Vilches."

Ottley held it up to the light.

"Nice-looking spic."

Steiner said nothing. "I am ready to shoot."

"How'd you learn English so good? I mean, I had French at Bayside High, you should hear me, though when I was in Paris this chick heard me, all right all right, no trouble there. How'd you learn English?"

"I apprenticed in London for two years in the twenties."

"Well, no wonder, no wonder."

"You will have to stand back. No reflected light."

Ottley stood up and looked down at the simulated spaghetti. "Hans, you're a genius. I'll get out of the way. Where's the can?"

After Ottley and his crew had left, Hans Steiner sat down and listened, motionless, to a Beethoven quartet on the record player. He felt a profound satisfaction.

# CHAPTER 4

Anton Speranski could hardly remember when last he had used a typewriter. But no one else—*no one*—would be permitted to translate the six sheets of paper he now had before him, delivered from microfilm developed and enlarged in the Special Services laboratory on the east wing of the fourth floor of the Lubyanka. Even though the technician knew no English, Speranski had stood over him—*ante partum, in partu, post partum*—the birth of a film the holy nature of which had been revealed to him three days earlier, when he received the cryptic message, the Annunciation, from East Berlin. He had cautioned the technician to be particularly careful. They entered the darkroom and the overhead light was turned off, replaced by the red bulb that enveloped the little room and its two occupants in the scarlet eeriness the technician was used to but which made Speranski, who hadn't worked in a darkroom since his very early days in the KGB, faintly nervous.

"You are certain the light is not too bright?"

The technician replied that he was quite certain.

Speranski could not conceal his nervousness. "You are to take *no chances*, understand?"

"Yes, Comrade Anton. I will make no mistakes."

In twenty minutes the negatives were dry. The technician took them to the enlarger. "What size do you desire?"

"Regular paper size . . . No. Larger: this size—" he spread his hands about eighteen inches apart. "But *don't take any chances.*"

The technician, an old hand, was exasperated by the suggestion that he was all thumbs with the precious negatives. He didn't reply, adjusting the enlarger to the required size and reaching for the box containing the larger-size paper.

Speranski stared as, under the light, the typewritten letters gradually reified into recognizable English characters. A minute or so per page; in ten minutes they were stacked together. The technician reached for a large envelope, inserted the prints, and handed the package to Speranski.

"Give me the negatives also. In a separate envelope."

He took them then to his study, into which the typewriter had been brought. Speranski's English was letter-perfect but he worked slowly, turning the English into the most faithful Russian rendition he could manage, occasionally crossing out phrases and whole sentences and rewriting.

An hour and a half later it was done, and he stared at what lay before him, very nearly breathless with excitement. He had intended to retype it all, so that he would have a clean copy for Shelepin and Malinovsky, but he could not contain himself. He seized the telephone and dialed the number of the Director of Soviet Security, Aleksandr Nikolaevich Shelepin.

"It's ready."

"Bring it in," the head of the KGB said. "Malinovsky is waiting."

The room at the corner was the most inaccessible in the Lubyanka, and even Speranski, notwithstanding the years he had spent proving to the same set of people that he was who he was, had to flash his identification to be admitted. It was not the large meeting room of the Director he went to, but the private office, with the small table around which not more than four people could sit on the stuffed red leather chairs circling the small but massively constructed mahogany table overlaid with a green cloth, with glass over it.

Malinovsky, Minister of Defense of the Soviet Union, flaunting only his Order of Lenin in addition to his marshal's stars, was seated. They exchanged perfunctory greetings.

Shelepin extended his hand. "Let's have it."

Speranski could hardly conceal his pride. He gave it expression by something he would not normally have done in such informal conditions. He clicked together his heels as he extended the envelope.

Shelepin sat, motioning the other two men to draw their chairs to sit, Malinovsky on his right, Speranski on his left.

Shelepin elected to read the papers aloud, and slowly. He lit his cigarette and cleared his throat. He began to read.

"Minutes. Meeting of the Executive Committee of the National Security Council of the United States, September 1, 1959. Present: The President. The Secretary of State, Mr. Herter. The Chairman, Joint Chiefs of Staff, General Twining. The Director, Central Intelligence Agency, Mr. Dulles.

"The President called the meeting to order at 3:20.

"The President said that it was clear from many reports that the invitation to Chairman Khrushchev to visit the United States on September 15 was not being met by universal enthusiasm. He cited the official position of the executive committee of the AFL-CIO announcing a boycott of Chairman Khrushchev, the delegation of Congressmen who had announced they would cooperate with the anti-Communist committees which had called for a 'day of mourning' on the day that Chairman Khrushchev arrived in New York. He alluded to several speeches, editorials, and columnists who had assembled Khrushchev's remarks during the past year threatening the peace of Europe by announcing the intention to make a separate peace treaty with East Germany, terminating Western rights in and access to Berlin.

"The President said that diplomatic objectives quite apart, it was important that the right tone be set in greeting Chairman Khrushchev. There would be none of the 'customary diplomatic affability.' He wished to establish a clear agenda, which would be communicated to relevant parties.

"The first and most urgent problem, the President said, was Berlin. The Soviet deadline on Berlin has to be lifted, the President said. He asked Secretary Herter whether the U.S. might come up with a face-saving concession that would permit Khrushchev to lift the deadline without appearing to be backing down.

"Secretary Herter said his specialists had examined the texts of Chairman Khrushchev's various messages but had come up with no formula that would be satisfactory to both Khrushchev and Chancellor Adenauer or to Western public opinion.

"General Twining said his own opinion was that Khrushchev had no intention of forcing the Berlin issue. That his purpose was merely to set the stage for what would subsequently be interpreted as conciliatory diplomatic action.

"Secretary Herter said that the numerous references to a summit meeting in May, 1960, could have the effect of tacitly lifting the deadline on the grounds that it would hardly make sense to meet in May, when the Berlin ultimatum was due to terminate one month earlier in April. The Secretary said he thought he and Ambassador Lodge—who would be Chairman Khrushchev's escort throughout his tour of the country—and the President himself, by guarded references to the forthcoming summit, might plausibly act in such a way as to invite the inference that Chairman Khrushchev would naturally not press the Berlin question until after the summit.

"The President asked whether the technical arrangements requested by the Kremlin had been completed, mentioning specifically the open telephone line from wherever Chairman Khrushchev would be, to his switchboard in the Kremlin.

"The Director said the arrangements had been completed by a special division of AT&T. He added that extravagant pains had been taken—in order that when the President visited the Soviet Union the following summer, the Soviets could not reasonably oppose what the CIA, the NSC, and the Secret Service would insist upon by way of communications made available to the President.

"The President then asked Director Dulles about the Soviet claim made in late July that a manned Soviet fighter had attained an altitude in excess of 94,000 feet. He asked to be refreshed on the altitude at which the U-2 aircraft could fly.

"The Director replied that the U-2's altitude depended on a number of variables, but that except in extraordinary conditions, it could maintain altitudes in excess of 70,000 feet. As for the claim made by the Russians on behalf of the T-431 piloted by Major Ilyushin, the Director said that the flight in question was under our radar surveillance, and that in fact the aircraft had not risen above 62,000 feet. The Director said there was clear agitation within the Soviet military at their continued inability to bring down our U-2 reconnaissance planes.

"The President asked how many sorties had been made over Soviet territory during the past period.

"The Director replied that no overflights had been deemed necessary during the past eighteen months, but that a number of special missions along the boundary were being made, and that these continued to collect important data. Other sorties continue, from bases in Turkey and Pakistan, over a wide area, from which we gather useful information about military movements in the Middle East and in southern Russia. The Director reported that without penetrating Soviet territory, it was possible for the U-2, in combination with U.S. radar, to check major developments in the Tyura Tam area on the basis of which Defense Department intelligence had come up with the conclusion that the Soviet Union has only ten fully operative intercontinental missiles.

"The President said he wished no sorties to be made by the U-2s during the period of Chairman Khrushchev's visit. Nor did he desire that any member of the executive branch or of the military should, during the period of Khrushchev's visit, entertain any question from a reporter or anyone else concerning the relative strength of the Soviet strategic arsenal and the U.S. arsenal.

"The President then asked for opinions concerning the stability of Chairman Khrushchev himself, noting that during a period of nine months there had been serious convulsions within the Kremlin, resulting in the ouster of Bulganin, of Marshal Zhukov, of Molotov, and others.

"Secretary Herter said his reports indicated that Khrushchev's power, while not absolute, was unchallenged at the present moment, but that he doubted that Khrushchev could on his own authority make significant diplomatic concessions while on U.S. territory. He would probably limit himself to procedural questions concerning the dates of summit meetings, etc.

"General Twining said that his opinion was that under General Malinovsky a strenuous effort was being made to emphasize the development of long-range missiles; and that General Twining was not himself satisfied by the reliability of the Defense Department's estimates concerning the number of missiles now deployed. He reminded Director Dulles that in July, U.S. radar penetration had resulted in considerable Soviet redeployment, away from Tyura Tam inland toward southern Siberia.

"The Director reminded General Twining that our U-2s out of Japan had noted the development, and that, in any event, missiles developed in Siberia would need to be brought to a geographical area closer to the continental United States in order to represent a threat; at which point existing technology of surveillance would detect such movements.

"The President said the Defense Department and the Joint Chiefs should iron out the differences in their estimates. He requested Secretary Herter to devise a formulation that might accompany a text announcing a future summit meeting, which text would be understood by the diplomatic community as having the effect of lifting the ultimatum on Berlin. Because as matters now stood, the Kremlin was saying it very clearly: Effective on the day we (the U.S.S.R.) make a peace treaty with East Germany, Western rights of access to Berlin are . . . forfeit.

"The President called the meeting to a close at 4:17 P.M."

Shelepin stopped reading. There was no comment. He reached for the red telephone and lifted it. "Shelepin, Comrade Khrushchev. I must see you right away." He looked at his watch. "Very well, I'll be there in ten minutes." He motioned to Malinovsky and Speranski to follow him.

# CHAPTER 5

Benni, as everyone called him then, was the guest of honor at the party—it was his birthday. The year was 1939. Benni was thirty-nine, and a considerable figure in Alturgia, the little suburb southwest of Rome where Benni was born, schooled, and now worked. Though still young, he had inherited his father's role as something of an informal ombudsman for the workers who kept afloat the massive enterprise that sustained Alturgia, a subsidiary of the giant firm of Etzione Srl. whose cash registers, to point to only one of Etzione's products, supplied half of Italy's needs, and were exported worldwide. These were made in Milan, but the firm had many products, including typewriters and sewing machines. At Alturgia the principal product was the renowned Etzione Stapler, and Benni was the shop steward of the craft union, which called on him to do much of the paperwork for the 600-odd employees who looked to him for help in those little matters that can mean so much, like getting an advance before the new baby. Benni would get it, and with the check, more often than not, came a letter offering, however prematurely, the congratulations—of the Italian Communist Party, Etzione Stapler division.

Soon after the advent of Benito Mussolini, back when Benni had just begun to work, the sales in staplers had risen dramatically. It was not only because under fascism the paperwork was enormous. Mussolini, who was given to variable and episodic enthusiasms, had on one occasion elected to dwell on the virtues of husbandry by speaking of the staple as a symbol. This had been during a long and robust address delivered over state radio and blared into all public buildings and town squares. His researchers, Mussolini had recounted, his voice rising with triumphant enthusiasm at the discovery, had calculated that for every paper clip, Italians could, at the same expense, manufacture *ten* staples. "I ask you, my fellow citizens," Mussolini had said, coming to the climax of his address, "I ask you, are you willing to serve the motherland to the extent of substituting a little physical exertion, in return for a saving of ninety percent?" Mussolini then dilated on the general theme of Italian physical culture, to which he was strenuously devoted. "Is it not," he asked in his most seductive accents, "something of a symbol to ask all Italians to exert themselves physically to the extent of applying a little pressure on a stapling machine, rather than to slither on a paper clip, requiring no physical exertion, causing the arm muscles to become flaccid, replicating the obviously degenerate ways of our anarchic neighbors to the west?" He ordered that henceforward the stapler should be recognized as the agent of the energetic in body and spirit. He did not want to see a paper clip in any office of the Italian Government, he warned, his voice now not only paternal, but menacing.

The next day the orders had, of course, outrun the capacity even of Etzione, and there developed a six-week delay in delivery; but the demand proved constant, and the Alturgia division flourished, bringing finally the promotion of Benni to the position his father had had when suddenly the old man died, in his sleep, from a heart attack. The handsome, diffident, hardworking Benni was all but unanimously elected, on the fourth round, and shortly after a visit to the only other contender by two heavily

muscled Party representatives from Rome, the other contender
announced that he had decided to withdraw from the race so
that Benni Bolgiano would receive the backing of all the
workers, united.

The negotiation process with Etzione followed a preset course,
every three years. The managers would meet with Benni and his
lieutenants and announce exactly what the terms of the new con-
tract would be. Benni would decide which terms of the new
contract the management should fail to enumerate in its public
message to the workers. Benni would take that clause—in 1938, it
was two weeks' vacation with pay after two years of work—and
publicly insist that the company yield on the point. Much pres-
sure would be mobilized. The managers would respond that the
concession was economically crippling, but Benni would stick to
his guns. Then, when there were only minutes to go before the
old contract ran out, management would tearfully yield and
there would be a noisy celebration among the workers. Benni
would join in their celebration, and make a speech about the gold-
enwork of the bargaining table. He was careful not to say what
actually was on his mind, namely that one day there would be no
bargaining table, because the workers would own and operate
the enterprise—that was for tomorrow, and at the last several
Party meetings in Rome he had been cautioned against any pub-
lic declaration that might attract the attention of Mussolini's fas-
cist police.

At the birthday party, Benni wished that the meeting in Rome
had been this morning rather than yesterday, because the other
historical event of September 1, 1939, was the attack on Poland
by Hitler. Benni was not certain how to instruct his friends in
the local Party on the proper reaction. Hitler was the enemy, of
course; but Mussolini had twice, in recent months, professed a
fraternal devotion to Hitler, and since the Party was cautious
about provoking the opposition, Benni thought it wise to caution
against any public comment, "pending developments." The great
Togliatti would have to instruct them on this one, for Benni
knew the importance of rank, and discipline. So when he raised
his glass, which he did frequently, both giving toasts and receiv-
ing others', he spoke the usual generalities, and when he got
home to his wife and ten-year-old son and saw that they were

safely asleep, Benni got down on his knees, secure from detection. Benni and the Party disapproved of prayers, but he was a man of some sentiment. "Although, Almighty God," he whispered tonight, "I know that you do not exist, there is no reason to hold that against you; and accordingly I address you simply as a matter of courtesy, to ask you to look kindly on the workers of the Etzione Syndicate, Stapler Division, to bless the efforts of the members of its affiliated unions, and to give special guidance, in his all-important role, to Comrade Stalin, to help him in his campaign to bring freedom and peace and justice and brotherhood to the peoples of this world. All this I ask, and especially that you look after my precious Maria and Michele." Benni now lapsed into the boilerplate of his youth, from which his mother, proudly Jewish, would ostentatiously desist when Benni's father conducted the prayer meetings, "through the blessings of thy son, our blessed Lord, Jesus Christ."

It wasn't until two years later that the Nazis came. They were technically there to help convert a part of the factory to the manufacture of parts for automatic weapons. At first Benni was treated with some deference, although he was not consulted on all of the decisions reached by the new military-technological hierarchy, even those decisions that directly affected working conditions.

He spoke to Maria about this one night in June, while Michele was fiddling with the radio. He said he would have to make an official protest, to which end he would have to see Captain Kreisler, who seemed to be the man to deal with, notwithstanding that he had no specific title; it was to his office that, increasingly, one went in order to get authoritative decisions. He would, he assured Maria, see him tomorrow—indeed, he had already made the appointment for three o'clock. Maria, pretty, always shy and a little frightened, turned her eyes toward Michele and asked Benni to be careful. He smiled, kissed her, and whispered that she might coach him better on how to behave—upstairs, in the bedroom.

Benni was astonished, on being admitted into the office of Captain Kreisler, that he was not invited to sit down. He stood, awkwardly, his opening remarks rather scrambled by the social clumsiness. Captain Kreisler, his black military jacket on, the heat of the afternoon notwithstanding, sat behind his desk, in front of a photograph of Mussolini and Hitler embracing at Munich. He had a sheaf of papers before him.

"I am glad you made this appointment, Bolgiano, because I had it down to see you."

Benni said nothing, but could not remember when last he had felt so awkward.

"You are the son of Eva Moravia Bolgiano?"

"That is correct, Captain."

"The records show that Eva Moravia was Jewish."

Benni, finding a sudden equilibrium returning to his body, looked down at the pale blond person with the wispy mustache and broad, hunched shoulders.

Benni weighed his words carefully. "What business is that of yours? Besides, my mother is dead."

Captain Kreisler's cheeks flushed.

"I am aware that she is dead. I am also aware that you are one-half Jewish. I am also aware that a Jewish conspiracy, world-wide, is engaged in attempting to frustrate the great war effort binding your country and mine. You are as of this moment relieved of your duties at the Etzione Company. Empty your office by five o'clock, and hand the keys to the clerk in my office."

Benni did not move.

Captain Kreisler looked up at him. "Should I make myself more clear? We do not want a Jew in our enterprise. Now get out."

Benni leaped over the desk as if catapulted by a huge sling. His hands were on the throat of the captain, who had gone crashing to the floor, toppling the chair and the typewriter table to one side. The captain screamed in German. Benni released one hand, closed it, and delivered a smashing blow on the nose which instantly swelled and bled. He had delivered four blows, and started a fifth, before they pulled him away and held him outside pending the arrival of the military police. Benni said not a word, lowered his eyes, and looked at the ground: he did not wish to see the faces of any of his co-workers; even as he knew that they, frightened, would not want to see Benni. The wait wasn't

long. There were three men in the heavy black car that drove
up. Two came out, and one of them with his stick, belted Benni
in the stomach. He doubled over, and the guards took the op-
portunity to toss him into the back seat, separated from the front
by wire netting.

The sergeant, preparing to enter the front section alongside
the driver, turned to the four men from whom he had seized
Benni.

"I am the adjutant of Captain Kölder of the military police.

"Send the official complaint by Captain Kreisler to the Office
of the Advocate General at the Palazzo Venezia. We're taking
him right to Rome."

During the next three days, in which twice each day he was
taken to the "courtyard," as the prisoners called it, and there
beaten, without any observable passion, by two huge young
loutish-faced men both stripped to their T-shirts, then dragged
back to his cell, no one asked him any questions at all, and to his
mumbled request to see a lawyer, a doctor, or a priest, no answer
whatever was given. In or out of his cell he felt only a single
pain: Maria and Michele. Michele, age twelve, would be—Benni
almost had to stop to calculate it—one-fourth Jewish. Would
harm come to him? To Maria? For having married a half-Jew?
His resentment during those days, which were followed by the
mockery of a trial (at which a gratifyingly mutilated Captain
Kreisler gave evidence) when he was unable to wrest from any-
one information about his family, let alone cooperation in trans-
mitting any communication to Maria, caused a radical change in
his easygoing nature. He felt hardening in him a resolve alto-
gether incompatible with anything he had felt before. A resolve
that left no room for compromise. It sustained him during the
trip to the penitentiary near Naples, administered now by the
Nazis, appearances to the contrary notwithstanding. He hardly
noticed his surroundings. What had been the sentence? When
last had he eaten? On the second evening Salvatore, his cellmate,
doused a piece of bread in the cold soup and flagged Benni's at-
tention. "Eat this for the sake of Maria and Michele." Benni was
startled. Who was Salvatore? How did he know?

Salvatore anticipated the question. "You talk about them in your sleep."

Benni looked at the mushy piece of bread as though he had never eaten before. He chewed at it, consuming about one half.

Salvatore spoke. "I have got word out on Maria and Michele."

Salvatore was speaking in whispers. "The Party will look after them."

"How do you know?" For the first time Benni felt he could focus on the problem. He looked at Salvatore, who was smoking a cigarette made from rancid prison tobacco rolled in newspaper. His voice was husky, but his words were authoritative in tone.

"I do not know. But the message has been passed along, and sometime soon you will hear."

Benni, unfamiliar with the sinfulness of being part Jewish, asked Salvatore, who was obviously more cosmopolitan, whether it was now the active policy of Mussolini's government to persecute the Jews.

"The answer to your question, Benni, is: Yes. It began with the October 1936 edict against Jews in the civil service and the armed forces. But the policy now fans out."

"Would it affect my son?"

"He would be better off elsewhere. His father," Salvatore spoke fatalistically, "is after all a political criminal who attempted to kill in cold blood the German representative of the Joint Military Command. They could have executed you."

"Why didn't they?"

"The workers at your plant stayed home until you were sentenced."

All this was news to Benni. "But it must have been—four, five days before they tried me?"

"Your . . . attack was on a Tuesday. You were tried on Friday. On Saturday morning the workers went back to work their half day."

Benni was visibly pleased, and proud; but then he wondered whether his co-workers' contumacy might enhance the danger to his family.

He asked suddenly, "What was my sentence?"

"Seven to ten years, in a labor camp. This is an administrative center. Soon they will take you away."

"And you?" Benni asked.

Salvatore, lighting another cigarette, said, "Me? Unhappily, I am to be shot."

Benni stood up, but dizziness and weakness brought him back to the bedside. He began to speak, but his voice failed to function. Finally he said in a whisper, "What did you do?"

Salvatore, twirling his cigarette in his hand, said, "I blew up the refinery at Ostia." He paused, and inhaled deeply. "It will take them three months to set it right."

"How did they catch you?"

"That is the only reason I will die without peace. It can only have been one man who betrayed me, and he will survive me. But not"—Salvatore crossed himself—"for long. I gave his name to my friend."

"What friend?"

"Never mind. The same friend to whom I gave the name of your wife and son. You must not ask for names in this business."

"What business?" Benni asked.

Salvatore looked pityingly at his cellmate. "Benni, we are both members of the Party. The Party was forced to make an ugly alliance with Hitler. But that alliance will not last. And what you must realize now is that there is only one thing that matters, and that is for the Party to prevail. *That* is our business."

Benni repeated, as if liturgically, "That is our business."

"Do you understand what I am saying?"

Benni said he understood.

"In that event, your imprisonment will cause you less suffering."

Benni then said, in accents he normally reserved for Maria and Michele, "Salvatore, what can I do for you?"

"Benni, you are a sentimental fool. What are you in a position to do for me? You cannot even provide me with a plate of fettuccine, let alone a bottle of brandy, let alone an hour with my bitch Teresa—curse her philandering soul—let alone cause these walls to dissolve, let alone bring on the death, by the slowest available means, of Il Duce and Der Führer." Salvatore paused. "You can tell them—don't ask who they are; they will make themselves known to you—that Salvatore Gigli died like a man, but that his soul will not rest in peace until his betrayer is brought to citizens' justice." Salvatore slowly, lasciviously went through the motion of cutting his own throat, sticking out his tongue as if in extreme agony. He was quiet then, and Benni did not want to initiate any conversation. He would not sleep for the few hours Salvatore had left to live, in case he wanted to talk. But he didn't; he simply smoked one cigarette after another, and when the smoke reached the level of the single window, ten feet up on the side of the wall, the moonlight illuminated it, rising torpidly in the night air in the hot, humid cell.

They came when the moonlight, though dissipated, could still be seen. An officer, six men, a priest. "Dismiss him." Salvatore pointed imperiously at the priest. "I am a Marxist, and need no opiate before leaving this wretched world." The lieutenant and priest spoke to each other in whispers. The priest drew back, but did not leave the detachment. His head was bowed in prayer. They put handcuffs on Salvatore, who turned then to Benni and said in a resonant voice, "The revolution will bury these bastards." They yanked him out then; moments later, Benni heard the fusillade and was sick, though all that came from his impoverished stomach was an ill-digested crust of bread. Was this, he wondered, what was meant by casting bread upon the waters?

Benni found, at the prison in Basilicata, that he was happiest in the company of those who discreetly shared his own secular passion. One month after his arrival the news had been passed that the Resistance, under Party leadership, had smuggled Maria and Michele to America; they were safe, living in Washington. From time to time the Red Cross would bring him a letter from Maria, reassuring Benni that she would wait forever for him, and that Michele—now "Michael"—was doing well in school.

The days and weeks and months went quickly—the summers hot, the winters cold, the food all but inedible, the spirits kept alive only by news, which would trickle in, of defeat after defeat, the deposition of Mussolini, then of course talk of a military invasion by the Allied powers, in anticipation of which the Nazis descended in large numbers. Would they—there were three hundred in the work detachment—be moved north? Perhaps even as far as Germany? Or might they be shot? That, Benni reflected, probably depended on whether the relevant orders were given by the Germans or by the Italians, whose loyalty in the southern provinces was less than rigorous. The Germans would be more expeditious in their approach, the Italians more nonchalant; besides, the Italians would be around after the surrender to answer for what they had done, while the Germans would be retreating to their northern fastness. All the talk was about what was looming; finally, during the summer of 1943, the guards permitted them to listen to the radio broadcasts. It was not difficult, after a week or two, to get the hang of it. The announcers spoke in an Aesopian mode: thus, "The Allied expeditionary force, led by General George Patton, suffered severe losses in the fighting outside Palermo, as the valiant armies of Italy resisted wave after wave of assault on the capital city." This meant that the next day the Americans would take Palermo. The prisoners did not bother to disguise their enthusiasm for the invading armies, and the morale of the guards was visibly disordered. By October all the Germans had been detached to the front in Calabria. The Italians did their work listlessly, under officers who at first were younger and of lesser military rank than their predecessors. These in turn were replaced by men who had clearly been yanked by the Nazis from retirement, and now the prison camp was under the command of Colonel Nicola Paone, who must have been overage in grade during the *First* World War. The colonel knew nothing about the manufacture of barbed wire, which was the principal production of Campo Spirito Santo, and there weren't enough old hands about to notice the general slowdown. The manuals had always specified that the barbs should be four-point half round, wrapped around both cable wires. So it had been from time immemorial, with the wire coming in from the die at one end of the long, ill-heated building. But the loss of supervisory controls began to bring on difficulties. The lubricant box was neglected, or the fiber washers went too long without replacement, or the holding screws were unregulated. At the other end, waiting for the naked wire, those in charge of the barbing process were often idle. And when the wire was passed through the feeds into the spinner head, as often as not a single worker would insert the barb, resulting in two-point, rather than four-point,

barbs. Instead of precisely measuring the specified eight cen-
timeters between barbs, the prisoner pulling the wire would
merely approximate the distance, then nod to the spinner opera-
tors. However, no one in Rome complained that production
quotas were not being met, indeed were down by fifty percent.

Benni, by now the ackowledged leader of the ideological mili-
tants, acted in effect as spokesman for all the prisoners, since it
was only the Communists who were organized; and it was he
who was called into the office of Colonel Paone on the evening
of February 4, 1944, and invited to sit down. Benni did so war-
ily, refusing the proffered cigarette. The colonel said that he had
listened to the shortwave radio the evening before and had done
considerable thinking. The war—at least the Italian part of the
war—was, he said . . . well, was over. In a matter of weeks, the
Americans would reach Rome—and here, at Campo Spirito
Santo, the prisoners were halfway between the beachhead and
Rome—what would be the point in pointless resistance? Benni's
heart began to pound, but he did not change his expression. The
colonel went on to say that American radio had put on the air a
general who, speaking in perfect Italian, announced that any Ital-
ian or German officers found guilty of brutality or acts of
savagery against civilians or political prisoners would be tried by
American military courts and held responsible for their acts.
"When we take Rome," Paone quoted the American general,
"we will have ammunition left over for firing squads."

Benni permitted himself to nod his head slowly, weightily, as
though the American general who spoke Italian had been metic-
ulously transcribing Benni's orders.

Colonel Paone then asked a direct question. He wanted to
know whether Benni would be willing to testify to the effect
that under Colonel Paone, he and his fellow prisoners had been
fairly and humanely treated?

Benni decided to take a long gamble.

"On one condition, Colonel."

"What?" Colonel Paone's voice was anxious.

"That you permit all prisoners to leave within twenty-four
hours."

Colonel Paone looked at Benni as if he were utterly mad. He

rang for the orderly, motioning him to lead Benni back to the barracks.

The next morning at dawn the usual bell didn't sound. The men began, out of habit, to stir. Most were fully dressed against the February cold. The prisoner nearest to the door which should have been unlocked at 6:45—so that they could walk, under the watchful eye of the guards with the automatic weapons, pacing up and down the elevated walks to the refectory—pounded on the door. "Hurry up! I'm hungry." There was no answer. Playfully, he pulled on the handle. The door swung open. The men fell silent. Apprehensive, he motioned to Benni, who walked purposefully to the gray-lit aperture, sticking his head out the door. The light was sufficient to see. He looked up to the commanding patrol tower. There was no one there. Benni looked to the right, toward the mess hall which would be bustling with the preparation of the soup and gruel they would be given for breakfast. It was silent.

And so he knew. Looking neither to the right nor left, and followed silently by his ragged barracks mates, he walked to the huge gate under the control tower. Confidently he turned the handle and pulled. It opened squeakily. For Benni, the war was over.

# CHAPTER 6

The President wiggled his index finger at his chief of staff, indicating that he should leave the Oval Office.

The Director had known the general many years, at historical and personal moments very high and very low. He knew the zephyrs, the williwaws, the storms, and the hurricanes. Observing him now, standing behind his desk, confronting the Secretary of State, the Chairman of the Joint Chiefs, and the Director of Central Intelligence sitting in the chairs to which they had been unsmilingly beckoned, the Director knew that this threatened to be a historic, typhonic low. Indeed, the President found it difficult to begin. His face was red, and the Director feared for his heart condition. They had come in by helicopter from Camp David that afternoon. He had said goodbye, after which Khrushchev went to a press conference, then to Andrews Air Force Base, and on to Moscow.

Finally, gritting his teeth and facing no one in particular, the President said:

"Ever see Khrushchev drunk?" He pronounced it Kroo-cheff. No one commented.

"Any of you, any of you. I'm asking you a question: *Did you ever see Kroocheff drunk?*"

Again there was silence.

"I suppose he doesn't drink vodka when he is merely in the company of underlings. Only with chiefs of state. Is that what your people report, Allen? Or do they report *anything?* Maybe *they're* all drunk. Why not, the good they do."

Everyone knew the President was on no account to be interrupted.

He lapsed again into silence, looking down at his desk.

"Know what the son of a bitch told me last night? At *my* lodge? At *my* presidential retreat? Named after *my* grandson? Know what he said? He said—now, I quote him e-x-a-c-t-l-y.

"He said, 'Ike, you should watch your language.' *Called me* 'Ike'!" The President's eyes very nearly popped out.

"I looked at the interpreter, I mean I looked at the son of a bitch and I said"—the President's voice turned to ice-coated steel—"I said, '*What did you say?*'

"The fellow looked at Kroocheff, mumbled something, Kroocheff mumbled back—fellow couldn't look me in the face this time—but he said:

"'The Chairman's words, sir, which he insists I translate directly, are: "Ike, you should watch your language."'"

The President resumed his agitated walk behind the table, his mind obviously reverting to the alternatives he had faced shortly before midnight the night before.

"I couldn't kick out the interpreter. That would have left me with that grinning son of a bitch with no way to talk to him. Oh, I thought of a few alternatives. The one that appealed to me most was to walk right up to him, eye to eye, then knee him one right in the crotch, then sit back and tell the interpreter to tell '*Nicky*' to watch *his* language. Oh, I'll dream of that opportunity every day of my life—don't tell Mamie. Every single day of my life I'll think about it, think about what I *didn't* do for my country. . . ."

There was silence. The Secretary of State finally broke it.

"Mr. President, what *did* you say?"

"What did I say, for godsake? I thought, this guy's got to be nuts. How many times have I seen him? Six? (Felt like thirty-six.) How many people were usually in the room? Except once, about a dozen. I didn't use any language which would have shocked—Mary had a little lamb. I mean, Mary. Mary's lamb. Oh goddammit, I mean, if I said '*Gee whiz*' in front of him I'd be surprised.

"Then I began to think. What I thought was, well, maybe the old bastard had read somewhere—you know, it's all over, in the books and articles they write about me—that I don't always talk —that people who've spent their lives in the army—don't always talk, well, you know, like nuns. So I asked him—very steady voice, and very formal language—'Mr. Chairman,' I said—twice I said Mr. Chairman, real cold, so he'd know how I reacted to the 'Ike' bit—I said, 'Mr. Chairman, where did you get the impression, Mr. Chairman, that I use improper language?'

"He says, 'When a report says, "*The President gave full expression to his displeasure*," isn't that the polite way of saying, "The President swore"?'

"So I said to him—I could have just changed the subject, but the son of a bitch had been drinking steady, like maybe eight, ten, fifteen vodkas, counting before dinner, so I wondered, well, where's this guy getting his information? So I said, 'Where did you see any reference to "The President gave full expression to his displeasure"?'—I figured somebody had given him an old column by Joe Alsop or somebody wanting to show off what an insider is—I asked him that.

"He giggled. Ever see his teeth up close, Allen? Help yourself to one of those telescopes you watch Mars with for signs of Soviet sub activity or whatever, and look at his teeth someday. . . .

"He giggled. Then he said—he didn't begin it with 'Ike' this time, he said 'Mr. President'—'Mr. President,' he said, 'we know everything that goes on, and we know how you "gave full expression" to your "displeasure" with Defense Secretary McElroy when you found out that what the Secretary had said about Soviet missile capability was incorrect.' He giggled again—I swear, I had to turn my face. Then he said, 'You remember,

Mr. President, how you spoke to Mr. McElroy after learning that we had many more than just ten missiles?'

"Son of a bitch," the President said. "Son of a bitch. I mean, that's exactly what happened, and if memory serves—and my memory does me pretty good service, no thanks to all that crap they print about the effects of my stroke—you, Dulles, and you, Herter, were in the room at the time. And maybe you, Twining, can't remember. NSC meeting. Was it in the Situation Room? I'd gotten that report of yours, Allen, about the Japanese U-2, and I chewed McElroy's ass out, *and he deserved it.* He admitted it to me later. In private.

"*In private?* Shit. 'In private.' What's that? *Tell me what that is, Dulles.*

"Now I've done a lot of thinking since midnight last night. I thought of calling McElroy in Paris. But think, now, how *that* would have sounded.

" 'Neil, this is Eisenhower.'

" 'Good evening, Mr. President. It's two in the morning! An emergency?'

"Me: 'No, Neil, not exactly. I'd like to ask you a very specific question. Did you ever tell *anybody*—wife, friend, anybody—that I chewed you out *using exactly these words:* "The President gave full expression to his displeasure"?'

"That would have been just great. I wouldn't have blamed McElroy if he thought *I* was drunk. Or crazy. So I didn't call McElroy. But—this was a coupla hours after Kroocheff went to bed—his aides came in, practically had to carry him out. I managed a smile. You know," the President's face lit up in a caricature, " 'the famous Eisenhower grin.' Take a good look, gentlemen, because you're not going to see 'the famous Eisenhower smile' again for a *long* time, I'm telling you, not for a *long* time.

"So at exactly 0235 I called Jim Lay. I said to him, 'Lay, get your ass down to the safe where they keep the minutes of the National Security Council meetings, wherever the hell that is, and call me back and read me what it says at the meeting back in —I figure about three weeks ago, sometime in early September— the meeting McElroy was at, and we discussed revised estimates of Soviet nuclear capability.'

"He told me he might have trouble getting into the safe at the

EOB this time of night. I told him the only trouble would be for whoever held him up from doing what I told him to do; I didn't care if he had to round up the Eighth Division as an escort, or get the Department of Engineers to bomb the goddam safe open. He got the picture. I gave him the number to call. He called me back in forty minutes, 0315, and here"—the President reached down to his desk top and grasped a sheet of paper on which, even at a distance, his audience could see his handwriting—"here is what he read me—I'm skipping the first part. Right to nuts and bolts." The President moved his trembling finger down the page to the passage: " 'After listening to the Director's report on Soviet nuclear missile capability, which conflicted with the earlier publicized estimate, *the President gave full expression to his displeasure.*' "

He threw the paper down on his desk, gripped the top of his chair, drew it slowly back, sat down, lifted his legs to the top of the desk, and leaned back.

His voice now was matter-of-fact.

"Herter, go back and study the minutes of all National Security Council meetings going back three months at least. Then assume everything we said is known to the Kremlin. Report back to me, and advise me how this will affect a) our policy; b) our negotiations; c) our public statements."

"Yes, Mr. President."

"Twining? Do the same thing. Plus make recommendations on how whatever we gave out that they shouldn't know can be confused; throw 'em off, that sort of thing. Get back to me by the fifth of October, or by the time their missiles land on us, whichever comes first.

"Dulles? Find the mole."

Without looking up, the President pointed to the door.

# CHAPTER 7

The last time the Director had called on Rufus, the Director had promised that never again would he trouble the man who had determined almost ten years before to retire. Not—the Director now said to Rufus, trying hard not to sound argumentative—not that it was obvious to him why Rufus, a younger man than the Director by seven years, should want so badly to retire; but that was his business. So when the Director had called this morning he simply hadn't bothered with the usual excuses. He'd just said, "Rufus, I've got to see you." Rufus's reply was as expected, and at a little after twelve Dulles's car reached the little farm in Maryland where Rufus devoted himself to his roses, while his wife Muriel seemed to attend to everything else, including discretion. The lunch was prepared and laid out in Rufus's study, lined with books on horticulture and philosophy, in three languages.

The Director had known Rufus since the war, at one tense moment of which General Eisenhower had insisted, with twenty

generals and admirals looking on, on hearing from Rufus person-
ally over the telephone that in his judgment the ruse had worked
on the Nazis, and that it was therefore okay to proceed with the
Normandy invasion. Rufus's reputation as a man of outstanding
ingenuity, tenacity, and discretion had actually got him notice in
a history book or two. There had been repeated attempts to in-
terview him, but these had now mostly died down, because
Rufus handled them uniformly and routinely: he returned all
mail, except that clearly marked as coming from his closest
friends, unopened, having first stamped it: "ADDRESSEE UN-
KNOWN." His telephone number was unlisted, and even so he
changed it every sixty days, at which point, in his methodical
way, he would mail eight postcards, on the back of which would
be scrawled merely: "New number: 325-1231. R." You couldn't
ever really tell, the Director thought, lighting his pipe as Rufus
poured coffee, but he supposed that Rufus was—not a truly
happy man. He was too philosophical to be happy. But he was a
man content; even fatalistic.

The Director liked to leap in directly—so to speak, without
warning. He turned from discussing his brother's funeral and the
distinctive roses, cardless, he had spotted at the church, to yester-
day's meeting with the President, which he described in detail.

Rufus could not suppress a smile. The Director, God knows,
was a man of this world, but neither he nor his brother, who had
resigned his post as Secretary of State as recently as April—wait-
ing until he was far gone in cancer before putting aside his work;
waiting until the last minute to advise even close members of his
family that he would soon die—neither of the brothers was at
home with profanity. They never quite got used to it, notwith-
standing the great doses of it to which they were subjected—
never (heaven forbid!) by their subordinates, but by a succession
of men who happened to serve as commanders-in-chief. The Di-
rector did not reproduce the President's exact language, but his
command over the conjugation of pauses was such as to permit
Rufus to infer exactly which of the usual inventory of expletives
the President had used as an intensifier in each situation.

Rufus, sitting by the window, turning his head slightly to
avoid the sun's rays, looked up at the Director.

"Allen, you're not asking *me* to find the leak, are you?"

"No, Rufus. If we can't find who, in the little circle of people who have access to the minutes of the National Security Council, is slipping the stuff to a Soviet agent, we'd better just all fly to Moscow, give Kroo-cheff (as our commander-in-chief persists in calling him) our swords, and hang it all up."

"You have a suspect?"

"No. But we'll find him. Or her. Yesterday was spent going over a) records of NSC members; b) the clerical staff of the NSC; studying c) the distribution of the minutes; and d) who actually handles the copies. I'm here to get your help in looking ahead; I want you to know what I've been thinking." Rufus seldom contributed any conversational momentum, like "Go ahead." He would say nothing, and his guest would proceed.

"Okay, let's begin. Either Khrushchev intended to let on that he was seeing the minutes, or he didn't intend to let on. It's pretty hard to figure out a motive for the former. We'll keep it open as a hypothetical possibility, even if we can't come up with an explanation.

"But we'll go with the hypothesis that it was a slip. This is consistent with what we know about Khrushchev, the man. He's often babbling and getting drunk, usually at the same time. For instance, the first we ever knew he was going to dump Zhukov was when he drunkenly whispered it to the wife of the Indian ambassador at a reception in Trieste, would you believe. Another thing: he loves to tease people, and loves to show off. What he said to Ike must have given him more pleasure than Disneyland. You read that the Secret Service wouldn't let him visit Disneyland? He was sore as hell. So *that* much fits.

"Next: Only Troyanovsky, serving as interpreter, was in the room. Troyanovsky's a plenty sharp guy. But he was brought in from the foreign service specially for the U.S. visit, and there's no reason at all to suppose that he knew that Khrushchev was making a fatal slip by teasing Ike about that 'full-expression-to-presidential-displeasure' phrase. For all Troyanovsky knew, Khrushchev was referring to some article he had seen or some book he had read. In other words, it's unlikely that Troyanovsky, back in Moscow, has told Khrushchev what he did, sounding an alarm.

"Next logical question: the next morning, did *Khrushchev*

know what he had done? I was able to go back to Ike yesterday afternoon and ask him, straight-out, whether when he said good-bye to Khrushchev he had managed to be civil, and ask him also whether he had done anything the next morning that might make Khrushchev suspicious.

"He did a lot of thinking, and then said that after the conversation he had told us about, Khrushchev had poured himself another drink, and started to ramble, at which point Troyanovsky briefly disappeared and came back in with Khrushchev's personal aide, who said something in Russian probably about how long a schedule they had the next day. Khrushchev then toasted Ike, the United States, peace, the revolution, and a few other things, and went out to his lodge a little unsteady, with Troyanovsky and the colonel walking close to him at either side."

"The next morning?" Rufus spoke for the first time.

"The President said he had decided, after figuring out in the middle of the night the gravity of the affair, that he had to keep cool. He fears that if anything, he overdid it. Talked to him in the chopper about their next meeting, about how he was looking forward to going to Russia. Nothing, in other words, that would make Khrushchev wonder what it was he had said the night before that might have . . . upset the President."

"So"—Dulles stood up, turning his back to Rufus, and looking out over the farm, and noticing the little fauvist signs of approaching autumn—"so the easiest thing to do, presumably, is find the leak and lock up a few people. I have something else in mind."

"So do I."

When Dulles wheeled around, Rufus was smiling.

"*Tous les beaux esprits se rencontrent*," Dulles said, returning the smile broadly.

"Yes," said Rufus. "But let's hope that either there aren't any beautiful souls in the Kremlin, or that if there are, just this one time they won't find our company."

The Director and Rufus talked another two hours.

# CHAPTER 8

It wasn't until the Kentucky Derby party that Blackford's exposure to Amanda Gaither was more than perfunctory. He had met her once or twice at one of the fancy affairs given by Mr. and Mrs. Roland Gaither in their neoclassic home in Chevy Chase, of which Roland Gaither was of course the architect. These functions inevitably had the requisite number of congressmen or senators or diplomats and, the last time around, even a Supreme Court Justice, who was seated opposite Blackford at dinner, whose name Blackford hadn't caught, let alone his station, and with whom Blackford had got into an argument about the *Nelson* decision in which the Supreme Court had ruled that state anti-subversive laws were presumptively preempted by federal laws touching on the same subject. Blackford, to whom the question had been originally tossed, gave the reason why he thought the decision nonsensical. The man opposite him undertook a spunky exposition of the Supreme Court's sophistry, to which

Blackford amiably responded that he "sounded like a Warren
Court," to which he had answered, "Maybe that's because I'm a
member of the Warren Court." The senator's wife had changed
the subject; Amanda, seated next to the Justice, threw back her
head in laughter, and Blackford's mind photographed the pose,
and he found himself thinking from time to time about the dark
voluptuous beauty, begot by Roland Gaither with his slight, shy,
Italian-born wife; and he went home that night thinking some-
thing pleasant, he forgot exactly what, about the melting pot.

But although Roland Gaither, just a few days after signing on
Blackford, had decided that here was the perfect bachelor to end
the protracted spinsterhood of Amanda (she was thirty-one), he
very soon discovered that Blackford was, so to speak, spoken
for; by a girl—he got this information from Benni, who had it
from his son Michael—called Sally Partridge, whom Blackford
had known more or less forever, i.e., since they were at Yale to-
gether. She, Michael had explained to his father, was actually a
little younger than Blackford, but since he had matriculated late,
having been delayed three years by the war, Blackford was an
undergraduate while she was in the graduate school. Were they
engaged? Gaither asked Benni.

"A kinda engaged . . . Roland." It took ten years for Roland
Gaither to suggest to Benni Bolgiano that he call his employer
by his first name, and it had taken another two years before
Benni found it possible to do so. No such formality, of course,
extended to his dealings with Amanda. She and Benni had met
within days after his arrival in Washington in 1944, when he was
reunited with Maria and "Michael," as even his father had now
come to refer to him. Michael and Amanda were the same age
and met at an office party to which all the employees and their
families had been invited. Maria had begun, in 1941, working as a
cleaning woman for Ambrose & Gaither. But the shortage of
skilled help induced by the war brought quick advancement to
those of natural talent and Maria, having mastered English with
little difficulty, became, progressively, telephone operator, file
clerk, chief file clerk, junior draftsman, and finally office man-
ager. She had retired early in the 1950s after her heart attack, at
the insistence of Benni, who had been given a job on his arrival
in Washington as a handyman of sorts but who, like his wife,

quickly proved his abilities and had now been bookkeeper for ten years.

Amanda and Michael, during their early teens, had been inseparable. What might have been Roland Gaither's instinctive resistance to a close social relationship between his only daughter and the only son of an immigrant Italian, by trade a professional union organizer or something of the sort, who had been in a fascist concentration camp, was diluted by his own history: as a young American studying architecture in Rome, he had fallen in love, courted, and brought to Washington as his wife a delicate Italian girl of considerable beauty.

Anita Gaither loved to talk in Italian to Michael, back when Michael was more comfortable in his native language. She encouraged his visits to the house, where he would play games with Amanda. Often they would go to the movies, mostly to matinees. There was great sadness when she went off to boarding school, but for a season or two she wrote to him, and always he replied. Valentine's Day had become something of a contest, and Michael, determined to outdo Amanda, would send, year after year, fancier and fancier Valentine presents, documenting the theory of incremental escalation because she would reply with like determination, and he finally gave up when, in 1948 during her senior year at the Ethel Walker School, she sent Michael by registered mail a human bone. Amanda's Italian uncle was a priest at the Church of St. Valentine in Terni, and he was never able to resist his sister's entreaties. Anita Gaither knew that all the bones of St. Valentine were collected in a single reliquary there, and that a single, small missing bone could not offend anyone as large-hearted as St. Valentine reputedly was, and so when Amanda said that she wanted one of St. Valentine's bones more than anything else in the whole world, more even than she wanted the election of Henry Wallace as President (this political infatuation was not advertised by Roland Gaither among his Washington friends), her mother relented, sending such a letter to her brother as he could not resist. So that Michael, now a freshman at Georgetown, sent a telegram to AMANDA GAITHER ETHEL WALKER SCHOOL SIMSBURY CONNECTICUT. I SURRENDER. A GOOGOL OF KISSES. MICHAEL. Amanda had had to look up "googol," and when she discovered that it was a digit followed by

one thousand zeroes, she was mildly irritated at a victory in the
Great St. Valentine's Contest that was less than total, since
probably not even St. Valentine himself had thought of sending
anyone that many kisses on his birthday.

But, as with Sally and Blackford, distractions ruled the day. It
was a coincidence that both Amanda and Michael went into the
Agency. But her job was in Washington, while his took him to
various parts of the world. On his returns to Washington, inevi-
tably Amanda would have taken up with another friend. Besides,
they had never been engaged; the relationship was primarily fra-
ternal, though not entirely, since their attraction to each other
was comprehensive. Sally, on the other hand, while not pressing
the point, would not contradict occasional references to Black-
ford as her fiancé. For several years she had given as her reason
for not marrying him his affiliation with the Agency, of which
she disapproved in terms exasperatingly chic, so much so that the
subject of the Agency seldom came up between them. After he
left the Agency to join Ambrose & Gaither, her friends more or
less supposed that the wedding would now be scheduled, but the
whole of 1958 and now much of 1959 had gone by, and occa-
sionally she was seen out with other men, even as he was seen
with other women; though mostly they were together, arresting
in their appearance: she as lithe as when Blackford had first met
her at college, her hair as always glistening, her gray eyes alight
with intelligence; he only just beginning to show a line or two
crowfooting from his blue eyes. When they danced, or merely
sat together at a table, many people would inevitably let their
eyes rest on them a grateful moment or two, as if to pay
obeisance to biological triumph.

The party was Amanda's idea because she dearly loved the
track, and beginning in January would avidly speculate on the
probable winner of the Kentucky Derby. She asked Michael to
bring "your beautiful suite-mate" and his girl friend, and she,
Amanda, would mix the mint juleps and serve them steak, corn,
and watermelon "and anything else I can think of that's terribly
American, maybe peanut butter?" on her little terrace. They
must arrive before five, because that was when the commentary
on the Derby would begin, and she didn't want to miss a word
of it, although actually she didn't see much point in even

watching the race, because Silver Spoon was obviously going to win it, never mind that First Landing was the favorite.

The afternoon was warm, but by no means uncomfortable, and though invited to do so, neither Blackford nor Michael bothered to take off their jackets, Michael's a canary yellow, Blackford's his customary khaki. Amanda was wearing slacks and a sleeveless blouse ("I need lots of freedom to mix my perfect mint juleps").

Sally arrived carrying a satchelful of books; she had spent the afternoon at the Library of Congress, was slightly distracted, and just a little bit irritable—Blackford knew the signs. She wore a blue-and-white gingham dress, and, as always, her single strand of pearls. She came in, was directed by Amanda to the bedroom, and emerged a few minutes later visibly freshened and with that perfume (she never divulged its name or the mixture to Blackford, and in her bathroom he always found it in an unlabeled bottle) that Blackford always associated with her, which even now, after eight years, quickened the circulation.

With considerable fanfare the mint juleps were brought out, the parasol tilted so that the image on the television screen could be seen. They would be permitted to talk, said Amanda, only during commercials. After the race, they could talk all they wanted. It was 4:55, and Blackford looked at his watch.

"Guess what," Michael said, sipping his drink.

"What?" Amanda was willing to play.

"Mickey Rooney just got divorced."

The groans were general.

"Guess what," Blackford countered.

Sally looked up at him. "Okay, what?—make it good."

"Elizabeth Taylor just got married."

There was a little chuckling, both events having taken place the previous day, followed by oohs and aahs about the mint julep, how strong it was, how bracing it was, how original the silver mugs. Amanda was visibly pleased.

"Guess what," Michael persisted.

"You can guess what for exactly forty-five seconds," Amanda said, fine-tuning the picture dial on the set.

"Khrushchev said No."

"Said No to what?" Amanda suddenly looked up.

"Just said No. I forget to what."

"Funny."

"Never said I was Bob Hope."

"Nobody ever suspected you were."

"Hey," Blackford said. "I thought you two were childhood friends."

"Michael *was* funny when he was a child; that means, right up to last week."

Blackford looked up at her. Something, he thought, wasn't quite right. Maybe she was tense about her horse, whatever his name was.

By the time the horses had got to the gate Amanda was quite simply agitated, her eyes riveted to the screen so intently that she managed to pour a part of Sally's fresh drink on Sally's wrist. "Oh, I'm so terribly sorry!"

"Forget it," said Sally, drying herself with the paper napkin.

"Quiet! Everybody quiet!"

They were off. Tomy Lee won. Sword Dancer was second. First Landing was third. Royal Orbit was fourth. Silver Spoon was fifth. Amanda was stricken. She turned to Michael: "Why did they put York, that burned-out case, on Silver Spoon?" Michael said he hadn't the least idea; perhaps she could ask her employer to find out the surreptitious motivation of the trainer.

Sally sensed an opportunity to make a grand slam. "That's a good idea. If we can get the CIA to focus exclusively on the Kentucky Derby, maybe we can make a few peaceful advances on the international front. Or would that hurt Mr. Dulles's feelings, Blacky?"

"Me Tonto," said Blackford. "Me no understandum forked tongue."

They were on their third drink, with Sally trailing by one, and the charcoal had been lit. Michael came in with what Blackford recognized as his Very Serious Tone.

"Aw come on, Sally," he said, his expression one of passionate concern. "Look what Khrushchev's just finished doing in Geneva. He's got Gromyko putting us in an intolerable situation. Unless we agree that when the Soviets make a treaty with Berlin we lose our rights in Berlin, he'll—"

"He'll what?" Blacky interposed.

more julep before the steak is ready." Without waiting for an
answer, she moved back and poured Michael a drink. Sally
declined a third. "I'll do the corn," she said, walking over toward
the grill. Blackford said nothing.

"Cat got your tongue?"

"Oh shit, Sally."

He was angry at her tedious disparagements of the whole of
the anti-Communist enterprise. And for her part, she would jolly
well let him simmer. She took no further initiative, so that while
he tended the meat and she the corn, inches from each other, not
a word passed between them, a cold war that went unnoticed in
the blare and jollity of the music.

An hour later Sally said she had to get home—term papers to
read. Blackford made no attempt to detain her. Michael, to
whom the rupture had become apparent, said the usual chattery
kind of thing and started to clear the dishes, but Amanda said to
leave everything, as Violet would be in first thing in the morning
to clean up. Michael gave Amanda the opportunity to suggest he
stay on, but the invitation wasn't proffered, a totally inoffensive
demurral as between two people who knew each other as sister
and brother. Blackford asked Sally if she had brought her car?
She hadn't. "I'll drop you off."

"You don't have to."

"I know I don't have to."

Michael and Amanda affected not to hear, slightly increasing
the pitch of their own goodbyes. Blackford extended his hand to
say good night. She took it and lightly stroked the palm with her
thumb. Michael was voluble in expressing his delight with the
evening; the others thanked Amanda. Sally consoled her on the
loss of Silver Spoon, and they walked into the pretty little house
to the front door that opened on P Street.

Blackford nodded in the direction of his parked Chevrolet,
and pointedly opened the passenger-door side for Sally before
going around to let himself in. He found his anger swelling,
though he recognized that the booze probably enhanced it; but
Sally had been, for several weeks now, quite simply bloody. He
was determined to take no conciliatory initiative. So was she. So
that when he reached her apartment house on Wisconsin Avenue
she simply opened the door, said "Good night," and walked,

"Well, you know what he says he'll do—he'll close the corr dor, and this time around deny us the airspace."

"And the cow will jump over the moon."

"Okay, Black, so maybe he's bluffing. But there's got to be some reason for all the concern."

"Oh?" said Sally. "Are the lights burning day and night at the Agency? Ooohhh," she shivered, as if a great cold had taken her. "My goodness, but I'm *surrounded!* Amanda—CIA. Michael— CIA. My Blacky—*ex*-CIA: because he did something naughty, and he never has told me what. Did you kill the wrong person, darling?"

Blackford looked at her, and his failure to reply was, by his standards, massive retaliation. Instead he took his drink and walked over to the grill to chat with Amanda, who was fiddling with the steaks. He left Sally and Michael talking heatedly.

Amanda joked with Blackford about popular misconceptions of the Agency, but kept her voice down. She had put on the record player, and Ella Fitzgerald was singing Cole Porter. Blackford responded amiably to her spirited dominion over the steaks, mint juleps, music and conversation, and again he remembered her, over a year ago, head tilted back, laughing, salvaging a tight social situation with voluptuarian delight. "You are an extraordinarily beautiful woman," he said impulsively as he stirred the charcoal. She replied, affecting the accent of Greta Garbo, "You should see the rest of me." He turned to her, her smiling face reflecting the torchlight, and knew that she had issued an invitation. "When," his voice was steady as he resumed his work with the coals, which he now found himself stroking, "is the rest of you visible?"

Amanda laughed softly. "I'll have to consult my astrologer. Besides," her head made the faintest motion in the direction of Michael and Sally, "just how much should a single man be permitted to see?"

"That depends on his reach."

She looked at him, this time allowing her eyes to descend slowly along his body. Blackford found it expedient to swivel to one side.

Amanda's laugh was now intended to reach her other guests: "Let's have another drink. Hey, Sally, Michael, time for one without even a ritual peck on his cheek, to the front door, opened it, and let herself in. Blackford was still standing by his car.

He was hot now with anger, resentment, and—he had known it was coming—lust. He drove down the street to the bar at the corner, ordered a bourbon and soda at the counter, and went to the telephone book. Gaither . . . Nothing under Amanda. A "Gaither" on P Street? No. Her number was unlisted. He returned to the bar and sipped his drink.

Blackford had the capacity not always to *control* his movements, but always to observe them with detachment. One thing he knew as surely as that the sun would in due course rise: namely, that he would succeed in getting the unlisted number of Amanda Gaither. He would not, of course, call Michael to get it. His mind raced for names of suitable friends in common. Why not call the old number? Oscar was still doing night duty, as far as he knew, and Oscar would give him the home number, for old times' sake. One possibility—No, he wouldn't call Roland Gaither. No, he wouldn't call. . . . He could, of course, just drive back to P Street. But there was an arrhythmic factor there he wouldn't stop now to analyze—it would disturb the cadence. No, he must telephone her. What the hell.

He went to the telephone. He knew his luck would now turn to his account, knew it as a certitude. But he mustn't wrench the thing.

The voice answered—always the same routine, giving the last three numbers dialed.

"Seven-three-four."

"Oscar? It's Black."

"How are ya, boy! Been a while. The missus was asking about you the other day. She always took a shine to you."

"Give Marge my love. Say, Oscar, I had dinner with Amanda Gaither—my boss's daughter, she lives at 1125 P Street. I left my damned briefcase there and I can't find her number. Unlisted. Do you mind?"

"Well, I don't guess anybody's going to fire me for giving you the number of your boss's daughter, so why don't you call your boss and ask him, ho ho ho. Hang on a minute, Black."

Blackford's pen was poised. He scratched down the number.

"Thanks, Oscar; good man, I'll give you a buzz at home real soon."

He hung up—but went back, then, to the bar. Times like this, Black old boy, you got to stop and *think*, if only so you can tell yourself that at times like this you stopped and thought, right? Right. Well, have you stopped and thought? Yes, he had certainly stopped and thought, so he went back to the telephone.

"This is me."

"Well, hello."

"I decided I would have that extra mint julep."

"So you want me to give you the recipe?"

"That's one possibility." Blackford had no remaining doubts. She laughed. "Come on over."

They went quickly into the bedroom on the first floor, where the only light was from the embers in the grill outside. He could not see her, not yet, but would soon, as his eyes adjusted. He took her voraciously, and she responded with unfeigned intensity. He tried to slake his appetite, and she hers, in silent and passionate exuberance, and as his eyes and hands discerned the contours he had up until a moment ago only imagined, he very nearly shivered. She, little by little, lost that trace of a smile as she turned up her head pleadingly, biting her lower lip, grasping him with both hands, kneading him now with the insulation of the gesture earlier in the evening gone, the circuit complete. She gasped, and now, finally, he closed his eyes, the moment frozen like a stilled motion picture; and then he collapsed. She raised her arms, and, tenderly, played with the hair on the back of his head, as if bent on braiding it. It was a half hour before she spoke.

"Is it me, or are you just taking it out on Sally?"

He paused. He enjoyed hyperbole—but not flattery. As a schoolboy he had had an aversion to any form of unction; he thought it servile. He came in on the question from a different angle.

"Why would somebody like you ever feel that anything other than you would be necessary?"

Amanda raised herself on one elbow, resting her head on one hand. She laughed. "Blacky, you're silly, but you're nice. I see your little analytical mind—I mean your big analytical mind—

working working working. Forget it. It was super, and there isn't any reason—you're right—to dissect it. After all, I suppose I could have said, 'Was that you, or the mint julep?' "

"I'd have said, in Kentucky, this is how well-bred gentlemen are trained to thank the ladies when the juleps are especially good."

She laughed again; and, with her free hand, began again to fondle him, traveling down the length of his body slowly, amiably, her fingers, closing casually on their prey, idling, teasing; no hurry.

"Dad says you're bored."

Blackford, his own hands now engaged, said, rather distractedly, "Oh? When did he say that?"

"The other day."

"What was he talking about?"

"You."

"Obviously. I mean, why was he talking about . . ." he lost, temporarily, control of his speech rhythm. Easier to start again. "Why was he talking about me?"

"He thinks you miss your old work."

"In a way I do."

"But he says if you stayed on, he'd make you a partner in a year or so."

"Maybe that was as of before toni . . . iiiyyyit."

Her laugh tapered off quickly. Blackford said, "I think you were commissioned to seduce me into coming up . . . with some monument nice . . . to . . . FDR."

The telephone rang. Startled, Amanda groped for it.

"Yes?" she said quietly.

"Sorry to bother you, ma'am. This is Oscar, at the Agency. Blackford Oakes called, asked for your number, and I gave it to him. Against the rules. Just wanted to check. Was that all right?"

"Oh, er—yes, yes of course. We're . . . preparing a little surprise for my father. Thanks for checking. Good night."

"I trust," said Blackford, "we're *not* preparing a little surprise for anybody. Let alone your father."

She laughed good-naturedly, content, and got out of the bed. Putting on a bathrobe, she said, "Let's go down and get that julep. But before that, stand up and move over, in front of the window. I want a good look."

Blackford obeyed. "Okay?"

"Not really. I could look all night. But—" she sighed exaggeratedly "—my mother taught me to be a good hostess. So put on your pants, and I'll go grind the damn mint."

"Knead the damned mint."

"Knead the damned mint."

# CHAPTER 9

It was hardly unusual to find Benni still at his desk even after the most junior draftsman had left the office. Ernie Johnson switched off the light in his own quarters and, passing by Benni's (the door, as always, open), said, "You *are* a grind, Benni. It's six-thirty."

Benni looked up from under the heap of accountants' pads on his desk and smiled. "It won't be so long now, Ernie. Good night."

Johnson waved, and went down the hall.

Benni waited ten minutes. He went then to the entrance door, locked and also bolted it. This was standard operating procedure at A&G, and on those infrequent intervals when only one architect, or one secretary, was in the office (it occasionally happened during the lunch hour), the remaining employee was encouraged to bolt the door to guard against the acquisitive who are not deterred by mere keylocks.

Benni then went back to his office and reached into a file drawer marked, "RECEIPTS, JAN–APRIL 1957." He took out the manila folder for February, opened it, and withdrew eight Xeroxed sheets of paper with closely, but neatly, typewritten material, single-spaced.

These he took to the blueprint room together with eight sheets of letter paper on which, during the preceding days, he had recorded miscellaneous figures, summaries of expenses, invoices—the accountant's equivalent of the lawyer's omnipresent legal pad. The paper in question, though not chalk-white like the stationery used by the firm, was not unusually dull. Benni was known to be thrifty in his own habits, and niggardly with the firm's money. He used dull stock for his work, less expensive than regular writing paper. It was, in fact, blueprint paper, taken from the roll of sensitized paper in the blueprint machine and trimmed to the standard 8 x 10. Benni's own typing and notes were carefully done on the desensitized side.

Now he placed on the belt one piece of his notepaper, sensitized side up, and from the other pile drew a single sheet, the typed matter face down. He flipped a switch and the conveyor belt moved the papers up under the glass plate and past the light source. Benni then retrieved both papers, aborting the passage of the sensitized paper which would otherwise have been guided by rollers into the water wash spray, then up and around the four heated drying drums. He repeated the operation seven times and turned off the machine. He now had exposed, but undeveloped, blueprints of the typed papers.

Then he went to the washroom and soaked the original eight typewritten documents in hot water until they were pulpy. He disposed of them in the toilet.

Back in the office, he inserted his eight sheets in a manila folder between other similar sheets of paper—more blank accountants' work sheets.

He looked at his watch. It was five minutes after seven. He waited five minutes and then at 7:10 he dialed a number in Brooklyn. He permitted the telephone to ring three times, then hung up.

That night he told Maria he would be traveling the next day to New York, to which he frequently went on Saturdays—to visit friends, and perhaps call on Salvatore's widow, who had helped to engineer Maria and Michael's escape. He usually took the train at eight.

A few minutes after two, he was in Brooklyn, at Prospect Park. He had with him a small brown bag, and sat on the bench eating his ham and cheese sandwich and reading that morning's edition of the New York *Daily News*. At the other end of the bench another man, wearing a light overcoat and a cap, also sat, reloading a camera. After putting in fresh film, he discarded the carton, leaving it in the space between him and Benni. His sandwich finished, Benni folded the newspaper and put it down, enveloping in his palm the film carton, which he eased into his pocket.

On the train back to Washington, Benni poked his finger into the carton in his pocket, drawing out a scrap of paper. Written in pencil was: "Popcorn Loew's 87th 4:05." Benni committed the data to memory, went to the men's room, and disposed of the film carton. When next he had materials to pass along, he would dial the telephone at the usual time on a Friday, and the next day at 4:05 he would be at the popcorn stand, establish eye contact, walk into the theater and select an uncrowded row. He would be followed by the man with the popcorn, who would sit two seats away. In due course Benni would leave an envelope with his work sheets in the seat between them. That envelope would be retrieved, and the half empty popcorn box discarded under the empty seat. Benni would pick up the scrap of paper lying on the uneaten popcorn, which would specify the site and hour of day for the next meeting. Both men would sit through the movie, but one would delay leaving until the first had gone, even though it meant seeing again a minute or two of film already seen.

After Hans Steiner picked up the papers in the park he returned to his studio. There he would work in his darkroom. First he developed the blueprint paper—this merely required washing it in clean water, thus producing the clear negative on a background of prussian blue. He then read over the material and made a judgment as to which of various means of transmitting it was appropriate. In recent months Benni had given him one or two items that needed to be transmitted with the greatest possible

speed consistent with security—for instance the order, which
Hans saw on July 2, dispatching a U-2 to overfly the Polish
border on July 4. Steiner had to weigh conflicting priorities on
that one. Steiner had thirteen effective agents, and had devised
contingent means by which he could sacrifice one without
endangering others, let alone himself. If a certain man in Ottawa
received a telephone call at the beginning of which the caller
identified himself as Max Schmeling, the obliging Canadian would
write down exactly the text of the message to be transmitted to
Moscow by cable. The Canadian, who worked in a travel agency,
would go to the Soviet consul to ask for blank visa application
forms; the assistant consul would be consulted about a hypo-
thetical problem involving a client of the tourist agency. The
troublesome Canadian birth certificate would be produced and a
Xerox copy made for examination by the consul-general. The
relevant information, taken from the birth certificate, would
reach the Lubyanka by code within three minutes.

But Benni's package today could go by one of the usual means,
which meant delivery in Moscow in four to six days. So Steiner
took the special camera, locked it into place, and filmed the eight
pages, then made the tiny negatives. The whole of the informa-
tion on the negatives would fit comfortably under two postage
stamps. He clipped out of the morning *Times*, after quickly
perusing it for material of plausible interest to an East German,
the notice of a statement by Dr. Nikolai A. Kozyrev of the
Pulkovo Observatory near Leningrad who had reported that
spectral photographs had proved the lunar crater Alphonse to be
an active volcano. The story went on to say that *Izvestia* had re-
ported the same day that the Lebedev Physics Institute had com-
pleted the most sensitive radiotelescope in the world and was
building "the world's largest," with a "crosslike" shape one kilo-
meter long and 131 feet high.

He inserted the clipping into the envelope, which he had
touched only with gloved hands. He carefully applied the post-
age stamps. Steiner was a perfectionist, and had fretted over the
matter of how to write the name and address. Certainly he
would never do so in his own hand. He had two typewriters, one
of them in his large workroom, a second, a portable, in the
hanging closet of his bedroom, a perfectly reasonable place in

which to store a spare. He had once or twice permitted himself to use this typewriter, long enough ago that he was satisfied that whatever risk he'd run had lapsed. Should he use it again? The alternative was cumbersome, namely to go into Manhattan to one of those pawnshops where there were always typewriters for quick sale, and go through the routine of trying one out, sneaking in one or two envelopes. He decided against it, brought down his portable, and typed out:

> Frau Ilse Müller
> 48 Mittelstrasse
> East Berlin
> German Democratic Republic

It wasn't as though he didn't have to go to Manhattan anyway. He went out the door, walked two blocks to the subway at Borough Hall, went up the Lexington Avenue line to Fourteenth Street, mailed the letter at the corner, and treated himself to a late dinner at Luchow's during which he read the latest issue of *Time* magazine, which carried a story on Chairman John McCone of the Atomic Energy Commission advising the Washington press that his tour of Soviet nuclear facilities had impressed him with the "remarkable" speed with which the Soviet scientists could organize and carry out new atomic projects. However, McCone reassured them, in every relevant field the United States was significantly ahead of the Soviet Union. "Maybe today, maybe not tomorrow," Hans Steiner said to himself elated, finishing his half-bottle of hock.

The letter, the following morning, was spotted, pursuant to the court-approved directive of the FBI that any mail addressed to an Iron Curtain country should be diverted. The order governed mail going out of Washington or greater New York. It was collected and sent once a day to an FBI office in midtown, where each envelope was steamed open, and its contents photographed, along with the face of the envelope. The time-objective was to delay the letter by no more than one day. The post office was instructed to postmark the stamp before delivering the letter to the FBI.

So that Benni's eight sheets were on a flight to Berlin not on Monday, but on Tuesday. Wednesday the envelope was delivered in East Berlin. It reached Moscow on Friday. That afternoon Anton Speranski, Aleksandr Shelepin, and Rodion Malinovsky read with fascination the minutes of a National Security Council meeting held the day before Chairman Khrushchev's arrival in the United States. There had been a detailed discussion of the U-2 flights, and the decision was made to step up the overflights on the Russian border and East European territory. There were scattered references to launch sites. The Americans were apparently now onto the Soviets' discovery that the CIA was using Giebelstadt in Germany as a base, and it was decided therefore to consolidate operations out of Pakistan and Turkey in Lahore, Peshawar, and Adana.

Once again, the KGB placed a call to Chairman Khrushchev.

Afterward Shelepin said, "He is a great joker," and putting down the telephone he shook his head, smiling. "He said, 'Aleksandr Nikolaevich, I am *never* too busy to read the minutes of a meeting of the National *In*security Council of the United States.'"

"What a wag!" said Speranski, who would not have used language that informal about the Premier of the Soviet Union before he and his agents had contrived to filch the minutes of the National Security Council, conferring upon Speranski certain social prerogatives.

# CHAPTER 10

"The detection of people who are violating American laws is a matter for the *Justice Department*, and the apprehension of such persons is the responsibility of the *Federal Bureau of Investigation*, and *that's all there is to it.*"

If the Director of the FBI said that once to the Director of the Central Intelligence Agency he said it—ten, fifteen times? The Director of the CIA replied, at first with his habitual placidity, that the resources of the CIA worldwide would need to be used, that it was there rather than here that we were likeliest to come upon the tripwire, that Rufus was ideally qualified to superintend the entire operation, that of course the CIA needed the aid of the FBI, but the matter was so delicate, in a way that involved foreign countries, that it really made more sense to put it under the direct responsibility of someone especially conversant with international intelligence and counterintelligence. And, finally, that the CIA had "designs" to turn to U.S. advantage the whole messy, dangerous business.

"Come to think of it," the Director said, sipping his scotch and soda in the comfortable study of his house, to which Rufus had come for a protracted evening, "I probably repeated *my* line as often as Hoover did his. I finally said, there's only one way to go. To the President."

" *'Not without the Attorney General!'* Hoover said. Of *course* he wants Bill there—Bill Rogers is scared to death of Hoover. For that matter, who isn't?"

"Are you?" Rufus asked.

"Absolutely. Don't know why, but he's the single most intimidating presence I've ever encountered."

"So?"

"So I finally said okay. Hoover went off and obviously gave Bill his orders. I called the White House and we got an appointment for four this afternoon. We went into the Oval Office, and Ike sat and listened. I waited till I thought the moment was just right, and then I said"—the Director was now clearly enjoying himself—"I said, 'Mr. President, I'd like you to know that I would like to put the whole operation under Rufus. I've been to see him and he's prepared to take it on.'

"You'd have liked his reaction:

" *'My* Rufus?' he asked.

" 'Yes, Mr. President,' I said.

"Then he turned to Bill. 'Bill' he said, 'it's obvious to me that what we got here involves two jurisdictions. There's a role in it for the FBI—that's for sure. There's a role in it for the CIA— that's also for sure. Now everybody in this room knows that any operation has to have a single boss. Just the way'—Ike's a cool one, all right: he was all of a sudden the same man who managed all those generals and kings and ex-kings and would-be kings in Europe. He nodded in the direction of Hoover—'just as Hoover, here, is *the* boss of his Bureau. Now, in this particular operation it is my judgment that the foreign thing outweighs the domestic thing. I mean, we're going to end up putting some sons of bitches in jail for violating American law. But the law they're violating is giving the Soviet Union the edge in a contest that could involve national survival.' Then he put on his glasses—you know the way he does, when he's laying down the line?—'Under the circumstances, I think we'll put the operation under Rufus. Mr. Hoover should appoint one of his most valued subordinates to cooperate in every way with Rufus, who will report to Dulles who will report to me. The FBI man will report to the Director, and then to the Attorney General. Now, Bill, have I said anything unconstitutional?'

" 'No sir.'

" 'Okay. Have I done anything unlawful?'

"Bill winced a little there, and looked away from Hoover. But he said, 'No sir.'

"Then Ike turned to us and gave us one of his pep talks. Hoover left that room profoundly convinced that America would live or die depending on his cooperation. We can complain about some things, Rufus, but Ike's sheer ability to handle people—what the hell. Let's get to work."

The Director had emptied three suites of rooms in a compound. Already he had amassed a sheaf of material detailing exactly the procedures to be followed by National Security Council members on receipt of their individual copies of the minutes of the meetings. The Situation Room had been swept, the sound deflectors checked; everything was secure at the mechanical level. The Director said he would be obliged if Rufus would take over the operation beginning the following day.

Rufus began at that moment. "How many meetings of the Executive Committee of the NSC have there been in the past year?"

The Director walked to his briefcase and brought out a sheet of paper. "First thing I checked. Here they are."

Rufus studied the calendar. "I see the longest interval without a meeting was about two weeks, but you've had them sometimes —here's a week you had three. Hmm."

"Of course. And we'll continue. We're going to have to keep feeding the mole. With minutes that'll satisfy the other side."

"That means," Rufus said, "we're going to have to give up a lot."

"Right. That's why we've got to compress the whole business as much as we can."

In the course of the next four hours they made many decisions. To begin with, the six members of the executive committee would need to be advised of the problem. They would be informed that the minutes they would hereafter receive would be blends of fact and fiction. Enough fact to persuade the KGB that the minutes were the real article. Until the crisis was solved, the committee members should follow *exactly* the same procedure as before in the handling of their copy of the minutes. In respect of policy implementation, they would have to rely on their own memories or their own notes, since obviously much that was important would be withheld.

Rufus would henceforward attend all executive meetings of the NSC and, in consultation with Dulles, would draft the "minutes" that would officially go out. This would require—in order not to alter external procedures in such a way as might tip off the mole—staying in the Situation Room together with Colonel Saunders, the man who kept the minutes. He had worked for the Agency since its inception, and before that for General Donovan. He would need to be apprised of the arrangements, so that, beginning at the point when he left the Situation Room to dictate the "minutes" to his secretary, no one would know that the minutes were doctored, save the selected members of the National Security Council constituting the unofficial Executive Committee.

An intense effort, beginning immediately, would be made at all the watering places of international intrigue to develop leads. Enticing money would be offered for defectors. Dulles agreed with Rufus that the probability was slight that the minutes were traveling from Washington directly to Moscow, although that possibility was also being looked into. The Soviet Embassy and known Soviet satellites were under electronic surveillance. The post office alert had been ordered as a routine check (during the past five years, such checks had been made four times), and a painful, meticulous effort was being made to check out correlations between outgoing mail and the dates of meetings of the

NSC. Rufus would appoint someone, probably from the FBI, to check on the mail to Eastern Europe and Russia.

"Here's a figure for you: last week, almost twenty thousand pieces of mail went out to the Communist countries. The sheer *scale* of the thing—going out there someplace . . . and wending the trail back here—is pretty intimidating." Yes, Rufus said, but the effort must be made; besides which, it would give us an up-to-date feel for pressures and counterpressures in the spy world.

The Director, his note pad filled, said he was tired—perhaps they should continue tomorrow.

"One more thing," Rufus said. "You know I like to work with people I've had experience with." Rufus, as always, was matter-of-fact. In the tone of his voice there was nothing anyone could interpret as a demand. And yet (the Director knew) Rufus was advising him what was necessary for the Agency to do in order to expedite—make possible?—Rufus's participation in the enterprise.

"I would like to have Singer Callaway, Anthony Trust, and Blackford Oakes working with me."

The Director paused. "No trouble on Callaway and Trust. But you know, don't you, that we had to drop Oakes?"

"Yes, I know. I think you made your disciplinary point. But I've worked with him on three assignments, and I'd like him back."

"I don't know whether we can get him back. He's working with an architectural firm, doing very well someone told me."

Rufus asked, "Would it be easier for you if I talked with him?"

"As a matter of fact," the Director said, "it most assuredly would be. I'll fix it at the administrative end; you take care of signing him on."

"Two questions: Am I to tell him that we want him for this assignment only, or that he is back in the Agency?"

The Director, puffing on his pipe, took a moment to answer. "I guess it's only fair, if you're signing him on for this particular mission, to tell him we're agreeable to taking him back. If he says he doesn't want in for the long haul, offer him a contract for this one assignment and he can go back to building bridges, or whatever."

"A minor point, but one he might ask: What grade?"
"Whatever he had before, plus one."
"Plus two, Allen."
Dulles smiled. "All right. Plus two."

Michael Bolgiano was the least importunate of men. Tenacious, yes, but that was always at his own expense. Requests made of others were always diffidently advanced, and accordingly Blackford was surprised when he got the call asking whether, even at the risk of inconvenience to himself, Blackford could join Michael for dinner on Tuesday. The call was placed on Monday morning, and Blackford was at his desk, engaged in making careful calculations on an aspect of the proposed subway, the contractors having retained A&G as consultants. He flipped open his calendar and looked under Tuesday, October 6. "Dinner—Sally." Ah, but that date was made before he got her note on Saturday morning at his apartment. The telephone in his left hand, he ran his pencil through "Sally" and wrote above her name, "Michael."

"See you then." He went back to his work.

But his mind wandered. He opened his middle drawer and took out the letter and read it yet another time. . . .

"Blacky, my love: So last night I bugged you again, just like last May, at that horrible Kentucky Derby party. We went a month—the whole of June, I think it was. Well, do we have what *Emma* (J. Austen, 1775–1817) felt for Mr. Churchill, namely a 'crystallizing incompatibility'? I don't know. I do know that what's going on now doesn't seem to work. I get so much pleasure from you, and you're the most *alluring* man I'll probably ever know. But your world and mine are rotating on different axes. I care mostly about literature, you care about who has the most atom bombs. Just writing that sentence makes me feel blue, because it's bound to infuriate you. What I don't want is the wretched business of last June—who will call who first; meanwhile we both are conspicuous in other people's, ah, company. I enjoy it when Austen's characters brood and fret and analyze their feelings, morning, afternoon and night, an evolution of glorious leisure lasting through chapters, even books. I love it; I write about it; I teach it. But not for me, Blacky my love. So:

I've decided that I'm going to give you up for October. No, let me be fairer and say I've decided you'd be happier if you gave me up for October. You know, like Lent. At the end of the month, we'll know more about each other, but not, this time, with the kind of awful agonizing we did during June. By the end of October I'll—no, I won't tell you now. I'll surprise you. By the end of October I'll be ready to talk to you. Now, if you want to interpret this letter as a terminal provocation, there's nothing I can do to stop you, except to say I love you, but if it wasn't meant to be, let's—let's *not* face it. Let's just drop October.

"See you in November, I hope.

"Love, Sally.

"P.S. You'll have more time to take riding lessons from Amanda. Though I could tell her you don't, really, need to practice what you're already perfect at."

Blackford could think of little else over the balance of the weekend, and a dozen times he had sat down to reply, but by Sunday night he had resolved that no reply was precisely the correct reply, so to speak, in the spirit of the moratorium she had decreed. The night before, to remind him of the suspended loyalty, he had greatly relaxed with Amanda. He was quite startled at a technique she had shown him, but stopped short of asking her who had given *her* her riding lessons. A nice young woman, exemplary family. He remembered that Byron had said that St. Augustine had taught him vices Byron had never known existed. Should he read the *Confessions?* Later, perhaps. Besides, Byron probably found what he was referring to in other of Augustine's writings. Without thinking he reached for the telephone and very nearly began to dial Sally, who of course would have known the answer to that question, until he remembered that he was under interdict. He went back to the subway designs.

The following morning it happened that he and Michael left for work at exactly the same time. As a rule, Michael—it was a part of that unending thoughtfulness to which Blackford had become shamefully habituated—rose very early and instantly made full use of the bathroom, so that by seven it belonged entirely to Blackford, whose rising hours were more flexible. Usually Michael was at his desk at 2430 E Street at 8; Blackford at A&G at 9. Blackford was therefore surprised when, at 8:30, he came out of his door at the same time Michael did.

They walked down the staircase, Blackford leading.

"What's up tonight, Michael?"

"If you don't mind, Black, I'd rather talk to you about it then, okay?"

"Okay. I'll be back at six. Got a little reading to do. Pick me up any time that suits you."

When, a few minutes before six, Blackford turned the key to his apartment, opened it, and saw the three men sitting in chairs boxing the compass of his room, he stopped. Slowly he shut the door behind him. Two of them were smiling, the third—something less than that.

"Son of a bitch. I *mean*, even Hollywood wouldn't do this! God*dam!*"

He embraced Anthony Trust, and had another bear hug for Singer Callaway. Rufus, he actually slapped on the back—before sobering up and extending his hand. He felt as if he had stolen a kiss from Marie Antoinette at Madame Tussaud's.

There was general laughter, and babble, and Blackford thought suddenly, "Is this my birthday?" No. He was born on December 7, a date that will live in infamy (over the years he had used that line more than a couple of times, often at marvelously appropriate moments of high salacious activity).

"Okay, okay, what's going on? Sit down. What do you want to drink? We'll start with you, Rufus. You would like, er, something that's one part clam juice, one part Perrier, with maybe a drop of rose water." Blackford opened the refrigerator and brought out a ginger ale, Rufus's drink. He brought gin, tonic, and white wine on a tray, with assorted glasses. He filled his own with wine.

And sat down. "So," he said. "What is it that brings to my humble abode three burglars? Or do you have a court order authorizing your illegal entry?"

Anthony Trust—a year older than Blackford, slim, intense, primly affectionate, a former classmate at Greyburn Academy in Great Britain, and at Yale—pointed to Singer Callaway. Age—

oh, fifty-five? Relaxed, loose-jointed, idiomatic, he'd have looked altogether at home performing behind a guitar in his native Ohio: Singin' a little ole song or two to his little old girl/ Waitin' for ole Singer/To stop singin', and come home. And Singer in turn pointed to Rufus. And that, always, was when the singing had to stop. They hadn't all convened at 40 Woodward Street to celebrate the sixth of October with an ex-agent who had been kicked out of the Agency.

So, Rufus got down to it. There was at hand a considerable crisis. As with some crises, this was one that bore an opportunity. Rufus had consented to take the command post. He had— "'specified' would be the wrong word," he said (but he did not go on to supply a substitute), that he work with three men with whom he had worked on a number of other assignments. Unhappily, the sheer scope of the enterprise would require that many men be involved. But he was here authorized to ask Blackford to accept recommissioning as an agent of the Central Intelligence Agency. Rufus thought it entirely inadvisable, on this or any future occasion, so much as to touch, let alone dwell upon, the reasons for Blackford's separation from the Agency. An earnest of the Director's confidence in him was that if Blackford agreed, he would be reinstated immediately as a Grade 16 officer. The invitation was, at Blackford's choosing, finite, or other than finite. Rufus hoped that whatever his ultimate professional plans, he would at least agree to interrupt them in order to help with the enterprise at hand; but he was here also to say that if he desired to stay on in the Agency, he would be welcome. He had already briefed Callaway and Trust on the problem, and had brought them along in order for Blackford to know that if he consented, he would be working with men with whom he had shared a number of experiences. . . .

Blackford said, "Let me think about it, Rufus." He paused, wrinkling his face in a caricature of concentration. "I've thought about it. The answer is yes. I assume I can give A&G a couple of weeks' notice?"

"We'd like you to start working—tonight."

A&G's subway . . . Was there anything, Blackford thought, that he and only he could contribute to the realization of the projected subway car? Yes, come to think of it. He had hoped to install a sauna in each car. But on the other hand, he could pass along that suggestion to his successor. Gaither would blanch. No, unfair. Roland Gaither, for all that he was occasionally a pompous old fart, was pretty decent, and, on the patriotic front, right up there with the Green Berets. After all, he had given his only daughter to the Agency. Given her, come to think of it, not only to the Agency, but to an ex-agent. At least, through October.

"Okay, Rufus. I'm all yours. What are we going to do about dinner?"

"Michael Bolgiano is having it brought in."

Blackford could not remember when last he was so thoroughly content.

# CHAPTER 11

It was cold in Berlin in January, and Blackford, walking now to the safe house he had occupied since early November, had braced against the cold which (what was it about the wind in Berlin? It always blew from the direction he wanted to go) roared down Hochstrasse. At the west end the buildings turned gradually to squat apartment houses. He entered number 322, taking the automatic elevator to the seventh floor. The elevator door opened, confronting him with the front door of his apartment—there was no hallway. With his foot he held the elevator door open while putting the key in the lock and stepping into the warm room, furnished with squalid, colorless comfort, heavy woods, gray-brown walls, carpeting, dusty books. There were two bedrooms, a dining room, and the large sitting room. In the dining room he had set up an office of sorts. It consisted of a file cabinet, a typewriter, what appeared to be a lifetime's supply of 3 x 5 index cards, and the most detailed map of Berlin outside the Berlin Museum. There were a few, not many, photographs. These were kept moving; at any given time Blackford husbanded not more than a few days' accumulation. In a separate pile were the photographs he got back from Washington with requests for more detailed pictures.

At 5:45 Günter came in, pounding himself to revive circulation. They spoke in German.

"Busy day?"

"Yes." Günter sat down at the dining room table, having taken off his coat. "I could use some tea." He was balding, chunky, red in the face, and well fed, but his movements were sprightly.

Blackford put the kettle on the stove. Günter drew four envelopes from his right inside breast pocket. Each had a name written on the outside. In each envelope were Günter's collected notes. Blackford would study these and decide which subjects, if any, warranted photographing. The decision made, Günter would work with Ada and Niklaus and, depending on the habits of the mark, the photographing would be arranged. Ada and Niklaus were in their mid-twenties. They could pose convincingly as newlyweds, and often did. Their "guide" Günter (he *was*, in fact, an official guide, registered as such and available from Cook's to take visitors anywhere in greater Berlin) would obligingly snap their photograph—at just the moment when they would suddenly pose—as the mark, the object of the photograph, turned the corner, or came out of the doorway, or whatever.

It was work at once dull and demanding, because almost every mark presented a different *kind* of problem. Take yesterday, for instance. They were to check one Anna Krindler who lived on Gartenstrasse. At 8:30 Blackford had presided over what was, in effect, a staff meeting. In the room was Michael, whose German was less than fluent, and who therefore attended to most of the paperwork westbound in English to Washington.

Anna Krindler. Why was she a suspect? She had received five letters from one Heinz Hary of Washington, over the two months since the postal reconnaissance had begun. The letters were simply signed "Heinz." The dossier from Washington contained a) photostatic copies of those letters, and b) a brief description of Heinz Hary. He was employed in Washington as a truck driver by a moving firm. Research indicated that he had been captured during the Italian campaign and transported to a POW camp in Augusta, Georgia. The war ended, and he registered his desire to remain in the United States, giving as his principal reason that if he were repatriated, it would be to East Germany, and he didn't wish to live under the Communists. U.S. regulations did not accept this as sufficient reason to warrant immigration into the United States, so Heinz Hary solved that problem by marrying one of the WACS engaged in administering the prison camp. With that, Heinz Hary became a legal U.S. immigrant. Five years later, he became a United States citizen. And five years and one month later, he divorced Mrs. Hary, who was now remarried to a postman. Mrs. Hary had been obliquely questioned about her former husband. The FBI agent, posing as a lawyer involved in a complicated distribution of death benefits, wanted to know whether the former Mrs. Hary knew anything about the identity or whereabouts of one Anna Krindler—was she related to her, or to her former husband? Mrs. Ancrum said not to her, or to Heinz, as far as she knew. Heinz often wrote letters to old friends in Germany, she recalled, but never talked to her about them. It would not be a close relative, because she knew that both his parents were dead, and his only sibling, a brother, had been killed in the war. The employers of Heinz Hary were approached, as if by a credit agency. They reported that Hary was a faithful driver, had his own little house, was quiet, withdrawn and, so far as they knew, kept a bank account and was current on unpaid bills—at least, no complaints from creditors had ever reached them.

Blackford had read over the letters to Anna Krindler the night before. They were most fearfully dull. He could not imagine that Anna Krindler could be as interested in hearing about Heinz's drives to Birmingham, Atlanta, Mobile (he was apparently stuck on southern routes) as he was interested in telling her about them. The Agency reported that the letters had withstood radiation tests—there was no secret ink. A superficial cryptographic reading had been given them—no peculiarities leaped to the eye.

So, then, Blackford had now to decide what kind of priority

he should give to developing information on Anna Krindler. He had handled 118 Anna Krindlers in the two months he had been in Germany, and struck out every time as he would on this one, spending two days on the enterprise.

But he felt no sense of futility. It was on Thanksgiving Day, as it happened, that the nature of the enterprise had dramatically changed. Rufus had sent Blackford to Berlin, in part from intuition, in part because Berlin contained, within a small compass, the highest congestion of agents in the world, and for the most obvious of reasons. The Agency maintained, moreover, a number of "assets" (as they were called) in East Berlin. Some of these were ideologically motivated; others were mercenaries. Both were useful. Much of the material they sent Washington was redundant, or pointless. But some of it was not. Rufus sent a second team to Paris, and still others to London and Rome, though the rigorous mail check was made only of letters going to a) West Berlin; and b) all addressees behind the Iron Curtain.

When Blackford arrived, he had made contact with the asset in East Berlin considered by the Agency its hottest property, in part because he was clearly motivated not by loyalty, but greed; was ever so careful to look after his own welfare, yet adventurous enough to take chances; and disposed of brilliantly useful contacts.

"It is this simple," Blackford explained at the Dahlem Museum where they had met, the requisite recognition signals having been exchanged, Blackford going by the code name Sebastian. "We believe it likely that someone in East Berlin is receiving information on a fairly regular basis from an agent in the United States, probably in Washington or New York. Obviously we want to know who that person is. But short of that, we care greatly to know whether the person we are looking for, whoever he is, in fact lives in East Berlin—or, for that matter, in West Berlin. Your assignment is to try to discover whether there are any signs within the KGB centers in East Berlin of any special activity— any special precautions, any unusual procedures or hustle and bustle such as would suggest that extraordinarily useful information is coming in."

What kind of unusual activity?

Blackford had replied that this was obviously for him to judge. "My clients would be willing to pay ten thousand DMs to anyone who assisted you in ascertaining whether we're working in the right city. We would express our gratitude to you with a like sum, and if we succeeded in locating our target, we would double it."

The man known as Reynard, pointing to the museum catalogue describing the corridor in which they strolled, said in a flat voice:

"There is something special going on. I know it."

Blackford, without changing the pitch of his voice, looked up at the "Man in the Golden Helmet" by Rembrandt and said, "Do you have concrete information?"

Reynard said, "A big man came in late June. It was assumed on an inspection trip. But he is still here."

"Do you know who he is?"

"No. I know he is a big man."

"You will find out?"

"I will try to find out."

"You will also try to find out why he is still here? Perhaps he has been demoted."

"I will try to find out. I will be in touch with you in the usual way."

The next engagement with Reynard was not at the museum. Reynard made it understood that he needed more privacy and a more extensive visit. And so it happened that Cabin B on the express train to Munich on Thursday November 26, 1959, was shared by two strangers, one American, one East German.

The conductor took the tickets, passport formalities were transacted. They traveled now, at 120 kilometers per hour, south through Leipzig. Passengers going by and looking in saw two men, both reading, the older, gaunt man smoking a cigarette. They went separately to dinner. While the passengers ate, they passed Plauen. At Hof, on the West German border, East German officials disembarked and West Germans boarded, jovial counterparts of the grim northerners, checking passports and asking the routine questions about cigarettes and liquor. The West Germans in turn got off, and the train roared on toward

Nuremberg and Munich. Blackford went back to the cabin, and Reynard joined him a few minutes later. He drew the blinds and locked the door. Reynard inspected every corner of the sleeper for microphones.

He then drew from his briefcase a notebook and began to read aloud. "You can take this down later, at your own speed, Sebastian. But I'll read right through it here. General Nikolai Kankrin, whose biographical history I have in detail, is one of the four principal assistants of Shelepin. He has been an inspector general for the KGB, survived the Beria purge, usually stays in Moscow, and makes occasional trips to different centers.

"He arrived in June. He displaced the regular man, occupying his quarters. Beginning one week or so after his arrival, procedures for relaying information to Moscow were changed. It used to be done by one courier taking the commercial flight to Moscow. The courier now goes by military jet."

"How often?"

"It varies. Sometimes every two weeks. Sometimes two or three times in one week. It is definitely irregular, it is definitely a change in procedures. I have the information from someone who coordinates between the general and the Air Force. I have pictures of General Kankrin and the military jet, and I would be obliged for twenty thousand Deutsche Marks. Only I want them in dollars or Swiss francs, which is one reason why I brought you to Austria."

After that, the business of looking into the Anna Krindlers in East Berlin seemed less academic.

The meeting, requested by Rufus, was held in the Cabinet Room. The appointments secretary had said three o'clock, and of course the designated participants were there—the Directors of the CIA and of the FBI, the new Secretary of Defense Thomas Gates; the chairman of the Joint Chiefs, Nathan Twining, was there with time to spare. The President, who had acquired his habits in the military, was on the whole punctual. When, seven years ago, he had found himself commander-in-chief, he permitted himself the occasional indulgence of being five or ten minutes late. He confessed it once to Mamie (it was the night of his reelection). . . . Although the early results portended a landslide over Adlai Stevenson, word from Stevenson headquarters in Chicago was vague as to just when the Governor would go to the ballroom of the hotel to concede defeat. When the President's jubilant campaign manager went to the presidential suite and told him that Stevenson had not yet set a time at which to capitulate and congratulate the victor, the President looked at his watch. It was 10:55. "Tell the son of a bitch I'm going to proclaim my victory at exactly 11:15, then I'm going to bed."

The message, bowdlerized, was instantly transmitted to Chicago, throwing Stevenson into considerable disarray, inasmuch as the convention was that the victor await the concession of the loser. Since Stevenson wanted above all to make a belletristic concession, he had to compose it. He could not bring himself to do so ahead of the event, notwithstanding the adamant despondency of the polls; and so now in the noisy suite, where his principal aides had begun to pay more attention to the bar than to the late returns, Stevenson retired quietly to an adjacent bedroom with only a yellow pad and a pencil, rejecting any offer of help. Of course, there was not enough time. Stevenson couldn't possibly compose something beautiful—something lapidary—descend to the ballroom, silence his lachrymose followers, and deliver his concession, all by 11:15. So that when he had it written out and it was being typed, along about midnight, and he asked anxiously where the President was, hoping that he would be photographed reacting in some way to Stevenson's eloquent message, it was perhaps the hardest blow of a hard evening to learn that the television cameras had followed Eisenhower from the hotel to the White House, where the door had been most conclusively shut to the press. It was then that his running mate, Estes Kefauver, weighed in with the elegant suggestion that the concession be made in the form of a telegram sent to the President at the White House, as though this were quite habitual. Sure, the commentators would catch it, but not the crowd inside. So that the words were quickly typed in, "I have"—here Adlai Stevenson stretched the truth a little—"one hour ago, instructed my office to send the following telegram to President Eisenhower, at the White House." One hour ago. Neat. That would have been *before* Ike's victory statement. . . .

It was later that night, with only Mamie and one or two others sitting about the living room of the family quarters, that Ike let off steam about Stevenson's tactics during the last weeks of the campaign, during which Stevenson had solemnly assured his countrymen that if they voted for Eisenhower, they would get Nixon. Without saying so in as many words, Governor Stevenson had implied that the medical statistics simply gainsaid any reasonable possibility that a sixty-six-year-old man who had had a heart attack and an ileitis operation would likely endure another four years of White House activity, in which case the catastrophe of a President Richard Nixon would confront the nation.

Ike had a glass of whiskey in his hand. "Every now and then," he said to his jovial and constant companion George Allen, "they say I'm 'ornery.' Well, every now and then I am. Right, Mamie? Shut up, Mamie. Every now and then I am, and this is one of those times. You know what? *I'll* attend *his* funeral. That's a promise."

Eventually only Mamie was left, and Ike was feeling pretty good. That was the occasion when, leaning back in the comfortable armchair and looking up at the discreetly lit portrait of Abraham Lincoln, he permitted himself to speak of the perquisites of his office. "I have to confess it, Mamie, when I arrive for a Cabinet meeting and all those people stand up, people who are tops in their own fields, I—well, it doesn't exactly annoy me. Took me a while before I remembered not to say 'At ease!' That was funny, that first time. Everybody laughed. Huh? Well, I guess just one more. Light. Don't get reelected President of the United States every day. Last time around for a Republican was 1900, McKinley. What? McKinley. William McKinley. The one who was shot by that anarchist. They strung him up in a hurry. Yup, four more years, Mamie. . . ."

The President entered the Cabinet Room, two doors down the hall from his own office, at 3:05. He greeted everyone in the room with a nod, with the exception of Rufus, whose hand he took. "Still got my dog tags, Rufus?"

"Yes, Mr. President." Ike had told Rufus in 1944 that if his predictions about Omaha Beach proved correct, Ike would give him the dog tags he had been issued when he graduated from West Point.

"All right. Rufus, go ahead." The President leaned back, thus exhibiting the confidence he showed only when he turned the meeting over to men of demonstrated economy of expression.

Rufus told the President that on the basis of extensive discussions with the Director of the CIA and the military, he had arrived at certain recommendations which, he felt, warranted presidential attention.

For three months, said Rufus, Operation Tango (thus had the enterprise been dubbed, when J. Edgar Hoover—J. Edgar Hoover!—had pointed out that it takes two to tango, and if *we* don't *take* minutes of National Security Council meetings, *they* won't *get* minutes of the National Security Council) has maintained the credibility of the Soviet mole by making certain to include in the minutes of every meeting of the Executive Committee of the National Security Council one or more pieces of information which are accurate, but which Soviet knowledge of hurts us only marginally. These tidbits have been put together on a random basis after careful consultation with relevant specialists, in most cases—in every case, excepting the Joint Chiefs and the two Directors—people who don't know what we're up to.

"But we're stretching it a little thin now. We run the risk of giving them frothy material, on the basis of which they might guess we've caught on to them."

The President interrupted. "I take it"—he looked at Hoover—"that we haven't actually got the mole?"

The FBI chief bit his lips and shook his head. He knew better than to proffer excuses. But suddenly he thought better of maintaining complete silence. "Remember, Mr. President, we can stop it overnight by merely overhauling the whole minutes distribution system. But the decision was made last September that we wanted to exploit this whole business, and that means keeping the leak open."

"Doesn't mean you can't find the goddam mole."

Hoover said nothing.

The President turned again to Rufus, who acted on the signal to proceed.

"I've studied the alternatives, and am here to make a recommendation. It's that we give out everything we've gotten from the U-2."

The President was genuinely startled, but said nothing.

Rufus laid it out as follows.

On the one hand, the U-2 had collected material of such importance as to redirect the entire U.S. strategic effort—away from bombers, toward missiles. "The U-2," said Rufus—but here he paused. He felt it appropriate that the Director of Central Intelligence, the agency responsible for the enterprise, should make the summary. He turned to him. "Allen?"

"Well, Mr. President, you know what it's done. We have a composite picture of military Russia, complete to airfields, atomic production sites, power plants, oil storage depots, submarine yards, arsenals, railroads, missile factories, launch sites, radar installations, industrial complexes, antiaircraft defenses. The U-2 has collected information with speed, accuracy, and dependability that could only be equaled by the acquisition of technical documents directly from Soviet offices and laboratories."

"It is proposed we give all this up?" the President said, turning to Rufus.

Rufus explained that very recent experiences of U-2s flying out of Turkey and Pakistan, north toward missile center Tyura Tam, indicated that Soviet SAM capability was coming dangerously close to achieving the 75,000-foot altitude necessary to knock down the U-2s, and that under the circumstances their days were definitely numbered.

"The idea, Mr. President, would be to ride the hell out of the U-2s for the next three or four months, giving us a comprehensive picture of what's going on. The integrated results of these flights can plausibly occupy a considerable part of the agenda of any NSC meeting—and constitute the bulk of the minutes. The Soviet Union is therefore learning that we know things about the Soviet Union which they of course already know. And the thrust of the NSC conversations can be that if at the coming summit meeting they throw the U-2 at you, you can say you went that route only because the Russians refused to cooperate on your open skies inspection proposal."

Ike smiled. He had always been proud of his proposal, made in

1955, that the two superpowers extend to each other the right to use freely the airspace over their territory in order to guard against surprises, and therefore mitigate the possibility of accidental war. He brought his fingers to his mouth, in the characteristic pose. "But so we go ahead and pass this on—where's the zinger? What's Operation Tango going to end up doing for our team?"

"Mr. President, I do have something in mind. But it isn't fully worked out. The timing is very important. And we can proceed only after we have fingered the Soviet agents operating here. Mr. Hoover is advancing on that with great thoroughness, and Tango has its own teams working in Europe, and we have some very good information. But the integration of the entire thing, with your permission, I'd rather put together later."

Ike let out a trace of a smile. He had heard the phrase "with your permission" a half-dozen times during the Second World War. It was Rufus's way of saying, "You can fire me if you want to or, for all I know, you can have me shot, but you're not going to get from me at this moment what I don't want to tell you."

The President spoke. "Very well. Now, on the matter of the U-2, I take it"—he looked about the table: the pipe-smoking imperturbable aristocrat in charge of intelligence; the ruddy, beefy, headstrong chief of American domestic security; the elegant Wall Street lawyer with the quick mind and decisive manner, now in Defense; the seasoned professional officer, whom Ike always preferred to see in uniform, but hardly ever did anymore— "I assume that on the matter of the fairly imminent obsolescence of the U-2, you are all in agreement?"

The Secretary of Defense spoke. "Perhaps this qualification should be made, sir. The Soviets are developing the technology to bring down the U-2. Correct. But it will take them anywhere from one to three years before they deploy that technology to keep any U-2 out of the Soviet Union. They're working on a prototype SAM, with infrared pursuit capability. But to surround Russia with these SAMs would be one hell of an effort. They'd begin by concentrating them around targets they want especially to protect from view. But the U-2 will still be useful until we get the satellite revved up: and then, of course, we can fly back, right over the SAMs—four hundred miles above them. Speaking for the DOD, Rufus's plan is okay by me."

The rest, by gesture, concurred.

"Is that all?" the President turned to Rufus.

"Not quite. I'd like to suggest that at the next NSC meeting you announce that you want to put in a lot of time with Secretary of State Herter on the Berlin question, and with State Department specialists, that you'll meet with them on an *ad hoc* basis in the Oval Office. The objective is to slow down the number of NSC Executive meetings, to maybe one every two weeks or so."

"Suits me." He looked about him. No one spoke. Simultaneously he depressed a button under the lip of the table, and rose. By the time he was on his feet, his appointments secretary had opened the door for him. The others stood and the President said, "Good afternoon, gentlemen. Nice thinking, Rufus."

# CHAPTER 12

It was Valentine's Day, and Michael reproached himself that he had not written to Amanda. He would write her tomorrow—tonight there was too much work to do, and he and Blackford had already had a long day. Perhaps he would spin Amanda a yarn about how St. Valentine's Day *really* originated not in Italy, as everyone thought, but in the Holy Roman Empire, in the northeasternmost part of which—Berlin—Michael was now situated, and here they were *very* strict on the point that St. Valentine's authentic birthday, given the Gregorian calendar change, should be celebrated not on the fourteenth of February, but the twenty-first. Oh well, worth trying.

He and Blackford, having dined at thirty different restaurants (they carried credentials from Temple Fielding, and were ostensibly collecting data for Fielding's annual guide to Europe), were full-circle back at the Alpach, on Uhlandstrasse, where they had eaten their first dinner out together in Berlin, back in

November. They cooked for themselves on odd nights, went out the balance of the time, and made it a point not to become fixtures at any single restaurant. It meant a lot of exploration, and they did a great deal of walking, otherwise using mostly public transportation. At the smoky, dimly lit, chanteuse-dominated Alpach, two girls had approached them and one of them, who looked startlingly like Marlene Dietrich in the *Blue Angel*, made all the requisite gestures to Blackford ("I can't understand why women gravitate to you, when I am the alternative," Michael had once commented). Blackford told the girls that, unhappily, he and his companion were waiting for their wives, and could not risk being compromised. Marlene Dietrich fluttered her eyelashes, puffed on her cigarette holder, slunk her tightly sheathed torso this way and that, and said that her girl friend and she were very much taken by the two young Americans, and perhaps they might care to visit them during the afternoon? She passed Blackford a card. He glanced at it: "Fräulein Nina Deutsch, Caterer. 24-hour service. Tel: 75-85-77. Address: 1161 Fasanenstrasse." Blackford pocketed the card and winked at her as, followed by a buxom blonde dressed like a Tyrolean doll, she slithered away. Michael sighed, "All work and no play."

Blackford looked up at him. "Here's the card," he slipped it to him. "Go on over after we line up the portfolios tonight if you want to. Want me to set it up?"

Michael's dark face very nearly blushed. But he took the card. "I don't know. Anyway, I wouldn't want to trouble you. My English combined with her German is probably enough to establish a connection."

"You'd better insulate that connection."

Michael smiled, and emptied his stein of beer.

Two hours later Blackford yawned, slid the carefully annotated index cards to one side of the table, went to the refrigerator and brought out a bottle of white wine. He opened it, moved to the sitting room and slouched down on the sofa. "Wine?"

"Sure," said Michael. It occurred to Blackford that in the four years he had known Michael, he hadn't once declined any suggestion. Blackford was tempted one day to say to him casually, "Suicide?" But the intensely lovable companion, with whom he had, after three months of constant companionship, what felt like an imperishable bond, would instantly have recognized the sarcasm. When you get a person of such thorough amiability, thought Blackford, you shouldn't tinker with the finished product; you might mutilate it. They had maintained the code, and Blackford still didn't know what the gentle Michael had done during his preceding travels for the Agency. He could not imagine Michael engaging in the kind of skulduggery that would hurt anyone.

The following morning, between eleven and twelve, could prove critical. True, twice before Reynard had summoned them, and twice before they had been disappointed. But Reynard, in that morning's telephone conversation, had seemed genuinely excited. "I think I've got her, Sebastian, I think I've got her."

Shortly after eleven the next morning Blackford would go to a designated address: an abandoned garage on Mittelstrasse—to which garage Blackford had the key. Reynard would be there waiting for him. Fifteen minutes later, Michael would arrive. From the loft of the old garage they would have a clear view of No. 48 Mittelstrasse. Reynard, without specifying, wanted them to see what he anticipated would take place in front of that building sometime between noon and two o'clock.

"God, I hope the trail is hot this time," Blackford said, staring at the ceiling. Michael poured himself a glass of wine and smiled. "I do too, Black. But you know, it hasn't all been dull."

"Goddammit, Michael, you're the most patient son of a bitch in the history of the world. If you were Sisyphus, you'd have accepted that rock with a shit-eating grin."

Michael—of course—smiled. "I don't know," he said. "I'm just —I guess—just happy. I'm working on the right team. I'm sitting a couple of miles from where Hitler finally blasted his own brains out. After initiating policies that, among other things, reminded my pop that he was half Jewish and therefore not quite human, and certainly not to be trusted to head a labor union. So I'm spending my life as a professional."

"What do you mean 'professional'?"

"A professional soldier. Working against . . . well, I guess I'd call them Hitler's successors—why not?—though in fact the Commies antedated Hitler. What the hell, five months ago you were designing buildings and subways. That must have been more fun than trailing innocent Germans around Berlin. But you choose to do this, right?"

Blackford said nothing. Over the years he had found that Sally had, however obliquely, intimidated him: so much so that he thought it, well, a little . . . vainglorious to suggest he was devoting his life to an idealistic project. Not because—his blood raced as he thought of it—*not that he thought he was engaged in anything less*. It was just that, oh well, anti-Communist activity is something other people, not quite PLU (as his mother in London would say), do; vaguely unpleasant, like making sausages. People Like Us occasionally use, not create, sausages. And you don't invite your butcher to tell you pantingly what he had to go through to make you those sausages. But he felt he had to say something.

"I know, I know, Michael. I'm not saying you're patient to engage in this particular profession, I'm saying you're patient about going so long without results. We engineers are spoiled that way. The first day we lay the first brick, the second day the second, the third day the third, the fourth day the fourth, and before too long we have a bridge, or a subway—"

"Or a monument to FDR."

Blackford smiled.

"But it's the same thing, isn't it, Blacky? Only we're constructing by a process of elimination. Just think of all the bricks we now *know* aren't the right bricks."

"Yeah. Unless the right brick put one over on us."

It was midnight, and suddenly Blackford felt one of those late night accesses of energy that from time to time galvanized him, routing torpor, fatigue.

"Michael?"

"Yeah."

"Let's have a look at that card."

"What card?"

"Marlene Dietrich's."

Michael rose, went to the dining room where his jacket hung, and returned.

Blackford studied it. "Whaddayasay?" His voice was a salacious imitation of Clark Gable's.

Michael's face brightened. He took a deep draft of the wine. "Why not? Who knows, we might make an important discovery."

Blackford went to the telephone. "Right. Besides, we have to report all opportunities for tourists to Temple Fielding. And anyway, our instructions were to effect deep penetration, right?"

"Right!" Michael, now standing, walked over to the bathroom. Blackford could hear the electric razor. "Hurry up with that call, Black."

A woman's voice answered the telephone. Blackford rattled away in German. While talking, he reached for his own tie and, by minor contortions of the neck and ear, managed to slip it on while still in conversation. "*Ja ja, zehn Minuten.*"

Michael said anxiously, "Okay?"

"Fräulein Deutsch is occupied." Michael's face fell. "But two of her associates are available and are equally skilled caterers. I said we were very experienced gourmets, and required the very best. She said the very best was what we would get." Michael's face brightened.

Blackford walked over to the map. He knew the street—he knew every street in Berlin. He looked at the number, and at the three-dimensional image of the building. "Looks like a boardinghouse. Pretty fancy address, though. Ah well."

In the taxi their conversation grew lighthearted, and then lightheaded, and by the time they arrived, they were both laughing loudly.

Blackford looked up at the building; all the shades were drawn. It was four stories high. He rang the bell. A disembodied voice answered, "Who is it?" Blackford gave the name he had used over the telephone. "We have an appointment."

The door opened and an unsmiling, trim elderly woman dressed in the uniform of a practical nurse bade them follow her.

In the reception room the barman was active, pouring champagne and whiskey. Seated behind a circular desk was a madam of adamant amiability, smoking a cigarette, a glass of champagne in front of her. Romantic music issued at considerable volume from an amplifier that seemed to be located across the wide room, overstuffed with couches and ottomans, on several of which there was muted conversation, with now and again a vaulting peal of laughter. There were two men at one corner. At another, a couple. On the larger couch, two girls and two men, a bottle of champagne on the coffee table in front of them. The girls' skirts were short, and the cut of their dresses accentuated their figures. But they'd have passed more or less unnoticed in church.

Michael left the arrangements in Blackford's hands, and in due course the two were led through a door, down a corridor decorated by fancily framed and lit pictures of the copulative ingenuities of mysterious India. The same "nurse" who had opened the front door now knocked on the door of a room designated as 12. A sultry voice said, "Come in." Blackford motioned to Michael, who smiled boyishly and started to head inside, stopping only for a moment to say, "Rendezvous?"

"Back at the house. Let's for the first time in three months do something out of sync with each other, okay?"

Michael smiled, straightened his tie, and the "nurse," announcing that Fräulein Naki awaited him, closed the door behind him. Leading Blackford still farther down the hall to the door marked 17, she knocked and told him that Fräulein Adele bade him join her. He walked through the door, which shut behind him. Sitting on a couch, a cooler of champagne in front of her, was a woman of very full bosom and shapely legs, platinum-blond hair combed straight, obscuring half of one of two beautiful hazel eyes. She looked at Blackford with her eyes wide open, her lips parting just enough to exhibit the succulent white teeth. With her right hand she stroked the glass on the adjacent desk, and maneuvered her body so that a plump and upright breast worked its way outside the folds of her nightgown.

Blackford went to the large bed, sat down, and began to laugh. For a moment he thought he might actually lose control of himself, and it was only when he saw that Adele, her expression now changed, was moving her hand in the direction of a highly visible bell on the wall that he took control of himself, rose, bowed gallantly, and said, "Permit me to introduce myself. I'm Adrian."

She hesitated. "At what were you laughing?"

"Oh," said Blackford, his mind racing, "it's—it's that you're wearing the absolutely identical nightgown my girl in Washington wears, and the coincidence was just too much." Adele smiled and brought Blackford closer to her, removing his coat and filling a glass of champagne, all this without moving from her languorous position on the couch.

Adele indeed. "Adele" had consumed—when you added them all up—probably thirty hours of Blackford's time during the past six weeks, ending only that morning when, reviewing Günter's step-by-step reconstruction of her movements over a period of three days, and examining her photographs, for which neither Berlin Station nor Washington had any counterpart, Blackford authoritatively struck her off the list of possible suspects. "She sees too many people," he told Michael. "Hell, she's probably a call girl." Michael, looking at the picture, said he doubted that. "Too much class. Maybe she works for a travel agency." By this time he knew a considerable amount about Adele's background, and everything about her regular and detailed correspondence with her sister in New York, which had put her on the suspect list last November.

Now, he figured, I can get a free ride by astonishing her, by telling her her fortune! No, Blackford, no, he said to himself. Then he wondered why he had overlooked asking Günter to get the results of her last Wassermann test. . . .

But that was his final preoccupation with business. Adele was more engrossing now than ever she had been when he studied her face in his room at Hochstrasse. He had, so to speak, spent weeks in disrobing her. Here, in a matter of minutes, she had disrobed him. He had spent hours attempting to penetrate her secrets, if any. In just a few minutes, he found her secret entirely, joyously, hospitably penetrable, and, after the first explosive round, his mind went back to the irony. Perhaps he might add an addendum to the report he had prepared for Rufus. Something like, "Checked her out all the way. Left no room for doubt."

Mustn't play games with Rufus.

Blackford rose at eight. He could easily remember mornings when he had bounded out of bed with less difficulty. Ah well, let's see, he thought, is entropy—the word was getting around—the right word for it? No, probably not, though it sounded better, to describe his condition, than other words that came to mind. He smiled at something Adele had said—but smiling and brushing his teeth were incompatible, and he decided he had better get on with his ablutions. It was his day to make breakfast, though as often as not he would rise on his duty day to find that Michael had already prepared it. Prepared breakfast and—supreme sacrifice—gone out to the corner restaurant to buy the morning paper. Ugh. He put the water kettle on the stove and, wearing only a T-shirt and pants, stuffed himself into his overcoat, rang for the elevator, and pitched himself into the cold, walking to the newsstand and picking up *Die Welt*. He fumbled with the change, head still bowed against the cold, turned back, and let himself in. The water was boiling. He broke four eggs and one tenth of a bar of butter into the pan, and added lots of salt and pepper. Time to wake Michael.

With a hot cup of coffee in hand, cream and sugar stirred, he kicked open the door of Michael's room.

"Wake up, Romeo. Izza dis my pretty-witty little Michelino? Michelino wantsa niza cuppa coffee, uh? All right, goddammit. Wake up." Michael shot up in bed, his eyes unfocused.

"What time did you get in?"

"In?" said Blackford meditatively. "Oh, I'd say about four and one-half minutes after I last saw you."

"Oh come on." Michael took the coffee. "What time did you get back here?"

"Before Romeo got back, because I looked in, and Romeo wasn't in his room."

"Aahhh . . ." came from Michael's lips after sipping the coffee.

" 'My ears have yet not drunk a hundred words/Of that tongue's utterance, yet I know the sound,/Art thou not Romeo . . . ?' "

"Black, would you cut it out? Please? What time is it?" Michael got out of bed.

"Eight-fifteen; eggs in two minutes."

At first Michael ate tentatively, but then greedily. By the time he had finished his third piece of toast, his color was restored. Blackford read the paper.

"Any news?"

"Yup. The State Department has revealed that it has denied

visas to East German reporters to cover the Olympics at Squaw Valley."

"That wasn't very nice of the State Department."

"Especially after what the Czechs did. Listen: 'American hockey coach Jack Riley of West Point credited Nikolai Sologubov, Soviet team captain, with first suggesting that the U.S. team take inhalations of oxygen to overcome fatigue after the 2nd period of its game with Czechoslovakia, when the Czechs led by 4–3. After following Sologubov's advice, the Americans rallied for 6 goals in the 3rd period to win."

Michael laughed. "Oh my God, poor Sologubov. Do they play hockey in Siberia?"

"Get this. 'The Russian coach, asked to comment on his team's performance, said, "They played like goddam amateurs!"'"

"*Imagine!* Sending *amateurs* to the Olympics! What *are* the Russians coming to!"

"We'd better get to work," Blackford said, emptying his coffee cup.

Blackford showered, dressed, and attacked the files. At ten he would check the mailbox. Michael, with a magnifying glass, was comparing sets of pictures. A few minutes after ten, Blackford came in with the mail. The Washington material was picked up from a drop, but it was time to hear from Sally, or his mother. He came with several letters in hand, tossing one to Michael. Blackford opened Sally's letter and experienced, as ever, a slight quickening of the pulse. It was a long, discursive letter, adamantly affectionate, with only a single inflection of the old hostility ("Will the Agency permit Senator Kennedy to run for President?"), a long and amusing anecdote involving a student who had written a term paper spelling the subject's name throughout "Jane Austin," and other levities, calculated to make Blackford laugh—and feel homesick. He heard a noise in the bathroom.

He walked over to it and opened the door to see Michael bent over the toilet.

"Michael, you okay?"

"Yeah."

Blackford could smell the nausea. Tactfully, he drew the door shut. When, after ten minutes, Michael had not emerged, he went back. This time he knocked on the door. The reply was a most uncharacteristic "Yeah?"

"Michael, are you going to be able to make it? To Mittelstrasse?"

Again, just: "Yeah."

Blackford stepped back. He was concerned. Michael had eaten a good breakfast, and seemed easily to have metabolized the dissipations of the preceding night. Blackford took the customary precautions, checking his pockets, taking his special wallet. And sliding the bulky envelope—fifty thousand Deutsche Marks, authorized only yesterday by code—into a tobacco pouch, the tightly packaged bills covered by loose tobacco and a small weatherbitten pipe, the whole fitting bulkily, but not obtrusively, in the deep pocket of his heavy woolen trenchcoat. Once again he approached the door of the bathroom.

"I'm off. Remember, you get to the garage at 11:14. The door will open to let you in. No knocking."

"All right." The tone of voice was metallic. Blackford was genuinely concerned. On reaching the door, he thought to return to the bathroom and have it out with Michael. He decided against it. But he knew that at 11:14 Michael would slide through the garage door.

Blackford turned right and, as usual when deciding to hail a taxi, went on a block or two and turned a corner or two. He entered a cab and gave his destination—the center of the Tiergarten, Strasse des 17. Juni.

In ten or fifteen minutes he was there, the center of Berlin's oldest park, the pride of the great city over a period of two hundred years. It had been something of a battleground during the war. On the park the Nazis had impacted their antiaircraft batteries, mutilating the grounds. Though ironically it wasn't until after the war had been lost—or, better, won—that the irreversible damage was done. In the bitter winter following the death of Hitler, Berliners cut down the trees, even as the French had done to the trees in the Bois de Boulogne during the siege of Paris seventy-five years earlier—to make heat. Trees that had taken one hundred years to grow. Much had been done to replace them, but the forest looked young as Blackford walked down the Strasse des 17. Juni toward the Brandenburg Gate.

On his left was the Soviet Memorial, a Russian enclave in West Berlin, guarded by two Soviet soldiers: a colonnade surmounted by a massive statue of a soldier, flanked by the usual artillery pieces and tanks. It was put together, celebrating the Soviet gift for cannibalization, from the marbled remains of the former Reichstag nearby, whose destruction by fire in 1933 gave Hitler the excuse he needed to suspend the opposition. Now it was redeveloped, at a cost of one hundred million DMs. Blackford could discern, though not easily, the Italian Renaissance structure built to house the Prussian parliament. He walked on to the Brandenburg Gate, just inside East Berlin, where the Volkspolizist extended his hand, examined Blackford's passport, and waved him on. Here was what had been the Arch of Triumph for the German capital, through which victorious troops had been accustomed to march. Only a year or two earlier had the famous quadriga been restored—the two-wheeled chariot, drawn by four stallions, that sits on top of the Gate. It had been destroyed during the war, but in 1957 West Berliners discovered the molds in which the original had been cast in the late eighteenth century; and, in a relatively uncharted venture of cooperation, East and West Germans worked side by side to restore the Gate to its former eminence. Blackford passed the Soviet Embassy, turning left on Schadowstrasse toward Mittelstrasse, a ten-minute walk from the Gate.

He went at a brisk but unhectic pace. In his gloved hand he clutched a rolled-up newspaper, in the fashion of bus and subway riders. He stopped outside a hardware shop to look in the window, in fact to look at his watch. At seven minutes to eleven Reynard would open the garage door. It was now three minutes short of that moment, and Blackford had two blocks to walk. He set out, slightly moderating his pace.

He turned the corner at Mittelstrasse. The street was dilapidated, but then so was the whole of East Berlin. On the south side there were row houses, opposite them a few makeshift buildings abutting a block-wide area that hadn't yet been completely cleared from the rubble of yesteryear's bombings. Fifteen years, and still uncleared! There was no comparable block in West Berlin. Blackford spotted, just beyond the derelict building without windows or shutters, a concrete garage with a prewar gas pump on its old tarmac, the rubber hose gray with dust and rot. Blackford edged closer to the buildings on the north side of the street. When he found himself abreast of the gas pump he paused, turned, and walked directly into the space that had opened up for him. The door closed behind him. There was light in the loft, insufficient to illuminate the area where he stood. Reynard turned on his flashlight.

"Sorry about the cold. Believe it or not, there's still electricity here. Otherwise I wouldn't be able to show you the little film I have to show you. Since we may be here for a while—in fact, you may have to come back tomorrow and tomorrow and tomorrow—we must struggle to keep warm." Blackford could feel Reynard's cynical smile, though he couldn't see his features. Why on earth, Blackford thought angrily, didn't I bring along a flashlight? Innocent stuff to carry in a greatcoat in midwinter, where the daylight goes before six. He wondered whether Michael would remember to bring his.

"What do you mean?" Blackford asked, while following Reynard up the ladder to the loft.

"They may not act today. But Monday is a very good day. Especially since last Friday and Saturday the postal workers were on strike. Today, the mailman will bring the mail for Friday, Saturday, Sunday, and Monday."

Blackford, gripping the ladder, was hardly helped by occasional bursts of the flashlight into his face—Reynard trying to be courteous. Not his style. Blackford subconsciously counted the rungs on the ladder—seven—before reaching loft level. He gratefully approached the little heater that gave off its orange glow in the dark. But then, he thought, probably he had reason to be grateful for the cold: it stood off the dissipated, but still mephitic, odors of oil, gas, rust, and rotted and burnt rubber.

"Come," Reynard beckoned him toward the semicircular mullioned window overlooking the street. "You will have to stand on the wooden case. When your friend comes, we can all take turns watching for the postman. Meanwhile I will show you the film. You brought the money, no?"

"Yup. I brought the money, Reynard. But unless I'm convinced you've got the right drop, the money stays with me."

"We will see. Today, I hope. If not, soon. I will show the movie," he stopped to look at his watch, "as soon as your friend comes. I will go down the ladder now. He will be here in two minutes."

With a single illumination of the ladder, Reynard turned around and, flashlight in hand, descended into the void. On reaching the ground floor he looked again at his watch. Blackford stood up on the case to see whether he could discern the approach of Michael, but the angle was wrong. In a minute he saw daylight below, and the profile of a figure moving in. The door closed and it was dark again.

"Your friend," said Reynard.

"How're you doing . . . buddy?" Blackford said.

"All right" was the reply. The tone of voice had not changed.

"Did you bring a flashlight?"

"Yes." A second beam pierced the darkness. Michael, with his usual thoroughness, did some instant reconnoitering. The garage was mostly empty, but there were some barrels scattered about, and workbenches, and rusty oilcans, and a few lengths of pipe and discarded hoses.

In German, Reynard told Michael to climb the ladder. Blackford no longer needed to translate functional German for Michael's benefit. Holding the light in his right hand, Michael worked his way up, followed by Reynard. The beams from Reynard's light never fell on Michael's face. Blackford was anxious to look him in the face, but didn't want to borrow the flashlight for that purpose.

"Now, either sit on the floor, or stand"—Reynard guided Blackford by the shoulders—"approximately there. Your friend at your side. All right? Now I will go to the projector."

A crude but serviceable screen—a bedsheet hanging from two convenient nails—had been installed. An 8-mm projector was brought out from behind a barrel. Flashlight in mouth, Reynard connected the cord to the electrical outlet. The projector creaked on, focusing on a postman arriving at a clearly visible No. 48 Mittelstrasse. He deposited the mail in a postbox situated inside the archway and perfunctorily rang the bell, resuming his rounds. The camera zoomed in on the postbox, and in an exasperatingly long couple of minutes the door to No. 48 opened and a woman's sweatered arm reached out through the opening and with a little key unlocked the bottom tray of the box, taking out its contents. The door closed. The screen went to white.

"Here," Reynard said, "obviously I did not keep the camera running. But I read to you now from my log, Sebastian. 'The . . . lady . . . opened her mailbox at 12:05.' What you will now see is the camera which I turned back on at"—his flashlight focused down on his notebook—"at 12:21."

The moving picture was now of a Wartburg, a driver, and a passenger in the front seat. The car stopped directly in front of No. 48. The front-seat passenger, a man of middle age and exaggerated paunch, wearing a brown fedora, groped his way out of the front seat and rang the bell. The camera focused closely on his hand. The doorbell he depressed by more than a single casual flick. Less than an elaborate code, Blackford noted: something simple, on the order, perhaps, of – – –. In less than one minute the door opened again; again, only partly. And the woman's hand extended through the narrow opening, giving the man an envelope.

He walked casually back into the car, and now the camera zoomed onto the license plate, IZ 58–23. The car drove off, and the screen went again to white.

"Now," said Reynard, his voice audibly excited, "now—watch this."

The screen showed 63–65 Unter den Linden, from a discreet distance—"You cannot, my dear Sebastian, place a camera too close. It is, after all, the principal KGB office outside of Moscow."

"That's good news," Blackford said. "I thought it was in Washington."

"I like your jokes, Sebastian. But now watch. Because my camera has a very highly developed telescopic lens. Watch now. And please understand, Sebastian, it took many hours of filming and watching to get this."

The camera—after blipping through a number of obvious false starts, filming sedans that turned out to be of similar model and color, but not distinctively qualified—now focused on a car that came to a stop, having paused first at the well-guarded sentry post under the portico of the recently rebuilt Soviet Embassy. "The time now"—Reynard beamed his flashlight on his log—"is 12:30—in normal circumstances, the time required to go, let us say, from 48 Mittelstrasse to 63–65 Unter den Linden." The camera brought in the sedan, and by the time it came to a full stop under the wide portico, its focus was exclusively on the license plate: IZ 58–23. "Now watch, watch," Reynard said excitedly. The camera lens had obviously reached the limit of its telescopic reach, but succeeded in discerning the profile of the man who opened the door and mounted the steps. That profile was distinctive.

The screen went again to white. And Reynard turned off the main switch, reducing them all to virtual blackness. Only the beam from Reynard's flashlight, muted by his fingers to prevent it from blinding, lit, barely, the surroundings: insufficiently to discern the features of any of the three participants. Michael had not said a word.

Reynard, who through the screening had relied on Michael to keep one eye on the street to catch the arrival of the postman, said he thought the evidence he had already shown them was conclusive, but the probabilities were high that the entire performance would be repeated any moment now, always assuming that the post brought something "from America." He did not need to wait long. "Come!" he hissed. The three men were now mounted on the wooden crate. The postman—the same man as in the moving picture—approached No. 48. His movements were identical. Moments after he left, the hand reached out with the key. And fifteen minutes later the car approached. Blackford could not make out the license plate, but Reynard handed him a set of pocket binoculars. Now he could see that the numbers were the same. And the courier, unmistakably the same. The Wartburg drove off.

"You are satisfied, Sebastian? But why should I ask if you are satisfied? I have risked my neck for your enterprise. I have worked for three months, for three months solidly. You have seen only one small portion of all the film I have had to make. Of course you are satisfied! It is I"—he rose, rather grandly, Blackford thought—"who now need satisfaction. Please, dear

Sebastian, and without further delay, we will go down to the garage floor, and you will give me the money."

Blackford didn't move. The silence brought Reynard back again to his seat on the wooden case from which he had operated the projector. "You have problems, Sebastian?" he said, fusing irritation and supplication.

"I think that you have done an excellent job and are entitled to be paid. But we must, Reynard, act as businessmen. For one thing: I must have the film."

Reynard paused. Blackford was certain that the pause was done for theatrical reasons. Clearly he had made up his mind, before the event, whether he would part with the film. But he believed, clearly, that grudging acquiescence should gain him bargaining points.

"I don't know, Sebastian. There is a danger. If it should fall into . . . enemy hands—who knows? No, I think I must keep the film."

"I'll have to have the film, Reynard, or you don't get your money, that's point number one."

Silence.

"Now, point number two: why didn't you film the sequence we just now saw?"

The astonishment of Reynard appeared to be absolutely genuine. *"Film what you have seen with your own eyes?* Sebastian, I must at this point wonder whether you are, as you put it, 'on the level.' If your own superiors will not believe what you have seen with your eyes, they are expected to believe a film which, theoretically—" Reynard stopped himself; what hazardous line of speculation had he adumbrated! ". . . that theoretically, *hypothetically*, could have been an imposture! I mean, it is risky enough to take films under any circumstances, but to take them merely to confirm evidence available from one's own eyes—I mean, Sebastian, you are obviously an experienced agent, but you cannot expect that I, as an experienced agent, would agree to any suggestion so, so—Sebastian, I do not want to offend you —so grotesque."

Blackford didn't move. Was this the right moment to bring Michael to life?

"What do you say—buddy?" Blackford took the conventional care to conceal his colleague's name.

The answer might have been delivered by a robot. "Whatever you say." Not even, "Whatever you say . . . Sebastian." He wished, how he wished he might have a flashlight, casually to pass over Michael's features.

He turned to Reynard. "Okay. My friend and I will go on down. You get the film rewound, and package it. We'll wait for you."

"You strike a very hard bargain, Sebastian," said Reynard, delivering the ritual lines. Blackford's consolation was that Reynard could not begin to know the true value of his information to Blackford's superiors.

So he descended the ladder. Michael shone his light down, obliquely, so that it would not blind Blackford, but would give him a sense of perspective. Michael followed his partner down, his flashlight pointing upward from his hand. On reaching the garage floor, he turned it off and said nothing. Blackford, waiting for Reynard, inched toward the door and, easing the bolt to the right, opened it slightly and surveyed Mittelstrasse from the visible west side. There was nothing there to attract his attention. He looked across the street, at such an angle as would have precluded a binocular from No. 48 from distinguishing him in the blackness of the interior. He looked for the telltale refraction of a light from a binocular, but saw none. Carefully he closed and bolted the door as Reynard, his flashlight on, descended the ladder.

Reynard took a nearby barrel, rolled it to a few feet from the entrance, and turned it vertically, where it served as a circular table.

On it he placed the reel of film.

"Your money please, Sebastian."

Blackford reached into his pocket and tossed the tobacco pouch onto the barrel.

Reynard said, "Your friend will perhaps be so kind as to shine his light on our little, ho ho, table, while I count the money? You understand I do not doubt you, Sebastian; it is that bankers sometimes make mistakes."

Michael obliged by turning his light on and directing it toward the barrel top. Reynard switched his off, put it in his pocket, and opened the pouch. He made a slight noise of disgust as he came on the loose and redolent tobacco. He took the pouch at both ends and turned it upside down. The pipe came tumbling out, a half pound of tobacco, and then a neatly bundled package of bills, bound in rubber bands. First Reynard counted the number of bundles. "*Eins zwei drei vier fünf sechs sieben acht neun zehn.*" Ten bundles. He then said to Blackford, "My dear friend, *you* point to the one I shall examine," giving off a philanthropic grunt that Blackford elected to ignore.

Mechanically, Blackford pointed to one of the ten piles. "That one."

Reynard picked it up. "Shine your light close, friend. Close, so that I can not only count, but inspect."

There were fifty one-hundred-DM bills, and he not only counted but felt them, one by one, calculating aloud monotonously. Blackford's impatience was not easily noticed since, standing outside the flashlight's beam, he was an invisible figure. Michael was, as ever, silent. Along about the time Reynard reached twenty-eight, Blackford permitted himself to say, "Oh shit, Reynard, can't you count faster?" Reynard merely smiled and, if anything, counted even more slowly. When he came to the end, he asked Michael to point his light even more closely at the tobacco pouch, so that he could stuff the bundles back in. In doing so—to the increasing exasperation of Blackford, who was cold, nervous, and apprehensive—he began to count the twenty bundles as he inserted them into the pouch. When he came near to the end he slowed down, as if to enjoy the experience to its fullest: 15 . . . 16 . . . . 17 . . . . 18 . . . . . 19 . . . . . . . 20! And with simultaneous motions he dropped the tobacco pouch into his left pocket and, with his right hand gripping his flashlight, knocked Michael's light out of his hand to the floor. His voice turned to steel.

"*Raise your arms!*" He flashed his light from Blackford to Michael and back. He exchanged the flashlight in his right hand with the automatic pistol in his left. He then shone the light on the automatic pistol. "Move back. Three paces. No more. Exactly three paces." Reynard's voice was entirely collected, entirely authoritative, entirely rehearsed. As Blackford and Michael cautiously retreated, he stopped to pick up Michael's flashlight, still lit. He turned it off and inserted it into his right-hand pocket. Blackford could see, now, only the light from a single flashlight. But, for the first time, he caught a glimpse of Michael's face, because now the beam irradiated light, however dim, over a broad diameter. He was hardly recognizable. He was white, and appeared to have aged. Blackford turned toward Reynard, lowering his eyelids to protect himself from the beam.

"Goddammit, Reynard, what the fuck's going on? You got your money, we got our information—"

"Yes, Sebastian. I do not cheat individual clients. I did not cheat you when you were my client. But the deal is consummated, and I have elected to have a fresh client. He—they—will be with us in . . . just a few moments. They will drive up to this door and take you and Michael away, and you will never again have to suffer such suspense as you have had to suffer in your present occupation. Oh my dear Sebastian, you must know that you are as valuable to me dead as alive. Well, I must be honest. *Not quite.* My alternate clients look forward to the opportunity to question you. But my fee will not by any means be . . . taken from me, if I should have the unfortunate obligation of delivering to them not a live Sebastian, but a dead Blackford Oakes."

It was hard, later, to reconstruct exactly. The whole of it could not have consumed five seconds. In his nightmares, Blackford saw himself as a movie director. *"Quiet on the set. Take one.* We'll walk through this one now, slow motion. Ready? All right, go ahead, Michael. Speak real slow, like one-half normal speed."

The shadowy figure, while the surrounding cameras whir in the infrared light, says in a loud but rhythmically slow voice, "Come . . . in . . . after me . . . Black." Then the considerable figure of Michael, at slow motion, dives toward the flashlight. Simultaneously two shots—the first . . . and then the second—sound. Michael is on the floor, Reynard under him. Blackford advances . . . slowly: hurling himself at the tangled bodies . . . reaching for the flashlight, wrenching it from Reynard . . . spotting the pistol, gripped by Michael's powerful hand against Michael's own abdomen so that it could not be aimed at Blackford. . . . The bodies writhe, but with the light, Blackford has the advantage, and—always slowly, balletically, with both hands, even though one also grips the flashlight—he reaches down to the barrel of the gun and twists it up, up, up, ninety degrees, so that it points now at the rictus of Reynard, and now he moves his hand down and, using Reynard's own fingers—Reynard's wrist has snapped—depresses the trigger once . . . *slowly, goddammit, the director says, slowly* . . . twice. Up the nose, already bloodied, of Reynard. . . . Heaving him aside, Blackford turns to Michael. He is still alive? He gasps out a single word, another, repeatedly, but the word is barely audible.

In the myriad reconstructions, the sound scratched at his memory. Blackford in due course concluded that what Michael had said was "Go! go! go! go! go! go! go! go! go!" It was a single syllable, and he remembered that a car was supposed to come. A KGB car, presumably. He began to lift Michael, but the very first motion precipitated Michael's unmistakable collapse. Blackford was standing. At his feet, Reynard was dead. In his arms, Michael was dead. Tenderly—slowly, in life as in his dreams—he lowered the body. A vague professional imperative asserted itself, and he took from Michael his passport and other papers. And, from Reynard, his papers, and the film from the table top. He rose to go, when he remembered. With grim hatred he kicked over the body, reached into the overcoat, and recovered —a pouch, smelly with rancid tobacco. Now he had instantly to go. He went to the door. Opened it slightly. Saw nothing. He turned in the direction traffic was least likely to come from. He took off his bloody coat, folding it inside out. Around the corner, three blocks down, he bought a ticket to the cinema. In the men's room, in the toilet, he examined himself. The overcoat was soaked with blood. Affecting to wash his face, he looked for other signs of violence on his person, found none. His overcoat artfully slung over his arm, he went down the aisle of the dark movie house and took a seat. He emptied the contents of the coat into his pockets and stuffed it under a seat in a remote corner, bought a box of chocolates from which, as he wandered coatless, distracted, down the street, he picked, cultivating the image of a vague poet, entering the store a block down where, complaining that he had mislaid his coat in the museum, he bought a coarse East German surplus army coat for fifty DMs. Back in the street, in stages, he transferred the booty from his overstuffed jacket to the deep pockets of his trenchcoat. He could not remember—not even in his recurrent nightmare—passing the two guards at the gate. He caught a taxi and made his way to 322 Hochstrasse, leaned on the doorway, barely able to manipulate the key and, as he very nearly fell into the living room, the telephone rang. Somehow, he knew that he must answer it, even though half the telephoning during the past two weeks had come from an enterprising advertising firm that had devised a computer assault mechanism for captive listeners to hear about the new coffee . . . peanuts . . . movies . . . condoms. "Yes," he said hoarsely.

"Günter here. Get out, and I mean get out quickly." The phone went dead.

Blackford knew that he would have to be deliberate. He and Michael had several times discussed procedure in the event of the need to make an emergency departure.

He walked, with near rhythmic exactitude, to the cabinet in the dining room and opened it. He poured a wineglass full of brandy and downed it. He stood there and forced his memory to reconstruct the checklist.

When he planned it with Michael, each would carry a suitcase. Would a single suitcase carry what he needed, or would he need to lug two? He forced himself to think methodically. There were no records anywhere in the apartment of the names or telephone numbers of Günter, Ada, or Niklaus. The photographs, about fifty, were of men and women he now knew *not* to be implicated—at least, not in what concerned Operation Tango. Wait—with the one vital exception. Did they have a photo of the inhabitant of No. 48 Mittelstrasse? He looked quickly. Negative. He could always just leave the other photographs. Still, they might be harassed. So he shoved the photographs and the accompanying dossiers into his suitcase. The contents of the file cabinets would now be meaningless. Not worth the time to burn them, time being important. He went to the bathroom and flung his articles into his toilet kit and it into the suitcase. He opened a drawer and clutched at a fistful of clean underwear and socks. He went to his bedside drawer where he kept Sally's letters and the Bible his mother had inscribed to him. Into the bag. No point in even trying to collect the books. The bag was not nearly filled— he left his clothing, all his suits, jackets, sweaters. He paused, and went then into Michael's room. He took the family pictures, tossing them into the bag. He opened Michael's bedside drawer and there found knickknacks—a key chain, a penknife, an address book—and, lying on top of a packet of envelopes neatly bundled together by an elastic band, a letter, together with the envelope it had evidently come in. It was crushed, as if Michael had at one point decided to destroy it. But it was there; so, along with the other letters, he tossed it in, closed the case, went to the elevator and depressed the button corresponding to the second floor. This was the landlady's floor, and he rang insistently.

Frau Burri, her hair in curlers, opened the door in evident astonishment. "Forgive me, Frau Burri, but I must see if my car is here." Without another word he went to her window and looked out in the waning light at the street below. It was apparently deserted.

"I'll be away for a few days, and so will my friend. But we will be in touch with you shortly." Impulsively he leaned down and gave her a kiss, an expeditious way of aborting conversation. She smiled through her surprise, said nothing, and led him out into the elevator. He walked out the door and five blocks before signaling a taxi, to which he gave an address four blocks from the safe house whose address he had memorized. Anthony Trust opened the door.

Three hours later a delivery van, with uniformed representatives of the Friedrich Schulze Spedition, a West Berlin moving company, drove up to an empty garage opposite 48 Mittelstrasse in East Berlin. Two men emerged and opened up the back of the van. The driver, Emil, complained to his companion.

"You'd think we were horses, they treat us like horses. We're supposed to get those spare parts into the garage, and I bet that package alone weighs sixty kilos." His companion grunted.

"I'll take a look inside, so we can see where to store them." Emil opened the garage door, and closed it. He flashed on his light. There was no indication that anyone had been in the room. Just two corpses, grotesquely dead, lying in their own blood. Emil went out, and in a normal voice said to his companion:

"Max, we're going to have to shove some things around in there before we can dump this stuff. Let's take the big empty trunk, and put the crap in it."

Max grunted, and pushed out of the back of the truck a large, steel-reinforced container used for transporting car engines, sliding it down the loading plank. Emil took one end of it and together they lugged it into the garage, again closing the door— but leaving their moving van casually open, the inside light on.

"We should try to get this done in less than five minutes," Emil whispered. They lifted both bodies into the trunk and sealed it. Looking about with his flashlight, Max saw a large barrel of old crankcase oil, half full. With Emil's help he rolled it to where the bodies had lain and then, with some care, spilled out enough of it to cover entirely the traces of blood.

"Let's go."

It was hard work. Reaching the outside, they complained again at normal volume about the hard manual labor imposed on them.

"Should have sent three men, bloody fools."

Using the winch inside the truck, they levered the trunk up a plank.

"All right," said Emil. "We'll get to the rest of it tomorrow. Time to turn in."

They drove through East Berlin to the Brandenburg Gate.

At the gate, Emil was questioned. He took out his bill of lading: delivery of various auto parts—to the garage that serviced the KGB.

"Bloody idiots," Emil cursed. "The garage was closed! And the gasoline station wouldn't take delivery. We'll have to come back tomorrow."

The guard ordered the van opened, ran his flashlight about the tightly packed interior, and told them to get moving. "Maybe next time you will make deliveries on time, eh?"

"We were only fifteen minutes late," Emil said, slipping his truck into gear.

Trust picked up the telephone. "Good. Good. Good." He turned to Blackford, who for two hours now had talked without stopping. He wouldn't even take the proffered brandy, or whiskey. He spoke about Michael. Trust had been listening with genuine sympathy, interrupting only to give instructions and receive bulletins.

He put down the telephone. "It was risky. But worth it. If Reynard's clients had been the KGB, they'd have picked up the bodies. It looks to me as though Reynard had a partner, planned to pick you both up, and maybe negotiate with the KGB—or with us—an agreeable ransom. So partner shows up, looks at the scene, and decides he'll sit this one out. Which means it's reasonable to suppose the mole in Washington or wherever will continue to send the stuff to Mittelstrasse."

# CHAPTER 13

Already, Rufus had given instructions to the FBI. He was to be called the next time any post office handled a letter addressed to Frau Ilse Müller, No. 48 Mittelstrasse, East Berlin. In two hours he had a call from New York. He gave instructions, and then called J. Edgar Hoover.

At 6 P.M. Hoover, Rufus, and three technicians were at the principal laboratory of the FBI, in the cellar of the vast building on Pennsylvania Avenue in Washington.

They stood, staring down at an envelope, steamed open, and its one-page enclosure—a newspaper clipping, at the top of which had been typed in German, "Ilse. Thought this would interest you." It was a report from the *Herald Tribune* by Red Smith on the Czech–U.S. hockey game.

Rufus said, "My guess is, with what we've been giving them, you're not going to find any cryptographic paraphrases. The

KGB will want the whole thing. It's got to be there. Micropho-
tography. Can't be anything else."

"Unless we're on the wrong trail," suggested the Director of
the FBI, never entirely reconciled to his subordinate position in
Operation Tango.

"That's correct. We could be wrong. But we have gone to a
great deal of trouble, and we have lost an agent, to identify this
woman. The photographs"—he pointed to the dossier that in-
cluded copies of past correspondence, almost always clippings,
directed to Ilse Müller—"wouldn't show up microphotography.
But now we have the envelope and the original enclosure. We
must proceed with total caution." He looked at the principal lab-
oratory specialist. "Everything we have planned depends on this
letter's being delivered to the address with minimum delay. *But
we must know*"—he pointed to the letter—"if that little piece of
airmail has in it five pages of minutes of the National Security
Council."

The technicians went to work. Hoover invited Rufus to his
august office. In order to reach the Director's desk it was neces-
sary to walk through the huge room, its walls sagging with pic-
tures, testimonials, newspaper headlines, plaques acquired by the
Director during the preceding thirty-five years. He walked
slowly, in the event Rufus wished to linger over the collection.
Rufus, entirely without mannerism save for the distressing habit
of relapsing occasionally into a totally impenetrable silence,
knew less by intuition than by craft the endocrinological re-
quirements of certain types of human nature; so that he said, his
eyes skimming the walls, "What a *very* impressive office, Mr.
Hoover. Abundant evidence of how greatly you have contrib-
uted to the national security."

"Well," said Hoover, his facial muscles now relaxed, "we all
have a job to do."

He sat at his desk, pushed a button, and a secretary materi-
alized as quickly as if she had been hiding behind the curtain.
"I'll take coffee. You, Rufus? . . . One coffee, one tea, and I
don't need to tell you to be quick about it."

They talked, but with increasing tension. Rufus had learned
early to steel himself against disappointment, and on one occa-
sion several years back had made a fairly respectable calculation

that in his own experience he had been disappointed about ninety percent of the time. But he would not apply that ratio to this operation, not after what he had learned from Trust. The groundwork had been very thorough. After a while there was simply no way of continuing a general conversation without making specific mention of what both men ached to learn. Hoover spoke first.

"The Russians. Do they have cameras as refined as ours for this kind of thing?"

"No. But the East Germans do. The Zeiss plant in Jena went to them. There's one instrument they've developed which can put an eight-by-ten negative in the diameter of a typewriter dot. The technique for implanting that negative on a piece of ordinary typing paper isn't easy. You need to increase the pressure on the typewriter key enough to penetrate the paper, leaving a tiny hole. On a manual machine, not so hard, you just pound. Harder on an electric machine, though not impossible, because you can turn on the index pressure for maximum carbon copies, make your dots, then reduce the pressure to normal. With tweezers, you insert the negative in the dot after coating the back side with an invisible colorless adhesive, to keep the negative from falling right through. Then you go back—the trickiest part —and type lightly over the hole. But there is a slight residual protuberance. Sometimes you can feel it with your finger. Other times you have to slide the paper through a nivellator, calibrated to measure differences in thickness up to one one thousandth of a millimeter."

"Yeah, I know all that," said the Director, who as a matter of fact didn't. It was then that his phone rang. He grabbed for it. "Director, here."

He listened for a moment, then put down the telephone without comment.

He smiled at Rufus. "The FBI always gets its man."

It was with visible excitement that even these professionals presented for inspection to the Director and Rufus the repristinated letter. By courier it would return to the post office on the upper east side, and the next morning wing its way to Berlin. Rufus had requested that only a single copy of the unearthed documents be printed. The Director was manifestly irritated by this (he liked to keep copies of everything), but Rufus's authority had by now been so markedly reinforced by the President that Hoover did not voice his resentment, instead authorizing by a nod of his head to his technicians Rufus's request. In a half hour, carrying his locked briefcase, Rufus bade the Director good night, thanked and congratulated him, and said he would be in touch presently. He went to the nearest pay telephone and rang the emergency number. In a few seconds he was talking to the Director of Central Intelligence. "Important. Can you meet me at The Quarters right away?" "The Quarters" was the designated term for the offices from which Rufus was running Operation Tango.

It was just after nine. Rufus kept some fruit in the corner of the room and when the Director was shown in, he found Rufus sitting in a chair staring at a piece of paper under a bright light while munching on an apple.

"Did I interrupt your dinner?" the Director asked.

"Yes."

"Sorry."

"You're going to tell me, I hope, that the envelope yielded the material?"

"I'm going to tell you more than that." The Director had pulled out his pipe and drawn up a chair opposite the little coffee table in front of Rufus.

Wordlessly, Rufus handed him the three sheets of paper.

The Director looked at them, and shot to his feet.

"Great God almighty!" There was a silence. "So help me, Rufus, sometimes I feel like giving up."

"I'll never remind you that you said that, Allen."

"But this means they're all over the place."

"Not necessarily. Might very well be the same one."

"You mean, the minutes of the NSC, all this time, have been leaking out of *my* office?"

"It would appear so. But you know better than I what distribution is given to these minutes in your office."

"The distribution is: one copy to me, one copy in the maximum security safe in my own office."

"What do you do with your copy after you have read it?"

"I personally insert it into the shredder behind my desk."

"Who brings you the copy?"

"It depends. In this case, the head of Canadian Operations. He'd bring in a single copy."

"How then would you make a copy for the file?"

"Through my own Xerox machine."

"Who operates that?"

"My Deputy's secretary."

"Isn't that, then, the likely place to look?"

# CHAPTER 14

It was agreed that the news of Michael would not be given to his parents until Blackford himself could do so, and throughout the first hours of the endless flight to Washington (though thank God for jet travel!) Blackford struggled with the formulation of an appropriate—or the least inappropriate—way to proceed. It was quite simply the case that Michael had given his life for Blackford. He had done this instinctively: Reynard had hardly given them time for deliberation. It was spastic heroism, un-cogitated love. Blackford's eyes went moist whenever he turned his mind to the episode, which he had difficulty keeping out of mind. Halfway across the ocean and well into a second bottle of wine, he suddenly perceived why his mind turned so constantly to those few seconds in a spirit not only of gratitude and love—but also of injury. It was that burr in the memory which at first he had passed over in consideration of the overarching drama.

But it stuck there, tenacious. It was, of course, Michael's strange behavior during . . .

Blackford took a notebook from his pocket, and a ball-point pen, and began to write:

> 8:00 Alarm rings.
> 8:10 Boil water.

. . . and so on. He characterized Michael's mood from the moment he brought him coffee through the next half hour, during breakfast, when he visibly recovered from his slight hangover. Then Blackford had gone for the mail—

Instantly he knew.

Only the congestion of events, he consoled himself, could so have distracted him as for him not to have realized earlier that Michael had received a letter, and that that letter—nothing else— must have brought on the torment that showed on his face the moment that Michael rushed into Reynard's discharging pistol.

He had slipped Michael's letters into a manila envelope, sealed it, and placed it in his own briefcase. The family pictures he had packed in his suitcase, checking it on the Frankfurt–Washington Pan Am flight.

He reached into his case, drew out the envelope, and sliced it open. The letters were as he had scooped them up: a collection of several months in one neat packet, and a single letter, crushed, clearly, within the palm of one hand. It was three pages, hand-written on both sides in a tight hand. It was in Italian. "*Caro Michelino*" it began, ending "*Col cuore affranto* [with broken heart], Mama."

Relying on schoolboy Latin, some French, a smattering of Spanish, he attempted to decipher it—but gave up after the second sentence. But he was too agitated to think about anything else. And so he set out to duplicate the letter (the words were entirely legible) in block letters on a legal pad of yellow paper.

He wrote one entire sentence in block script on his pad. Then he would drop four blank lines, and write out the second sentence.

By the time he was through, he had used up eight pages. He left out all proper names, coding them.

He then called the stewardess.

Most stewardesses were extra-attentive when Blackford Oakes rang the call button. They would often attempt conversation, but this one—plump, vivacious, efficient—could see that the handsome young American was preoccupied.

"Can I help you?" she asked, turning off his call button.

"I have an unusual request. I'm really sorry to bother you with it. But I would be ever so grateful if you would ask on the public address system if anyone on board is carrying an Italian dictionary."

She laughed. "Of course I wouldn't mind. Is it a particular word? I speak Italian. My mother was Italian."

Blackford looked up at her. His impulse was to turn over the note pad—but of course he must not.

"Well thanks, and maybe if I get stuck with a particular word I'll call on you, but if there's a dictionary around, that would really help."

"Attention, ladies and gentlemen, this is your stewardess, Corina. There is a gentleman in distress on our flight. He needs to borrow an Italian–English dictionary. If anyone has one and would be willing to part with it for a few minutes, Pan American would be very grateful."

To her astonishment, no fewer than four signal lights flashed on. Corina went the rounds, making little notes of which dictionary corresponded with which passenger. Three were useless —assorted word guides fashioned for tourists, one of them giving perhaps five hundred words, the largest of them twice as many.

But the fourth, apparently belonging to a man whose name and address were written on the flyleaf: John T. Bergin, 1908 Hall of Graduate Studies, Yale University, was a well-thumbed onionskin Cassell's Dictionary designed to handle everything short of the comprehensive dictionaries. Blackford returned the three to Corina, keeping the Cassell's.

Knowing nothing about Italian declension or conjugation, Blackford—as obsessed now with the assignment as if the safety of the flight depended on it—began by writing above the Italian word the English equivalent, when this was unambiguous. After a few sentences, he found this method tedious. He decided instead to alphabetize all the Italian words. So he grouped the A's, then the B's, on down the alphabet. Then he sub-alphabetized each to the second letter. Now he copied them out on yet other yellow sheets so that, turning now to the dictionary, he could do so in an orderly way, hunting down the English equivalent. For several words, no English was given. (Either the words were extremely uncommon, or else they were slang, or else a part of a private vocabulary.) After wrestling with a few verbs, he began to feel an instinct for the tense. In just under an hour, he had an English word for almost all the Italian words.

Now, using his guide, he went back to his original pages and reproduced the letter. It was over 1,500 words long.

Again he rang for Corina.

"What does the word *squaciata* mean?"

"Can you show me the context?"

Somewhat guardedly, Blackford showed her a line on his yellow pad, making it difficult for her eyes to rove above or below that line.

"That," said Corina, "means 'torn apart.' "

"Thanks. And here's the dictionary for Mr. Bergin. I wrote a note in it. Could I have some more white wine?" Corina smiled and went off.

Blackford carefully folded the original letter, within the folds of his numerous yellow pages, closed his eyes, tilted back his chair, and imagined what Michael must have experienced yesterday morning at breakfast.

The letter had spoken of his mother's suspicions that her Benni had taken a mistress in New York. Ostensibly his trips were to visit the widow of Salvatore and old friends from the concentration camp. But the trips had now become weekly. She tracked down the telephone number of Mrs. Salvatore Gigli, and by deft questioning established that Benni had seen her only once in the past four months.

So: Maria had undertaken to discover what was taking Benni to New York with such frequency.

In the past few months he had also taken to staying late in the office on Fridays, almost without exception, and she resolved to begin her investigation by inquiring into the reason for this.

No one knew the offices of Ambrose & Gaither better than Maria. Accordingly she dropped by one Friday afternoon, as occasionally she did on weekdays while passing the building, to greet her old friends. But instead of leaving through the front door, she let it slam and slipped into an adjacent stationery closet, behind whose shelves were old files never consulted. By these files, she waited. When the last person but Benni had left the office (she had left the closet door slightly ajar), she saw Benni bolting the door. Then heard his footsteps. He stopped at his cubicle, then walked away, toward the blueprint room.

She followed him and, opening the door slightly, saw that he was diligently using the blueprinting machinery. She could think of no reason for him to do this. Moreover, he withdrew from the machine not the characteristically large stretches of blueprint paper, but letter-sized pieces. She ducked back to her hiding place.

That night, after he had gone to sleep, she went downstairs and looked through his briefcase. The texture of a half-dozen pieces of paper was different from the others. She knew those to be blueprint paper. The next morning she left a note for him on his breakfast tray: she had risen early to go to a baptism, and would see him on his return from New York. She was, in fact, on his train ("I disguised my face," she had written). She followed him to a park in Brooklyn where he left a newspaper on a bench which a stranger picked up. That night she searched his briefcase again. The blueprint papers were missing. The following Saturday she repeated the procedure and—though this time the reunion was at a museum—again, he had trafficked with the same man. This time she followed the stranger, who returned in due course, by subway mostly, to a commercial photographic studio in Brooklyn.

Her last words were: "My darling son, I am seized with terrible suspicions. Your father always thought the Communist Party was the savior of all of us, and although he said he left the Party when he came to America—now I am not too sure." There followed the phrase, "I am torn apart."

Michael, Blackford assumed, would have guessed that the woman they were setting out to finger at No. 48 Mittelstrasse was the recipient of the favors of no less than Michael's father.

# CHAPTER 15

During the world war, while the wholehearted, hyperkinetic Amanda Gaither was at boarding school at Ethel Walker's in Simsbury, Connecticut, she felt out of things. Her roommate Jane had two brothers in the army; Jane's younger sister Trish would lose, that summer, not only the brother who had been her constant companion from childhood, but also her young friend in South Carolina, who was going off to Annapolis. Amanda had no brothers in the service, and her father was too old to serve (he had been decorated in the first war). During a school debate in 1943 on the question "Resolved: This house believes the Allies should launch a second front in Europe now," Amanda spoke emotionally in the affirmative, and during the rebuttal one of the girls, defending the negative, made a devastating reference to the understandable bellicosity of those who had very little of a personal kind to lose from premature military operations.

Amanda compensated for this awful disability during her last two years at preparatory school and during her early years at Vassar by two means. She joined student peace movements wherever she could find them. She accustomed herself, without strenuous effort, to the relevant terminological protocols. On the whole, everything was "peace"-oriented, even when the Soviets were calling for second fronts or more intensive bombing raids. She learned how, in pursuit of *peace*, she should argue for *war*. . . . This wasn't difficult, and she quickly learned to master the dialectic, mysterious to some, as when her roommate asked her why the Soviet Union should be so hot for us to strike a second front in Europe, while they failed to take action against Japan. To which Amanda was able to answer that the leaders of the Soviet Union were beyond infantile leftism, an answer that left her roommate, though not exactly satisfied, at least dumbfounded; and that was good enough for Amanda.

On a typical weekend, enjoying the considerable liberty given to seniors on the honors list, she would take the bus to Hartford, and then head for Boston or New Haven or New York to convene with, or march with, those who demanded a second front; and, in due course, with those who demanded that the United States give up its nuclear monopoly; and soon after, though based now at Vassar, she would join those who demanded that the United States recognize the Soviet Union's natural sphere of interest in Eastern Europe, and reject counterrevolutionary movements typified by Mikolajczyk in Poland, Stepinac in Yugoslavia, and, later, Masaryk in Czechoslovakia.

By the time she was in Vassar, though a mere second-term freshman, she was elected secretary of the Vassar branch of the Young Progressives of America. One of her clandestine assignments was to join the school newspaper, *Vassar Miscellany News*, and use her influence—if possible, by becoming its editor—in order to cause the paper to endorse the presidential candidacy of Henry Wallace. She did not succeed in becoming the editor, but she was confident that her considerable passion for the transcendent imperative of peace and her encyclopedic knowledge of the militaristic and commercial background of the men who surrounded President Truman gave her a missionary's touch in dealing with pagans. Her fellow students, while falling short, for the most part, of endorsing Wallace, were easily stirred by declamatory demands for a higher idealism that would bring an end to war.

The second means by which young Amanda Gaither thought to aid the war effort was by being ever so obliging to soldiers, whether soldiers back on furlough or leave, or freshly discharged. She owed them a considerable debt, she reasoned. Moreover, if they were most acutely pleasured by familiarity with her body, she was prepared to make that "sacrifice"—to use the conventional formulation, which she decreasingly did. The first time was after a senior dance, away at Millbrook School. Her blind date was an attractive enough sixth-former who, however, for reasons she finally abandoned exploring, kept bringing up the subject of snakes. Jim had, it appeared, a considerable collection of snakes in the school zoo, each one of which—while Jim and Amanda ate, and while they danced—he would describe to her, including its eating habits, the do's and don'ts of feeding them white mice, the age at which his boa constrictor would acquire the strength actually to choke the life out of a grown man ("not for at least three years"). Amanda had to keep reminding herself that Jimmy in a matter of weeks would go to midshipman's school, and from there to roam alien seas, where the reptilian monsters that would strike at him would most likely do so from underwater, spitting out their toxic missiles in the North Atlantic, or in the South Pacific. Amanda could get very emotional, and she could see Jim gurgling his last, going down into the vasty deep, worrying about who would look after his snakes. Amanda became so carried away by this that she came very near to promising Jimmy that if anything ever happened to him, she, Amanda, would adopt his snakes. Fortunately, at just that moment, a young man in uniform cut in.

"I'm Brian, Jim's older brother. And the rules say a) you can cut in; and b) even if the rules didn't say that, I'm bigger than Jim so I'd make up my own rules." With which he swept her away, indeed quite off her feet.

It was against the rules to return to Ethel Walker's other than on the school bus, but by the next afternoon, when the time had come to leave, Amanda and Brian (he had more or less dismissed Jim, who resignedly spent Sunday morning at the zoo) had solved that problem to their satisfaction. Carol, Amanda's seat-mate in the bus, would bend her head over as though playing a game of checkers with Amanda, which she frequently did, and when Miss Otis, going down the roster, called out Amanda's name, Carol would answer, "Here." Brian, who was headed for Hartford where he was attached to the Signal Corps unit at Bradley Field, would have Amanda safely back at Ethel Walker's well before the bus got there, except that as it happened she was not "safely" back three hours later, but was a changed woman.

Brian was easygoing, slight of face, quick to smile, a good listener, and his eyes were both amused and passionate. He was a second lieutenant, a station which hugely impressed Amanda, who studied his bars and emblems. He had the weekend off and decided to spend it at the school from which he had graduated the preceding year. He talked easily about the training he received, and the responsibilities he would inherit probably in Europe ("most of the Pacific Signal Corps people are training in California") and, carefully watching her responses, he said he had of course to be fatalistic about his chances of returning whole. "The casualties among Signal Corps men," he said as he drove sixty-five miles an hour up toward the Berkshires before swinging northeast toward Simsbury, "are very high, because among other things, we have to be there to give the signal to retreat!" He laughed, with genuine amusement Amanda thought, admiring extravagantly his debonair attitude toward a life that might, so soon, come to an end. Without slowing down, he reached over to the back seat and fished up a bottle of beer.

"Want one?"

Amanda had never tasted beer before. She found herself saying, "Of course."

The right hand disappeared again and came up with a second bottle. "The opener's in the glove compartment."

They reached the outskirts of Simsbury one hour before the pokey bus would, and Brian asked if she knew any place they might park in privacy and "just talk." Indeed there was; she knew the whole of the area, after four years, intimately. It was dark, but without difficulty she guided him by the farmers' road to a forest, from a little clearing in which they could look up at the twinkling lights of the huge main schoolhouse, so grandly situated up the endless grass slope, and, beyond that, the house on the hill, still higher, where the senior girls lived.

Brian then spoke in earnest about the impact Amanda had had on him. Up until knowing her, he had been lackadaisical about his future, but in the past few hours alone, his perceptions had changed. He must, he said—his arm around her neck, his fingers probing—he must go abroad with an entire memory of this beautiful girl.

Amanda knew all about the techniques of love, knew that sooner or later she would be initiated in them, and resolved early on—she had said as much to her roommate—that when the time came, she would not feign a reluctance she did not feel, or a passivity assumed by nineteenth-century novelists to be the generic behavioral responsibility of the female species.

"Do you see this?" Brian said, extricating a small package from his back pocket.

Amanda fingered it.

"They are condoms," she said, her voice entirely steady.

"Do you think you could take one and put it . . . on?"

Amanda swallowed, her determination to be poised notwithstanding. She found herself saying, "Yes, but it's dark."

"That doesn't matter," said Brian, his voice now hoarse. "You'll see. I'll guide you."

The deed was done, and he led her to the back seat, leaving his trousers and shorts in the front seat. Throughout, he talked to her, and told her that now he had a real reason for surviving the war. They caressed passionately. The wrench came suddenly and she cried out, but only briefly, and felt no resentment for Brian; on the contrary, she returned his post-coital kiss ardently. He reached down, took the towel that had encircled the bucket of beer, and gently stroked her.

"Brian," she said, practically, "I'm going to have to have some light."

"All right," he said. "I'll turn on the car light, and walk away, and come back in a couple of minutes. That way you can tidy up."

She made maximum use of her two minutes, stuck the towel into the bucket, got into the front seat, and tapped lightly on the horn. Brian reappeared. He kissed her, started the engine, and drove her to the senior residence, telling her that she had made all military sacrifice tolerable. She was silent. By no means shocked, or resentful. She had not enjoyed herself, but for this she had been prepared by her reading. They agreed to meet again the following Wednesday night. She would sneak out during the late study hour, at 9:45, and come again to the identical place—could Brian find it? "A Signal Corps man," he replied, "can find anything. Besides," she could see the boyish, yet cosmopolitan smile on his face now as they approached the road lights, "your . . . body issues a little beep, and my . . . body could home in on it no matter where you were hiding." They kissed. Amanda hid in the gym until the bus drove in, at which point she joined her class, mostly silent after the long ride, facing the decompression from a weekend at a prep school and long hours with algebra, Chaucer, irregular French verbs, and the Lincoln–Douglas debates. Amanda was visibly animated, her face flushed with excitement, and Carol said, "You look like you've opened a second front."

"I have," said Amanda brightly. "I mean"—she checked herself—"I have a feeling we'll open one soon."

At Vassar, Amanda's promiscuity was somehow brought off with a kind of professional dignity. Her preference—not exactly advertised, but manifest—was for fellow workers in the Progressive Party movement. Her fastidious roommate Maureen pointed out to her that it was an awful pity that the young men who declared for Henry Wallace were not more attractive biologically, and Amanda replied that she knew more about them biologically than Maureen, thanks very much. Among her friends it was quietly accepted that Amanda—whom they were greatly attracted to by reason of her cheerfulness, her vivacity, her idealism, her openness, her spontaneity—was perhaps something of a "nymphomaniac," but at one point, when the suggestion was raised, Maureen, who though not a Progressive was a feminist, denounced the very use of the word as signifying that women took pleasure from sexual union even as men did. "You can bet Johnny D [all the girls knew Johnny D] isn't called a 'satyr' by his friends at Yale, yet the two words are complementary.

Amanda is wholehearted in everything she does, and she enjoys everything she does. I doubt if she has had any more pleasure out of sex than she had when she deposited one thousand signatures with the Town Clerk to put Wallace on the ballot."

The humiliation of Henry Wallace had been crushing to Amanda. That spring, the Soviet Union had staged the Czecho-slovakian coup. And during the summer, the news magazines came out with exposé after exposé, convincing the majority that Henry Wallace had become the tool of the Kremlin ("Josef Stalin's Mortimer Snerd," Clare Boothe Luce had unkindly put it in her keynote address at the convention in Philadelphia that nominated Thomas E. Dewey). Suddenly the crowds thinned down, and at what was planned as a monster rally in Poughkeepsie in October, featuring the candidate himself and pitchman Frank Kingsley, plus one or two Hollywood speakers—victims of the House Committee on Un-American Activities such as Albert Maltz—the crowds had been discouragingly small. The organizer of the rally, a woman sent out from New York with experience in such matters, had noticed the wholehearted work and devotion of the enthusiastic and voluptuous junior. She asked Amanda whether she might manage to go to New York to meet her to discuss a matter "of vital importance to world peace." Amanda, in her outgoing way, said this was easily arranged, took the name and address and the time of the meeting, and walked back from the rally all the way to the campus, instead of taking the bus. She reflected on the motives of "Andy," as they all called the organizer. "I bet," she thought, "that Andy will try to recruit me to join the Party." She would certainly accept, she said to herself. Her disappointment with the rally, and her suspicion that the following Tuesday the candidate for whom she had worked so very hard would be crushed, were somehow discounted by her own resolution. Let the American public bend to the will of the usual types who have buggered up the century with world wars, racism, and materialism. Some people will stand up against it, and I'll be one of them. She would, however, need to tell Andy that her membership in the Party would need to be surreptitious, because life at home would simply be impossible otherwise, and she had no particular ambition to embarrass her father, a prominent Washington architect, or her godfather,

Dean Acheson; or her mother, whose interest in politics terminated with the death of Mussolini.

She need not have worried. Andy, who introduced her to "Klaus," had in mind for her something very different from public agitation. Indeed, it required that slowly, but convincingly, during the year and a half she had left at Vassar, she distance herself from her former political passions—not so difficult, since the migration away from the Progressive Party was, on the collegiate scene, very nearly total. Indeed, by the end of her senior year, she must associate herself not only with such causes as the United World Federalists, but with those wings *within* those causes that sought to exclude Communists from membership.

Amanda traveled frequently to New York, always seeing Andy, sometimes seeing Klaus himself. And they told her that, after she had graduated, she would be given an assignment. To this she looked forward eagerly, and as she read the headlines— the heightening of the Cold War, the emergence of McCarthy, looming confrontation in Korea—she took solace from the knowledge that she had a secret, and that history would vindicate her. The commencement speaker was Mrs. Agnes Meyer, the wife of the publisher of the Washington *Post*. She urged the young ladies to face life boldly, to be willing to make personal sacrifice, to pursue their ideals.

Amanda smiled. "She's describing me," she thought, contentedly.

# CHAPTER 16

Rufus, who had permitted himself to wonder how it was that between October and February the FBI had not managed to come up with the mole, even though transcripts of the NSC documents passed through fewer than forty hands, had to admit that Mr. Hoover's agents, moving in force now on the basis of the information in the letter to Michael, did so with a quite dazzling thoroughness.

Happily, an acre-by-acre search for the photographer Steiner had not proved necessary, although, Mr. Hoover assured Rufus, even without the intelligence discovered by Maria Bolgiano, in due course, checking every commercial photography outlet, they'd have fingered Steiner—but that would concededly have taken time. As it was, two of their top agents cased his studio while a third, radio in hand, stood outside in the event Steiner should be seen returning. A fourth agent followed Steiner from time to time, satisfying agent No. 3, who satisfied agents No. 1 and No. 2 that Mr. Steiner was at this moment on a bus heading up toward Fordham. Any sudden materialization at 252 Fulton Street, Brooklyn, was ruled out.

The agents admired the order in Steiner's studio. His was no brummagem enterprise, light veneer for spy work. He had lists of patrons, carefully kept ledgers, considerable files containing copies of work accomplished. They found, without great difficulty, the Zapp microdot machine that permitted microdot photography. The mere ownership of such a machine would not, of course, constitute evidence of felony. A professional photographer is not obliged to describe the uses to which he puts esoteric equipment.

They swept the place clean. In his upstairs closet they discovered a portable typewriter, and only after carefully studying its position in repose, including that of the zippers that enfolded the case, did they take it out to get samples of the typeface, as they had done with the principal typewriter below. They took fingerprint samples as targets of opportunity; they had been told that the envelope bore no fingerprints of the sender. They searched in vain for an address book, for anything at all that might give them a clue to the extent of his apparently extensive network.

"Let's face it, Rhubarb"—agent No. 2, Ollie, was unaware that his colleague, the senior FBI investigator-technician in New York, had often ruminated on the probability that his failure to achieve more dramatic advancement traced to his inability to get anyone at all, even the Director, to call him other than by the preposterous nickname he had been given at age three, when he contracted chickenpox—"if this fellow's got microdot technology and wants to hide a neat list of his agents, including home telephones, girl friends, and birthdays, he doesn't need a nice red leatherbound appointment book."

"That's right," Rhubarb said. "At the same time, and for the same reason that microdots are useful, they're delicate, and you'd go to considerable pains to keep them in some kind of classified shape. My guess is that they're in the library, tucked into his books, and that he has somewhere a key to their location. But this isn't anything we're going to find out today. Realize this cat's been operating *twelve years!* Oh, man, I can see the Director handling that one in the press!"

Ollie, while looking tenderly under the blotter on the main desk, said in heroic accents, "FBI ARRESTS MASTER SPY. Washington. Director J. Edgar Hoover announced today before a crowded press conference that after twelve years of investigation, during which his agents had gone over an estimated 118 million pieces of information, using the most modern technological equipment in the inventory of counterintelligence, the FBI had arrested Hans Steiner, a German-American residing and doing business as a photographer at 252 Fulton Street, Brooklyn, charging him with violating eleven federal statutes governing stolen secrets and unauthorized traffic with a foreign country. . . ."

"Right on," said Rhubarb, looking up at the congeries of floodlights, most of them affixed to flexible stems in order to achieve any desired configuration. "What the Director *won't* say is that the technological datum that brought us here was a jealous Italian mama."

"Is that right?" Ollie commented.

"Shit," said Rhubarb.

"What's the matter?"

"I shouldn't have told you that."

"I've forgotten it. Steiner was fingered by a jealous Hungarian vamp."

"I'm serious, Ollie."

"Okay, mum's the word. You can look at my bank account and tell I don't have any press contacts."

"I know, I know."

They were gone an hour before Hans Steiner returned, in time for his four o'clock appointment with Pepperidge Farm. In a half hour, his studio smelled like a bakery, and he remembered the distinctive smell of fresh bread at the farm in Thuringia where his mother always rose before the dawn to make it.

The Directors of Central Intelligence and the FBI sat with Rufus going over two sets of documents, the first relatively dated, the second fresh as last week.

The first pile was from the dossier "GAITHER, Amanda."

It contained the notorious forty-page questionnaire completed by applicants who desire to serve in the Agency, together with reports from FBI agents and special CIA agents. Few routine files in Washington are more copious, and Rufus sighed at the prospect of going over it, but much of it, of course, he could skim. The three men sat alongside each other at The Quarters, and Rufus would pass along a document to the Director of the CIA, who would then pass it on to the Director of the FBI. To review the first pile took over an hour. They all took notes.

Rufus addressed them. "It is clear that Miss Gaither was an enthusiastic supporter of Henry Wallace and was deeply involved in the Progressive Citizens of America, an operation dominated, particularly in its last period, by the Communist Party, and from whose ranks the Communists did their most vigorous recruiting during the late forties."

"Yep," Hoover added. "But most of them dropped out."

"We are not talking about most of them," Dulles said, with just a touch of stiffness.

"By the time she left Vassar, she seemed to have gotten away from the hard-core apologists for Stalin; in fact, she appears to have quarreled with them. In any event, the next three years, spent here in Washington with the Spanish Tourist Office, don't seem to suggest any residual political obsessions. All her teachers and friends seem to like her."

"Her boyfriends certainly seem to like her," Hoover said gruffly.

"There is that," Dulles agreed; "and the usual blackmail opportunity. But—do you realize that I have known her since she was approximately four years old?—to the great distress of her very proper parents, Amanda has never made much of an effort to conceal her . . . capacity for total infatuations. Nor does she appear to have been attached for any very considerable time to any one person, the ironic exception being Michael Bolgiano— with whom, however, there is no trace of a relationship going beyond the fraternal. She was often in the household of her godfather, Dean Acheson. I telephoned him a day or two ago and asked about her."

"Did he say he would never turn his back on Amanda Gaither?" Rufus asked.

Dulles's eyes moved quickly to ascertain whether the FBI Director had got the quip; he hadn't.

"He said he found her consistently lively, amiable, and rather apolitical and apparently satisfied with her job."

"Very well then," said Rufus, "let's look at the second dossier. It is—correct me if I am wrong, Mr. Hoover—a minute-by-minute account, to the extent possible, of her activities during the past week, correct?"

"Correct."

Experienced eyes, trained to brake at the anomaly, read quickly through such material. Rufus wanted to focus especially on just where she went upon leaving the office of the Director of the CIA, and what she carried with her. The answers were there: no fixed pattern as to where she went. Monday it was to Camalier and Buckley, where she made a purchase. Tuesday it was to a bridal shower, Wednesday a Vassar tea, Thursday to her father's office, Friday directly home to prepare dinner for six guests, none of them members of the Politburo.

She carried with her, on leaving, only her raincoat and a purse.

They studied a picture of her emerging from the office building.

"That purse isn't large enough to contain a wad of papers," Dulles observed.

That sort of thing went on for another exasperating hour, until finally Rufus, calling first for fresh coffee, said:

"Gentlemen, let us reason *a posteriori*. If we can rule out that the Director here is a mole, or his Deputy, then the transmission is necessarily being done by one of the four women in the office. The only one of these four women who operates the Xerox machine is Amanda Gaither. Moreover—I grant this could be coincidental—it is an employee of Amanda Gaither's father who has been photographing the materials and serving as courier to our spymaster in New York. There cannot be any reasonable doubt that it is *she*. If we cannot deduce how it is that she actually takes the documents out of the building, why can't we devote an effort to discovering how she takes copies from the Xerox machine? Mr. Hoover, is it feasible to install a moving-picture camera trained to film the Xerox machine when it is operated by Amanda Gaither?"

"Of course. It will be done tomorrow."

Two days later they were again at The Quarters, one room of which had been turned into a makeshift theater with screen and chairs, blinds drawn. The Director of the FBI had not only provided a moving film, but one with sound.

It began with voices of women saying good morning and vague and garbled requests for coffee. The camera, recessed overhead, was tilted to capture the whole of the Xerox 914 and the desk of Amanda Gaither, a few feet away.

Oh my God, thought Dulles, reflecting on the renowned thoroughness of Mr. Hoover. Was he, the Director of Central Intelligence, the eyes and ears of the free world, going to have to sit through, minute by minute, Amanda Gaither's eight-hour day? He decided to give the whole thing ten minutes, then go and leave it all to Rufus to endure.

But the camera was selective. There had been a live and discriminating operator, working from a monitor, who turned the camera on and turned it off, according as there was any action to record; an operator, moreover, who dominated the camera in its various capacities.

There were two OUT baskets so labeled on Amanda's desk. The Director explained that the one colored red was one whose contents were designated for the Director himself. Any document placed there was instantly to be Xeroxed and the original deposited in the corresponding red tray in the Director's office. If his door was closed, the document would be placed on the red tray on the Deputy's desk. The single Xerox copy was taken directly to the safe and inserted into a slot designated merely by the date: February 23, 1960. The exception was NSC transcripts, which were inserted into the slot marked "NSC." These documents were retrievable only under supervision, by security specialists who had the combination locks to the relevant lockers.

The camera proved versatile. A stopwatch signaled the hour on the film. At 9:43:03, a bouncy clerk came by Amanda's desk and dropped two pieces of paper into the red basket.

"How's Indonesia?" Amanda asked cheerfully.

"Bloody. They need clerical help. I've submitted your name."

Amanda smiled. She finished the paragraph she was typing, then rose and took the two documents in hand to the Xerox machine. With her right hand she checked the on-off switch and evidently assured herself that the temperature was warm. She leaned over—the camera zoomed down on her fingers—and turned the numbers switch to "1," signifying that a single copy was to be made.

She went then to face the machine. She pushed the triggering mechanism and the machine whirred, though to no apparent effect, because no copy was disgorged. But Amanda was patient, and in a few seconds it whirred again, and this time a copy slid out on the tray.

She picked it up, along with the original, and walked directly to the safe, looking down to locate that day's designated slot. She inserted the copy and then disappeared from the camera's ambit, to reappear in a few moments and resume typing. Her telephone rang. Clearly a social call. She put off what must have been an old college friend. It rang again. This time she was faintly furtive, and her voice dropped while she took from her drawer that morning's Washington *News*, folded at the relevant page. "Bowie, fifth race, five dollars across the board on number five. Got it?" She hung up and resumed her work.

A half hour later (by the camera clock—the sequence was immediate) a young man came with a pile of papers perhaps an inch thick. These he placed in the gray basket.

"Those are unclassified area reports," Dulles filled in. "Résumés of foreign press reports from remote regions, Third World stuff mostly. My Deputy looks at it and decides whether there is anything I should look at. If so, he marks it; if not, he puts it back on Amanda's tray and she sends it over to USIA— saves them a lot of work."

"How does she send it?" Rufus asked.

"I don't know. By courier, or by mail, I suppose. USIA is over at 1776 Pennsylvania. My guess is we mail it. Nothing urgent. If there were, we'd treat it specially."

Three more times Amanda was called on to use the Xerox machine, and the procedure was duplicated. The stopwatch showed 4:45 as the final time she approached the machine. This time she appeared to have a little difficulty with it, and bent down apparently to clear the paper passageway. When she stood up, she lifted the copies off the tray, added them to those in her hand, walked into the safe, came back past her desk, and, as if distinguishing one set of papers from another, put one pile into her gray basket, and went with the other into the Director's office.

"Let's have that one again," said Rufus.

After running it over three times, it became clear that Amanda was retrieving papers from a bottom cavity, and putting these to one side on the gray tray. The film went on. Immediately after returning from the Director's office, she took from the day's accumulation one pile and with a bold pen, using the Agency's regular unmarked stationery, addressed it to United States Information Agency, P.O. Box 772, Benjamin Franklin Station, Washington, D.C., Attn. Mr. Rattner. The second pile she addressed to Department of United Nations Affairs, P.O. Box 1334, Benjamin Franklin Station, Washington, D.C., Attn. Mr. Elgar. To her own bundle she now added the outgoing mail from her three co-secretaries, dialed a number, and a messenger came to deliver the lot to the Agency post office.

It was another session with the technicians, and Rufus and the FBI Director stood while the two agents and the supervisor from Xerox examined the disassembled machine.

"It's breathtaking," the laconic Xerox official, perspiring from his excavations, seated on Amanda's chair, began his summary. "With one hand on the calibrator you can add a number to the apparent number of copies you ask for. Then, standing in front of the traveler, she'd nudge the knob with her foot. The first copy slides down into the bottom chamber, which is really just a storage compartment. Then, once a day, she stoops down there, picks up her copies, and sends them to—? To where was that?"

"Never mind," said Rufus. "Now, it's important that you restore the machine to exactly how it was."

"That's simple. The only difference from the other ten thousand models is the rift in the traveling mechanism."

# CHAPTER 17

The day was now set: Saturday April 2, 1960. The timing, everybody kept saying—was the thing. Hoover's men had been superbly productive during the three weeks since No. 48 Mittelstrasse. "Goddamdest thing I ever saw, Rufus"—the CIA Director was at The Quarters, reading the latest FBI reports— "this fellow Klaus, as they call him, is the biggest Mr. Big since Sorge in Japan. Klaus now has"—his pencil ran over the neat typewritten page—"*thirteen* people reporting to him *that we know of*, though none on the clockwork basis of our friend Benni. Hmm. I see two of his agents are with the Soviet delegation at the UN—that figures; two with *Pravda* in Washington; two with the Soviet Embassy, a couple in Ottawa, and five Americans. A nice catch. *One hell of a catch.*"

Rufus nodded. "There's fresh news you don't have. I had it over the telephone from Hoover just now. They've isolated a ham radio set in Canada run by one of Klaus's agents—a set rarely used, but used periodically, the boys are convinced, to transmit Moscow-talk. We now know that Klaus is supposed to monitor that frequency at certain times."

"How do we know?"

"We recorded a fragment in his studio this morning. It was interrupted by sharp static, but what we caught was plain."

"What was it?"

"What was it? Well, of course it doesn't make any sense, just a few words pulled out. But he was obviously trying to bring in the signal. It was a message for Klaus, in my opinion."

"For God's sake, Rufus, what did it say?"

"Just five words . . . MARCO POLO, IF YOU CAN."

The Director smiled. He stayed silent, experiencing the pleasure. The Marco Polo diversion had evidently worked.

"The wording of the NSC meeting for the twenty-ninth has got to be *just right*."

"I have a proposed draft," said Rufus. He handed over a sheet of paper. "I would propose that the first part of the minutes be devoted to a discussion of the agreement of Khrushchev to the summit conference in May in Paris, then to general talk about the agenda in Paris, then to specific talk about the Berlin question, a brief report from you on fresh revelations from the U-2 operations, and then—" he pointed his finger to the typewritten sheet.

"*The President asked the Director of the Central Intelligence Agency if he had any reports on the progress of 'Marco Polo.' Mr. Dulles reported that there had been a considerable breakthrough at Islamabad, that he expected that later that same afternoon he would receive the relevant documents, which he would distribute with the minutes of the meeting in the form of addenda. The President advised the Secretary of State that the Marco Polo development would have considerable implications for the Summit Conference and that every means possible would be taken to keep it confidential. . . .*"

"Sounds right to me," said Dulles. "Have you checked with the Attorney General on cordoning off Steiner's studio?"

"I have. Apparently no problem. The prosecution will take the position that the entire studio is a part of the prosecution's case, and that under the circumstances no one, Steiner's lawyer included, can have access to it."

"Is the man who'll be tailing Steiner on the Saturday we pick him up equipped to hear what Steiner says over the pay phone to Canada?"

"He'll have the best equipment we've got. Hoover says his gizmo will pick up a conversation in a pay phone from two hundred feet away. Fine. But even if it doesn't, a second agent, two minutes later, will get on the identical phone and establish which was the most recent number called. If it's our Ottawa number, we can pretty well assume what it is that Steiner will have relayed."

Dulles leaned back in his chair and puffed away. Rufus looked drained.

"Have we overlooked anything?"

"No," said Rufus. "But we haven't done everything I think needs doing."

"Oh God," said Dulles. "What else do you have in mind?"

"A flight on a U-2 piloted out of our base in Japan along the Sino-Soviet border." There had been quarrels over the question whether Rufus had ever been known to smile; a photograph of his expression at this moment would have won the argument for the affirmative. "My proposal—this one obviously has to be cleared by you, and then by the President—is really straightforward. The addendum we will attach to the NSC minutes will detail a specific agreement concluded after much negotiation between a special representative of the United States and a special representative of the People's Republic of China, meeting in Islamabad. Concretely, the United States agrees to make available to the People's Republic of China *four* of our U-2 aircraft over the next year, and to provide covert training for Chinese pilots and support personnel. As an earnest of our good faith, we shall send one of our own most skilled operatives to fly from South Korea to Turkey one day during the first week in April. The photography resulting from that flight will be made available to the representative of the PRC in Pakistan, from which he will derive firsthand knowledge of the miraculous capability of the U-2 aircraft. Given what we know about the mounting tensions between Mao and Khrushchev, the intelligence the PRC will then have concerning Soviet troop deployments will be of vital interest to the PRC."

"What does the United States purportedly get in return?"

"We are, by the terms of the written 'agreement,' to get copies of all the information Chinese pilots subsequently collect while flying the U-2s from their own bases, reaching parts of the Soviet Union not accessible to us. It will of course be obvious to the Soviet Union that what we are really after is a rift in the Sino-Soviet alliance."

Dulles neglected even to tamp his pipe. Finally he said, "It is a most . . . audacious . . . idea."

"If it works," said Rufus, always objective, "it will be of considerable consequence. Among other things, it could bring about a significant redeployment of Soviet military strength—away from Eastern Europe. And, Berlin being the great question during this period, the less concentrated Soviet strength in Eastern Europe, the better off Europe is."

"And we are."

"And we are. . . . In order to persuade the Kremlin that we have actually concluded such an arrangement with the Chinese (the Chinese will of course deny it, but would in any event), we must contrive to give the Kremlin access to the Marco Polo Protocols. These, I fancy, should be *quite* detailed. They should, for instance, quite specifically detail the route of the special demonstration flight in April. As though the route had been negotiated with some reference to plausible Chinese curiosity," Rufus turned to the map behind him, ". . . it should cover, I'd guess, the industrial cities north of the Mongolian line—Chita, Ulan-Ude, Irkutsk, and then—oh, Semipalatinsk, the Tarbagatay Range, Alma-Ata—which would put the pilot within reasonable distance of our base in Peshawar in Pakistan."

"Does the U-2 have the range? I mean, what the hell, I know the range of the U-2. I mean, what sort of distance are you talking about?"

"Great circle," said Rufus. "Seoul to Peshawar is 2,692 miles. The route I have suggested, which would be most likely for an intelligence operation, would take five or six hundred miles more. Well within the range of the U-2."

"We all know, Rufus, that the Soviets are closing in on our

U-2s. But they haven't been able to knock any down yet, and their advanced technology for doing so doesn't sit on that Sino-Soviet route. Their radar probably wouldn't even pick up our U-2 flight. So that the flight could be relegated in the Kremlin to sheer fancy."

"Yes, I thought of that," said Rufus. "My proposal is that our pilot go down."

"That he what?"

"That he go down. Suffer a flameout—in the area of Semipala-tinsk—and be taken by the Russians."

At this point Dulles simply put down his pipe, as if permanently abandoning it.

"Oakes?"

"Oakes."

"How do you propose we get him back?"

"How do you propose the Soviets will get back Hans Steiner?"

"I give up, Rufus. Have you discussed the matter with Oakes?"

"No," said Rufus, looking rather absentmindedly at the map. "It's on my list of things to do."

# CHAPTER 18

Blackford Oakes found the U-2, notwithstanding its eccentricities, the closeness of cockpit conditions, and the wretchedly uncomfortable skin-tight air suit, an exhilarating machine to fly. The idea of combining a jet with a glider was, he felt as he looked out, discerning the Pacific Ocean on his left, and to the northeast the Rocky Mountains, an insight of engineering genius. He was flying at just under 70,000 feet. Sixteen miles high. Five thousand feet higher than the official record, then held by a Brit called Gibb, flying a Canberra B Mark II. The machine was skittish, and although in one week he had logged over thirty hours in it (you could fly only every other day to guard against denitrogenization), he knew not to accept it nonchalantly. For one thing, every aircraft was in some slight way different from every other. He had flown three, and knew this to be true. But all of them had problems in common. One was what the instructor called the "coffin factor," a graphic way of reminding you that you had better stay well aware of it. At the highest altitudes the atmosphere gets so rare (at 70,000 feet, he was in the upper five percent of the earth's atmosphere) that small variables in speed could leave you in an—unmanageable situation. If you went too fast, you ran into the Mach "buffer"—and the whole light-skinned soaring plane (that, really, was what it was) could simply decompose. On the other hand, if you didn't maintain enough speed you would stall. Recovering from a stall in an airplane is routine stuff, but you have to have that nice palpable a-i-r to dive into, not the wispy stuff you get sixteen miles up. Diving down to recover from the stall meant risking those high speeds again.

And twice he had experienced a flameout. The atmosphere is so attenuated, the engine just loses its fire every now and then, and before you can spark it up again, you have to slither on down to where you can feed the jet a nice gulp of good, wholesome, combustible air. He recovered from the first flameout at 65,000 feet, from the second at 60,000 feet. He had, of course, a particular interest in flameouts, because he was scheduled to have a most inconvenient one, near some goddam city in the Soviet Union whose name he kept forgetting. But don't worry, Blackford old shoe, you'll have a nice map strapped to your oxygen suit, and you won't make any mistakes when the time comes. He would flame out, come down and rekindle, then suffer successive flameouts, and finally—finally, well, time enough to work out the details.

Blackford's high-performance experience had mostly been in fighter aircraft, during the war, though his father was always letting him horse around with the latest models, and he had flown jets several times. His navigation was a little rusty, and the day after tomorrow he was scheduled to make an eight-hour run without the use of conventional navigation aids, using only a long-wave receiver, picking up regular radio programs issuing from radio stations en route, whose signal numbers were being assembled. These and, of course, the sextant and the compass. That was it.

Well. That's what the fellers have been using, he thought, over Russia and the Mediterranean, and over the China Sea, flying out of Atsugi near Yokohama. There had been casualties, but none the result of defective navigation. So that it was merely a matter of applying himself, and pre-calculating, to the extent possible, the sextant work, so that he would in fact be confirming his estimated position, rather than figuring out *ex nihilo* where he was; compensating—that's what he'd be doing—for such anomalies as wind drift.

He knew he could do it. Getting to that Russian place, whatever it was called, didn't make Blackford question himself. It was what would happen after that. Rufus had had some zany ideas in the years Blackford had worked for him, but this particular one had to have more moving parts than a pinball machine. And if anything went wrong, why, all he'd have to do was figure out a way of escaping from the Lubyanka.

How different the sensation from the noisy old Grummans! In those days—it was only fifteen years ago—when he set out, he set out to kill. Not this time. Like so many others, he had been arrested by Yeats's poem on the unmotivated quandary of the Irish airman:

> *I know that I shall meet my fate*
> *Somewhere among the clouds above;*
> *Those that I fight I do not hate,*
> *Those that I guard I do not love . . .*

How applicable was that, he wondered, soaring peaceful as a seagull up above forests and deserts and mountains? He loved very much, he believed, those he thought himself as helping to guard. And he hated, very much, those against whom he guarded them, the grim men whose enemy is the human spirit, who blind the artists, mute the poets, deafen their musicians, take parents from their children and children from their parents, and lie, with that awful tenacity that severs those painfully fragile threads that inhibit men from giving way to their beastliness. What a marvel, this vessel! he thought yet again; and thought of the closing lines of the Irish aviator. What had driven *him* to the air, if not a public cause? It was:

> *A lonely impulse of delight*
> *Drove to this tumult in the clouds . . .*

Except there was nothing tumultuous about it, up here in the cold calm, flying a plane so high it was invisible from the earth, while the sky above was a deep, mysterious purple. The tumult would be below. Soon now. The first good flying day in the first week of April. The instructor had said there was little more he could teach him. At the simulators, Blackford's reflexes had proved as sharp as when he flew at age nineteen. The navigational work would be done mostly in Japan, and on exercise pads.

On the ground, he talked casually to the instructor and the briefing officers, rattling off the routing data and submitting to the customary physical. No question about it, you came down tired. Life at Watertown Strip, located in southern Nevada, was calculated to intensify the diligence with which pilots mastered the arcana of the U-2. There was—nothing, at Watertown Strip, except the PX, the mess hall, and his little room.

It turned chilly in March, and one night after eating he put on a sweater and walked, alone, down the length of the strip. One could hardly tell where it ended. It stretched almost seamlessly into the desert, flat, uninviting. He walked an hour before turning back, at which point he could barely make out the lights from the little cluster of buildings. He homed in on his own, took off his sweater, sat down in the little armchair and began to read Buckley's *Up From Liberalism*. But his mind wandered. Hardly Buckley's fault. Blackford felt he had to talk to Sally.

So he went out and walked to the dusty corner, to the pay telephone. Exasperated, he shook his pockets for change. The PX had closed. He would have to telephone collect. He didn't like doing that, even though Sally didn't mind. But there was something about a conversation introduced with the phrase, "Will you accept a collect call from Mr. Oakes?" that had a way of pre-pitching the conversation. He vacillated . . . and returned to his room. He wrote her:

> Dear Sally: I shall in a fortnight or so be going away on one of those you-know-whats. I wonder, what would you think of spending the weekend before I leave (March 26–27) in Bermuda? The weather wouldn't be ideal, but swimming with you in Bermuda wasn't what I had in mind anyway. Now now. That *of course:* don't we belong to each other? Even if we haven't made it formal? But besides *that,* we should talk. Talk and talk and talk, endlessly. You did a

fine and nice thing last October during your interdict, read-
ing all those books by the dissidents. And when I told you
about Michael, your reaction was very different, I think,
from what it would have been even a year ago. You under-
stand that Michael *didn't* waste his life. (He certainly saved
mine.) Why did he do it? Why do I feel, more and more,
this compulsion, not to build bridges, but to make it safer
for people who want to build bridges? That's the kind of
thing we need to talk about. That, and—oh, your stunning
academic promotion, your stunning unacademic bustline,
your dismayingly learned piece in the *Sewanee Review*. And
—now, this is very important, so don't let me forget when
we get there—there is the question of what we should name
our children. Michael is—you will agree?—obligatory for our
first boy. Things like that. Say yes, call your former room-
mate Betty at her travel agency, and book us at the Coral
Beach Club. They have those little cottages. I know it's a
private club, and you probably don't know that dear old
Mum keeps up her membership. I'll call you on the tele-
phone the day after I figure you'll receive this letter. Mean-
while, be sure to have a letter waiting for me when I get
back, telling me how much you love your

                              Unruly but devoted,
                              Blackford.

# CHAPTER 19

J. Edgar Hoover, jut-jawed, beefy, all business, sat at the center of the ten-foot-long table. At his right sat Rufus; at his left, the chief of Cointelpro, Lewis Nichols. Opposite them was a screen. The slide operator could, by computer, summon onto the screen a photograph, at the desired scale, of every block or group of blocks in Greater New York. As the men sat, the area shown was the block of which 252 Fulton Street in Brooklyn was a part. The time was 12:31. A loudspeaker at the upper corner of the room was activated: someone was about to transmit.

"Control One. Able One is emerging from railroad car and making his way into main terminal."

Rufus glanced down at the typewritten sheet in front of him:

> Able One-Benni Bolgiano, Washington, followed by Cover One.

*Able Two-Hans Steiner, Brooklyn, followed by Cover Two*
   *and Intercept Two.*
*Able Three-William Stockley, Bell Labs.*
*Able Four-John O'Brien, Aberdeen Proving Grounds.*
*Able Five-Esther Meyerson, Edwards Air Force Base.*
*Baker One-Nikolai Muraviev, United Nations.*
*Baker Two-Josef Golitsyn, Pravda, Washington.*
*Baker Three-Vladimir Arakcheev, Soviet Embassy.*

Nichols drew the table microphone close to his mouth, depressed the transmitter signal, "Control One, roger."

Hoover, the fingers of his left hand tapping the table, snapped his right fingers at an aide stationed in the corner who nodded, touching a buzzer. In a few moments a secretary appeared with a tray, placing sandwiches, tea, coffee, and three plates with napkins within reach of the three men. Absentmindedly, Rufus shook the salt cellar into his coffee. There was total silence.

Again, the sound of transmission. The voice of an old-timer: "Control One, Able Two is emerging from residence, heading west.

"Control One, Able Two has descended subway at Borough Hall."

The screen opposite magnified the subway station.

"Control One, roger." And, to his colleagues at the table, "he'll be headed for Manhattan." Nichols raised the cup of coffee to his lips.

"Control One, Able One has emerged from Penn Station and is walking south on Seventh Avenue."

"Control One, roger."

The right half of the screen now showed an overhead view of Seventh Avenue from Pennsylvania Station stretching south about five blocks.

"Control One, Able Two is walking out of subway at Twenty-third and Park and walking south toward Gramercy Park."

"Control One: roger, Cover Two."

"Control One, Able One has turned on Twenty-first Street and is walking east."

"Control One: roger, Cover One."

"Control One, Able Two is walking west on Twenty-first Street."

"Control One: roger, Cover Two," and to the Director, "they're heading toward Broadway, looks like."

The screen now showed New York's Twenty-first Street, from Seventh Avenue to Third. At the right edge of the screen Gramercy Park was visible.

"Control One, Able One has stopped at newsstand at corner of Twenty-first and Broadway. He is looking at the papers on the racks."

"Control One: roger, Cover One."

"Control One, Able Two is approaching newsstand at corner of Twenty-first and Broadway." The camera descended on the corner of Twenty-first and Broadway.

"Control One, Able One has inserted the newspaper he was carrying into rack, has pulled out another paper."

"Control One, Able Two has picked up newspaper from rack and left other paper. Able Two has gone to vendor, left payment. Has put newspaper in pocket. Is walking back east."

"Control One, Able One has paid for paper, is walking north up Broadway."

Hoover turned to Nichols, and with his index finger, signaled an X.

"Control One to Cover One. Suspend further contact. Acknowledge."

"Cover One to Control One. Acknowledge, suspending contact."

"Control One to Cover Two. Continue to advise."

An aide at a switchboard at the right-hand end of the room, beside a table around which three officials sat, sent over a Telex dispatch.

"ABLE THREE REPORTED AT HOME. ABLE FOUR DITTO. ABLE FIVE IS DRIVING DIRECTION LOS ANGELES, CONTACT OKAY. BAKER ONE LUNCHING IN WASHINGTON, CONTACT SECURE. BAKER TWO, DITTO. BAKER THREE AT HOME, BAYSIDE, CONTACT SECURE."

At 1:35: "Control One, Able Two has reentered residence."

"Control One to Cover Two, roger."

Hoover spoke for the first time.

"The three times we've observed him, he stayed two to three and a half hours after contact before going out and posting."

"Yes," said Rufus. "But we're guessing that he'll probably call Ottawa on this one. And he may decide to do that even before making the negatives."

"Seat-of-the-pants stuff from now on," said Hoover.

"Assuming he goes right to work and skips lunch, he'll develop the minutes and the protocols in a half hour. Say he takes twenty minutes to read them. Say he decides then to make the call. He'd leave within an hour. That would be 2:30."

"Control One, Able Two is leaving residence." The time was 2:15. "He is proceeding west. He has flagged a taxi." There was a brief silence. "Control One, instructions to taxi driver intercepted. Destination Grand Central Station."

"Control One to Intercept Two, roger." Nichols was beginning to perspire. "Cautious bugger. Probably wouldn't use a neighborhood phone if he read we were sending over our missiles at two-thirty. . . . If he uses one of those phones in the open banks in the terminal, it's going to be hard as hell to intercept."

This, for Rufus, was a moment of high tension. Everyone knew this. Even so, he couldn't help saying it, "Mr. Hoover, we *cannot* risk blowing this. Do you think you should cut out the intercept attempt and hope the phone company comes through?"

Hoover snapped, "I'm using skilled men." Even so, he said to Nichols: "Warn Intercept Two: No risk; repeat, no risk."

"Control One to Intercept Two: No risk; repeat, no risk. Acknowledge."

"Intercept Two to Control One. Roger, no risk."

"Control One, Able Two paying taxi and heading toward Lexington . . . Walking up Lexington . . . has passed entrance to station. Is headed for pay phone at corner Forty-third and Lex." The screen zoomed down on the corner, the pay phone easily visible.

"Able Two in booth." Rufus held his breath. The switchboard operator had instantly relayed the location of the telephone, and within six seconds the AT&T computer flashed out the number:

MUrray Hill 4-3414. The number was flashed to the relevant intercept switchboard, and the recording unit began to turn.

"Control One, regret no intercept possible account street noise plus security."

"Control One to Intercept Two: Roger." Nichols turned to Hoover questioningly.

"Dismiss him," Hoover said.

"Control One to Intercept Two: Discontinue operation. Acknowledge."

"Intercept Two to Control One: Discontinue, roger and out."

Rufus now tapped his fingers. Steiner had been on the telephone approximately one minute. Probably the recorder had begun logging forty-five seconds after Steiner picked up the telephone. What it would catch would depend entirely on the speed of the conversation at Steiner's end and at Ottawa's.

"Control One, Able Two has put down telephone. Is leaving booth and flagging taxi."

"Control One to Cover Two: Roger."

"The taxi trip from Fulton Street to Grand Central took twenty-five minutes," Rufus said. "Will we get the telephone tape before he gets back to Fulton Street?"

"The lines are laid on," Hoover replied. "We should get it right away, if we got it at all."

At that moment the switchboard operator signaled, "Sir, Elgin, at Tel-Lab. He's got the tape. Want me to put it through the loudspeaker?"

"Yeah," said Hoover. "We won't need anything from Cover Two for the next minute or so."

Again, the pre-transmission hiss. The sound was strained, but the voices audible. The tape had obviously begun to roll after the conversation had started, but not much after.

"Yes, Klaus," a high-pitched voice said. "How's the weather down there?"

The guttural accents of Hans Steiner complied with the coded request. "Windy, east by south. And up there?"

"The weather is changeable, but nothing important."

"Do you have a pencil?"

The credentials had obviously been established.

"Yes, proceed."

"The message is: 'I have the Marco Polo Protocols. Will forward as usual.' Please repeat."

"'I have the Marco Polo Protocols. Will forward as usual.'"

"Thanks very much, Willi."

"Any time, Klaus."

The click was heard.

Hoover tried to look blasé. But Rufus—Rufus!—could not contain himself. He smiled. He then reached absentmindedly for a coffee, took Hoover's cup and began to drink. Hoover looked over in dismay, raised his eyes in the direction of the overattentive aide, who nodded. A fresh cup was brought in.

"Control One, Able Two has gotten out of taxi two blocks from residence. Is paying taxi. Proceeding by foot."

"Control One, Able Two has entered his residence."

All three men wrote down the time: 3:10. Rufus had said it all before, but he found it easier to say it again than to say nothing.

"We must assume that he will proceed directly with the microfilming. Two pages of minutes, six of protocols: total, eight pages. Our telephone call should be made at four-twenty. We agreed on seventy minutes to make the negatives and the microdot reductions."

"Right," Hoover said.

At 4:19 Hoover lowered his index finger, giving the signal. A large lady of Slavic countenance was now sitting at the switchboard. She dialed a number.

Hans Steiner picked up the telephone.

"Steiner Photo. Yes?"

The woman spoke in German. Her words were enunciated distinctly, telegraphically.

"*Klaus. They are coming. Conceal all evidence.*"

She hung up. Hoover nodded at her.

Rufus again spoke out loud. "He'll be hiding his negatives now. We want to give him time to do that—fifteen minutes. But of course you are ready if he attempts to break?"

"Of course," said Hoover. He nodded to Nichols. "Make contact."

"Control One to Cover Two. Are forces in position?"

"Cover Two to Control One: Roger."

"Control One to Cover Two. Proceed to surround building. Entry to be made at four thirty-five. Acknowledge."

"Cover Two to Control One. Roger. He will be detained before four thirty-five only if he attempts to escape."

Hoover spoke. He faced the switchboard corner. "All right, proceed with arrest of Able Three, Able Four, and Able Five. Report progress on Channel Two, keep Channel One clear for Cover Two."

"Yes sir."

Hoover turned to a second aide: "Inform Secretary Herter all clear to serve expulsion papers on Baker One, Baker Two, and Baker Three."

"Yes sir."

Two agents of the FBI knocked at the door of 135 North Martine Avenue. A tall black woman opened the door.

"Ma'am," one of the officers said, "is Mr. William Stockley home?" The agents knew that he was.

"*Billy?*" the woman roared. "Someone here to see you."

A huge black man, dressed in khakis and T-shirt, appeared.

"Yeah?"

"Mr. William Stockley, we're agents of the FBI and we have here a warrant for your arrest. You are charged with violating the espionage laws of the United States. You have the right to remain silent. Anything you say can be used against you in court. You have the right to talk to a lawyer and to have him with you during questioning."

Five minutes later the car drove off to the Federal House of Detention on West Street in New York City.

In Baltimore, John O'Brien was walking with his wife and children in the spring sun to a matinée, to see David Niven's *Please Don't Eat the Daisies*. A man approached O'Brien and asked if he might talk to him privately for a minute. A moment later John O'Brien, scientist with the Aberdeen Proving Grounds, said to his wife that she was to go on without him to the movie; something had come up, and he would be in touch with her. He took a twenty-dollar bill out of his pocket, and the children tugged at their mother to get on.

Esther Meyerson, a clerk at the Records Section of the Edwards Air Force Base, couldn't understand why the police car was signaling to her to pull over. She checked her speedometer—60 miles per hour. She pulled over to one side, determined to be argumentative on the matter: she was within the speed limit.

As she drew to a stop she noticed that behind the state trooper's car was a second car. Two men came out of it, and the three approached her. She put up a struggle and was therefore handcuffed, taken to the second car, and on into the Federal Detention Center in Los Angeles.

Nichols looked at his watch, then over to Hoover. Hoover nodded.

"Control One to Cover Two. Proceed with arrest."

Three men walked up the concrete steps to the door of 252 Fulton Street and rang the bell. On the street, six agents were strategically deployed.

The door was opened by a slightly bald man in his mid-fifties, precise in his movements and neatly dressed, wearing slacks and a sweater.

"Hans Steiner, we're agents of the FBI and have here a warrant for your arrest for violating the espionage laws of the United States. You have the right to remain silent. . . ."

At the end of the ritual sentences Steiner's eyebrows rose. He reached out for the document. "I wish to examine it."

The agents had been instructed to give him ample opportunity to read the warrant. A second document authorized a search of his premises and a sealing off of the premises pending prosecution and trial.

Hans Steiner asked if he might collect his toilet articles and perhaps some reading matter—"It will, I suppose, require a little while to establish my innocence of these outrageous charges."

The arresting official answered crisply: "My instructions are to take you directly into custody."

Twenty minutes later Hans Steiner was in the Federal Detention Center on West Street, and Hoover and Rufus were at 252 Fulton Street, together with two technicians. Rufus desired merely a feel for the place. There was a smell of smoke in the bathroom. Ah yes, but what had been burned had first been photographed, and Rufus knew that the negatives must be somewhere in this house. The house would of course be searched. But even if it happened that the searchers were so lucky as to come upon eight negatives, each one of them the diameter of a typewriter dot, Rufus would see to it that they were delicately returned to wherever Klaus had recently hidden them. The Protocols of Marco Polo would not leave 252 Fulton Street until Hans Steiner himself retrieved them. But no one would be permitted to set foot in 252 Fulton Street before then. It was sealed now, order of the federal court. No innocent cleaning woman. No lawyer representing Steiner. No one who didn't take his instructions from Rufus.

Benni was back, sitting in his favorite chair. He had adopted the American habit of drinking beer while watching televison. He tuned in to the news.

He saw it all. More than five minutes was given over to it. Pictures of Klaus (his real name apparently was Hans Steiner) . . . of a technician at Bell Labs . . . of a scientist at the Aberdeen Proving Grounds . . . a clerk at Edwards Air Force Base . . . pictures of Soviet diplomats . . . a statement from the Secretary of State . . . protests to the Soviet Ambassador . . . talk of a trial that would expose the largest network—the words were those of John Edgar Hoover, who appeared before the camera, advising that his agents had been working "months and months" on the case of Hans Steiner—the largest spy network in postwar history. . . . The government would ask for the maximum penalties against Steiner and his agents. . . . Life imprisonment. Conceivably, death—if atomic secrets were involved.

Maria wasn't home. Since Michael's death, she had taken to spending most of her time at the convent on Thirty-ninth Street doing volunteer work. Sometimes she wouldn't come home at all. Benni went to the telephone. He dialed Amanda's number. "Are you alone?"

"Yes," she whispered.

"You saw it on television?"

"Yes," she said.

"They don't . . . know about us."

Amanda's voice broke. "How can we be sure?"

"We'll know soon."

"Benni, I don't think we should talk over the telephone."

"All right. On Monday, you come by the office—to see your father. We can have our usual cup of coffee."

"I'm scared."

"Don't do anything unusual. And don't use the machine."

"Don't worry." She hung up.

# CHAPTER 20

On receiving the news by teletype, the KGB duty officer telephoned Colonel Anton Speranski. It was just after 2 A.M. Speranski had gone to sleep only a half hour earlier, after a long evening celebrating—what *was* he celebrating? . . . he tried to clear his mind—celebrating Saturday night, he supposed. The duty officer's words sank into his mind like a poison pellet. Then, the little stab of pain, and as the poisons began to course through his consciousness, the disastrous implications of the news—they had arrested Klaus—were little by little conjugated. He had, up until now, presided over the most strikingly successful intelligence operation in Soviet history—certainly the most spectacular penetration since Kim Philby, and before that Richard Sorge. And what with the message—was it only three hours ago? (*that* was what he was celebrating! he suddenly remembered)—that Klaus had actually got hold of the Marco Polo Protocols, he had silently drained that last glass of vodka to celebrate what would surely develop within a matter of months, perhaps weeks: the highest honors, a promotion, his own dacha.

And now . . .

He kept the duty officer on the line while he gave thought to the single question he must answer without delay. Should he awaken Shelepin?

What could Shelepin do? It was too early to get fuller reports. Should he be awakened—no doubt in his congenitally fearful mood, aggravated by this terrible reversal—in the middle of the night?

On the other hand, if he *didn't* wake him, Speranski ran the risk that tomorrow Shelepin would be enraged at not having been given the news immediately. Conceivably he would even call Malinovsky now. Conceivably he would even call Khrushchev!

Speranski thought back, his whole frame shivering, on the single occasion when he had been present at one of those notorious late-night meetings at Stalin's dacha. It would not have been necessary to wake *Stalin* at midnight—for *him*, that was early.

Speranski was the juniormost KGB official in the room that night, and it had struck Stalin's fancy to say—nothing. He simply kept Beria and the two generals and, of course, Speranski, standing there while he sat in his couch, the great bear rug under his feet, looking absently at the big log fire. The head of the KGB had finished his report, and Stalin made no comment. No gesture of dismissal. And so they stood. Twenty minutes later Stalin, without looking up, said to his aide, "Tell them to go."

"Good night, Comrade Stalin."

"Good night, Comrade Stalin."

"Good night, Comrade Stalin."

Never before or since had Speranski suffered so. Was he too unimportant to bid Stalin good night? Might it be considered . . . forward? He had seconds in which to decide. He compromised.

He turned toward Stalin, and bowed his head deferentially. Stalin looked him full in the face. And then, that bolt of lightning shooting through the room.

"Good night, Captain Speranski. I have heard about your fine work."

Speranski had opened his mouth, dumbstruck. Should he reply? Say, "Thank you, Comrade Stalin"? Instead, he merely repeated his bow, only this time he bowed even more deeply. Outside the inner sanctum, the door having been gently closed by Stalin's aide, his senior colleagues looked at Speranski in utter amazement. Wordlessly, they put on their coats and went to their waiting vehicles. Beria thought to himself that only a man as perverse as Stalin would have done such a thing after so pointedly humbling Speranski's superiors. Speranski had not slept that whole night, experiencing multiple orgasms of pride and excitement and pleasure, one after another. . . .

But he was daydreaming, and the duty officer had permitted himself to clear his throat at the other end of the telephone. Speranski drew a deep breath:

"Get me the Director on the line."

He shivered as he waited. A minute later he heard Shelepin's voice. Clearly he had not been awakened. "Yes, what is it?"

"I am sorry to disturb you, Aleksandr Nikolaevich, but there is a bulletin from Washington. They have arrested Klaus."

First a silence. Then, "Just Klaus?"

"No. There were multiple arrests."

"You know of course why it is vital that we should have the exact circumstances."

"Of course, Aleksandr Nikolaevich. Right now we have just the bulletins. We have the alternative of waiting until fuller reports come in from regular channels, or making our own inquiries."

"Meet me in my office."

"Yes, Aleksandr Nikolaevich."

Speranski had further to travel to the Lubyanka than Shelepin or General Malinovsky. Both were at the Director's office when breathlessly Speranski arrived. They were reading the news from the ticker. An aide brought in another installment. The story was being reported in considerable detail. Speranski sat, and took the sheet of paper already read by Shelepin and Malinovsky. In ten minutes they had all read what had been transmitted by Tass. Shelepin instructed an aide to rouse a translator and have the Associated Press wire story rendered in Russian. "And bring tea." Which meant vodka as well.

Shelepin said, "It is quite extraordinary. They do not appear to have arrested our principal Washington assets."

Malinovsky commented. "Perhaps they have, but haven't announced it."

Speranski felt obliged to make a clarification. "General, in the United States they don't make secret arrests. At least, I never heard of one. Arrests are made only pursuant to court orders, and these are instantly published."

Shelepin tapped his fingers on the table. " . . . Is it *conceivable?*" he was talking, really, to himself; " . . . Is it conceivable that they did not pick up the Washington penetration?"

"Sir," Speranski said, "it is surely *conceivable*. Because they have picked up fewer than half of Klaus's assets."

"The Protocols," said Shelepin. "The bloody Protocols. Did Klaus dispatch them before he was arrested?"

This, of course, was the question on which Speranski had most vigorously concentrated in reading the dispatch. He had already drawn his gloomy conclusion.

"It says here, Aleksandr Nikolaevich, that Klaus was arrested at his studio in Brooklyn at 4:35 New York time. We heard from Ottawa at 2:45. I greatly fear that he would not have had time to execute the usual arrangements before 4:35."

"I greatly fear you are correct."

Malinovsky: "Where, then, *are* the Protocols?"

Speranski spoke. "They were certainly at the Fulton Street house at the time of the arrest. We do not know whether they were apprehended by the FBI. If Klaus proceeded instantly with the microphotography and destroyed the originals, then quite possibly the FBI did not find them. Klaus is a cautious man, and he could certainly have hidden negatives less than the size of a postage stamp before opening the door."

Shelepin: "On the other hand, if they found them—perhaps they were still in the developing room, or in the camera—then the FBI is almost certain to trace the source. Worse, Washington will know we have been seeing the minutes."

Shelepin rose. Characteristically he did so only when he was ready to give orders.

"It is obvious that we need, instantly, to advise one of our law-yers—you know which one, Speranski. Instruct him to appear instantly—instantly—at the detention center and announce that he is the attorney for Hans Steiner and demand to see his client."

"Sir, if we get that lawyer, it will be rather obvious that Steiner is our man. . . . "

"Bulldung, Speranski! The FBI will not have brought in Hans Steiner without plenty of evidence. I grant that the use of that lawyer will confirm the public position on Steiner, but that is of little concern at this moment."

He resumed. "Get him. What's his name?"

"J. Daniel Umin."

"Of course. Bright fellow. Now listen, get Ottawa to call Umin. Steiner will know not to disavow Umin. Probably he has made no motion yet to get a lawyer."

"Probably the government appointed a lawyer."

"Steiner can dismiss him, after having a word with Umin. Now we want Umin to get from Steiner the answer to three questions—you are listening, Speranski?"

"Of course, Aleksandr Nikolaevich."

"One, did he send the Protocols? Two, if he didn't, did the FBI get them? Three, if the FBI didn't get them, where are they?" Shelepin took a deep draft of vodka. Malinovsky, as if to be companionable, did also. Speranski lifted his glass, but before it reached his lips—"Now move, Speranski. Report back here after Ottawa talks to Umin. I really cannot see why, if you apply yourself, we shouldn't have an answer to those three ques-tions before dawn. Ottawa has all Umin's numbers?"

"Of course, Aleksandr Nikolaevich. I trained Ottawa myself."

"Use my line, next door."

"Remember, sir, it's Saturday night."

Shelepin stared at his associate. Speranski bolted out the door.

J. Daniel Umin's name made judges with cast-iron stomachs and nerves of steel moan. For twenty-five years he had defended Communists, crypto-Communists, saboteurs, seditionists, terror-ists. His intrusion into a case meant a volcanic tremor, felt up and down the judicial vertebrae from jail guards to Supreme

Court Justices. He was inevitably insolent, studiedly impolite, routinely obscene. There had been a dozen meetings, mostly surreptitious, among judges and officials of the New York Bar Association to inquire into the possibility of successfully disbarring him. That his contempt for the courts, his abuse of process, his outrageous personal behavior, would objectively justify removing him was not doubted by anyone who consulted the record (or read the papers). But J. Daniel Umin had acquired a perverse immunity. He had industriously advertised himself as a friend of the helpless, of the politically oppressed, as a bastion of political liberty, the prime mover in the anti-McCarthy movement in America; and as such he regularly worked the college circuit. He delighted in taking a judge—whoever had most recently ruled against him—and devoting an entire lecture to the judge's background, making sexual insinuations, accusations of outright incompetence, innuendoes about the judge's drinking habits, about scandals involving his brothers, sisters, mother, father, children, godchildren. He did this with such utter, righteous, communicable high-mindedness that he succeeded in causing several distinguished men of the bar to have nervous breakdowns and two to retire; one died of apoplexy, right in the courtroom. Umin never appeared anywhere without a) a cigar, b) a poetic tribute to the First, Fourth, Fifth, and Sixth Amendments, c) a warning against the ideologization of justice by the military-industrial complex, and d) the suggestion that behind it all was: the Central Intelligence Agency, primeval enemy of Thomas Jefferson, Abraham Lincoln, Martin Luther King, and Lillian Hellman. Notwithstanding that he was a traveling spectacular—the indigenous equivalent of Moscow's May Day Parade—he was a careful scholar and brilliant legal parliamentarian. At Yale as an undergraduate he had had a distinguished career, during which he had shown no radical tendencies. But in his junior year he accepted election to the senior society Scroll & Key. More than one biographer of J. Daniel Umin had suggested that his rejection by the *leading* senior society at Yale was the root cause of his anti-American resentments. Soon after graduating from the Yale Law School he came out for abolishing all private colleges as "citadels of privilege." He had a speech on just that subject which he delivered at least once to every college generation at Harvard, Yale, Princeton, Columbia, Cornell, and NYU, regularly receiving standing ovations.

It was a few minutes after ten when the door at 427 West Street of the Federal Detention Center opened in response to the buzzer. Umin strode in to the big receiving desk. The lieutenant at the desk looked up and thought to himself, Oh my God. Him.

Umin, a portly, hairy man with an elegant mustache, always wore black, a striped shirt, and his Phi Beta Kappa key. He was followed by an acned assistant carrying his briefcase. Outside the building, a congregation of reporters and photographers, spotting Umin, instantly began to photograph him, but he had said he would return presently to conduct a press conference.

"Lieutenant," said J. Daniel Umin, drawing on his cigar, "bring me somebody important."

The lieutenant bristled, but was hardly surprised. "What is your business, sir?"

"I demand to see my client, the latest victim of American fascism, Mr. Hans Steiner, the distinguished artist."

The lieutenant had been briefed: anything to do with Hans Steiner was to be referred instantly to an on-duty assistant U. S. Attorney. There would be one on the premises around the clock.

"You'll have to talk to Mr. Lichtenstein," the lieutenant picked up the telephone and dialed a number.

"Tell him to hurry up."

The lieutenant spoke into the telephone. In a few minutes a slim young man wearing glasses and a rumpled brown suit and carrying a clipboard emerged from the elevator. He approached Umin. "I'm Steve Lichtenstein."

"It is of no interest to me who or what you are. I am here to see my client, Mr. Hans Steiner."

"Mr. Steiner has a court-appointed attorney who has advised him of all his rights. Inasmuch as Mr. Steiner has not discharged Mr. Johnson, my answer to your request is: Mr. Johnson is Mr. Steiner's attorney of record."

"Young man," said J. Daniel Umin, chewing his cigar, "have you by any chance ever read the Constitution of the United States?"

Lichtenstein ignored him and began to walk back toward the elevator.

*"Stop!"*

Lichtenstein turned. Umin snapped his fingers. His aide opened a briefcase and took out a telegram. Umin snatched it. "This telegram was delivered a half hour ago. Assuming you can read, you will see that it is quite straightforward." The assistant U. S. Attorney took it and read:

"J. DANIEL UMIN TELEPHONE PLAZA 2-1220. DESIRE YOU TO ACT AS MY ATTORNEY BEGINNING IMMEDIATELY. NEED URGENTLY CONSULTA-TION. PLEASE DISMISS COURT APPOINTED ATTORNEY. HANS STEINER."

It did not surprise Lichtenstein that Umin was in the act, but it considerably surprised him that he had gotten into it quite that fast. He inspected the telegram.

"When was this delivered?"

"It was not delivered. It was telephoned in. I sent my clerk to the Western Union office for a copy."

Lichtenstein decided to consult with the U. S. Attorney. "I'll have to check on this, Mr. Umin."

"I will wait five minutes, after which I will file to vacate the arrest on the grounds that my client is being denied his consti-tutional rights."

While Lichtenstein went upstairs, J. Daniel Umin went out and delivered an impromptu press conference to the reporters on creeping American fascism, the revival of McCarthyism, the se-nility of Eisenhower, and the repeated rejection by the U.S. of peaceable initiatives by the Soviet Union.

Back in his office Lichtenstein dialed the number where, he was told, his superior Howard Trent would be at this hour. He told him what had happened.

"We could play around a bit," Trent mused over the phone, "waste a few hours, but what the hell. Umin was meant for this case. But this *will* give us a chance to test Steiner's reflexes. Ob-viously he didn't send the telegram. Go into his cell and ask him, 'Have you made a request for another lawyer?' Just that, see what he says. Call me back."

Lichtenstein went to the carefully guarded eleventh floor. There were three barriers, of men and of steel, between the ele-vator and the little cell in which Hans Steiner sat on a wooden chair, reading a book. Any instrument by which he might have committed suicide had been taken from him, his shoelaces included. As additional precaution, in the empty cell opposite, the cell door open, a police official sat, charged with constant visual monitoring of all of Steiner's movements. The officer rose to admit Lichtenstein into the cell. Lichtenstein motioned that this wasn't necessary.

"Mr. Steiner," he said, talking through the bars, "I'm Steve Lichtenstein, the assistant U. S. Attorney. I'm in charge of this case until relieved. Did you initiate a request for any other attorney?"

Hans Steiner, still sitting, put his book to one side. He hesitated.

"Would you be more specific?"

"Have you asked for any attorney in place of Mr. Johnson, your court-appointed attorney?"

It became clear that Steiner's reflexes were in excellent condition. He replied, "I managed to get word to a friend to retain a suitable lawyer for me. Can I assume he has arrived?"

Lichtenstein knew the game was up. "I'll advise you in a few minutes."

He reported the conversation to Howard Trent, who groaned. "Okay okay. They can have an hour. Get a written statement discharging Johnson and appointing Umin."

Five minutes later, J. Daniel Umin walked triumphantly into the corridor. "The Nazis had more civilized prisons," he sniffed. "Open the door," he wiggled his cigar. Lichtenstein would have liked, more even than professional advancement, to have poked J. Daniel Umin in the nose. But who then would care for Steve's widowed mother?

"He'll have to sign an order discharging Johnson and appointing you."

"Very well," said Umin, nodding at Steiner. Steiner studied his expression, and then accepted the paper from Lichtenstein, signing his name.

"Him"—now Umin pointed to the police officer, who after opening Steiner's cell door had resumed his seat opposite. "Him. That creep. Get him out of here."

"No, Mr. Umin. The sergeant's orders are to maintain Mr. Steiner in sight at all times. He will not be able to overhear your conversation."

Umin sensed that this wasn't one he would win. So he motioned with his cigar that Lichtenstein was to remove himself.

Umin then went to the far corner of the bed. Sitting on it, he was cheek by jowl with Steiner.

Umin reached into his pocket, and brought out several 3 x 5 cards. On the first was typewritten: "Instructions to defend you came to me from Ottawa, telephone 613-Central 2-4232, Willi."

Steiner read the card and nodded.

Umin flashed the second card. It said: "*You are to decline to answer any questions by anybody on any subject. The next card contains my telephone numbers, name, office, and home address. I will leave that card with you. When interrogated, about anything except what you want to eat, point to the card and demand my presence.*"

Steiner nodded and pocketed the card.

The fourth card he handed over with a pencil.

Neatly typed was:

"*We must have the following information immediately. 1) Did you mail the Protocols? 2) Did the FBI get them? If not, 3) Where are they?*"

Umin sat while Steiner moved his pencil about the card. Without looking at it, Umin put it back in his pocket. He brought out the final card:

"*I will make an appointment for tomorrow. You will have all resources working for you. Now I must go.*"

He rose. "You," he said to the sergeant. "Open the door." To Steiner he whispered, "Good night, comrade."

It was dawn in Moscow, and Shelepin was talking to Malinovsky, who, however, was not entirely attentive, the bottle of vodka having been emptied. While Shelepin reminisced, Malinovsky dozed. But then the door opened with a bang. Malinovsky awoke with a start. Speranski was very nearly breathless.

"In answer to your questions, Aleksandr Nikolaevich, 1) Klaus did *not* have the opportunity to dispatch the Protocols. 2) Klaus has reason to believe the FBI did *not* come upon the Protocols. 3) The Protocols are in Klaus's studio."

"Where in his studio?" Shelepin asked, almost in a whisper.

"In the Encyclopaedia Britannica. On the page that gives the biography of Marco Polo."

# CHAPTER 21

The relatively inconspicuous American Air Force base at Atsugi, fifteen miles east of Yokohama, was being used among other things for general reconnaissance flights along the South China Sea, and there had been occasional light penetrations over China. The U-2 detachment there, formally under NASA, was ostensibly engaged in high-altitude meteorological work even as its sister detachments, flying out of Peshawar in Pakistan and Adana in Turkey, used the same cover story. No aircraft had ever before taken the route that Rufus, after considerable consultation with area experts, had laid out for Blackford. The question Rufus had asked them was, at root, simple: "If you were the chief of staff of the Armed Services of the People's Republic of China and coveted knowledge of Soviet military arrangements along Russo-Chinese borders, where would you route a preliminary reconnaissance flight, on the understanding that the maximum range of the photographic 'vehicle' was four thousand miles?" The primary question was whether to fly along the northern border of Outer Mongolia (officially an "independent" country—"The People's Republic of Mongolia," actually a satellite state) or south of its border, on the grounds that effective military control of Mongolia by the U.S.S.R. really made this the relevant geopolitical frontier.

The decision was to go north. Piecemeal intelligence already in hand hinted that there was no significant Soviet military activity within Mongolia, where military arrangements along the southern border were at least informally familiar to the Chinese. By contrast, the 1,500-mile-long border to the north was utterly unfamiliar. The route would take Blackford across the Sea of Japan, south of Vladivostok, over Harbin in Manchuria to Zabaykalsk, at which point the borders of the Soviet Union, Outer Mongolia, and China join. Thence he would follow the frontier, heading west over 1,300 miles of border. He would develop his engine trouble in the area of Alma-Ata, where the dizzyingly high mountain ranges would exclude any possibility of landing to the south, outside Russian territory (as though he'd get a friendlier reception from the Chinese!). The hypothetical flight plan called on him to dip south at Alma-Ata, overflying Kirghizia and Tadzhikistan, to safety at Peshawar. The radio signals had been collected, and neat and graphic charts laid out, together with the running instructions governing the operation of the camera. It would be a considerable, but by no means heroic, enterprise, requiring the pilot to be in the air approximately six hours and forty minutes.

Blackford arrived in Tokyo on D minus 5 and was met at the airport and driven to a small suite of rooms kept for visiting dignitaries by Colonel Robin Sharples, who headed the detachment. Colonel Sharples had been put in charge of assembling navigational information for the Marco Polo flight. He had not been informed of the ulterior purpose of the flight, or that it was designed to come down over Russia. Arrangements had been made at Peshawar to radio Atsugi news of the arrival of Flight 1107, as it had been designated, nine hours after takeoff, which would result in a routine "mission completed" check going into the relevant dossier. The commanding officer in Peshawar was quietly instructed not to inquire into the meaning of the fake signal he was to send. As a trained operative of the CIA, he accepted his instructions matter-of-factly.

On D minus 4, Blackford took up the aircraft that had been designated for his mission. It was free of any external markings, painted entirely black. He headed south and for an hour or so attempted to tease out of the aircraft its distinctive mannerisms. He found nothing idiosyncratic in its movements, and after the hour regularly required to accustom himself to the tight oxygen suit he found himself relaxed, in fact serene. He made a lazy turn, brushing by the northern islands of Okinawa, then over toward the southern island of Kyushu. He passed over Nagasaki, and closed his eyes in a gesture of piety. From there he could easily see Hiroshima, across the Suo Sea. Then Osaka and, a half hour later, he was down. An assistant helped him to remove his helmet. He checked in at Communications.

There was a telegram for him. SEE YOU TOMORROW. SINGER. He felt a flush of pleasure. He had experienced acute loneliness since arriving in Japan. Intuitively the other fliers, officers, and officials sensed that "Sandy"—that was the whole of the name given him—was on an offbeat mission. It was known when he would fly out (the meteorologist approving), and that therefore he would be around for only a few days. Accordingly, no one took aggressive social initiatives, which in any event he would not have welcomed. One day he spent in Tokyo, mostly walking about, revisiting buildings and museums he had seen on previous visits.

He devoted his spare hours to writing. He wished to compose a personal memoir of Michael Bolgiano, to give to Maria, whose devastation on learning of Michael's death had very nearly paralyzed Blackford. He had seen her alone twice since giving her the news, and had already sensed that her life with Benni was over. Blackford told her that Michael, before his accidental death, had discussed his mother's letter with him. For Michael's own sake, Blackford stressed, she must not reveal to Benni that she had any knowledge of the real purpose of his visits to New York. She promised, but also told Blackford that whatever happened to Benni (she supposed that, at the convenience of the authorities, he would be led off to jail), she had decided to associate herself with the Sisters of the Holy Child Jesus. She thought herself too old, and perhaps unsuited, formally to join the order, she said, but since her retirement she had worked as a volunteer, and she was prepared now to propose to the sisters that she live on the premises of the convent and assume a greater share of the administrative work. "You don't have to worry about me, Mr. Blacky"—as she had always insisted on calling him—"because I don't spend any money. Besides, I have my savings from when I worked, and social security." Blackford didn't tell her that, in due course, she would be receiving the life insurance the Agency pays to the next of kin of those who die in the line of duty. She said she harbored no bitterness toward Benni—he had always been an idealist, and his early commitment to the Party had apparently survived all that he knew or had read about since the war. At the same time, she found she could only with intense self-discipline endure his company. Blackford would now, in his memoir, disclose the truth, giving Michael's mother an accurate account of those final hours. He need not disclose to her the chronology, which would give her grounds to suspect her son might be alive but for her letter. He could, and would in some detail, let her take pride in her son's heroism. It was better, he knew, that she should have those details after she had effected her separation from Benni.

Singer materialized at noon, greeted Blackford happily, but asked only one favor: that he be permitted to sleep, to recover from the endless flight traversing ten time zones. Blackford gave him the second bedroom in the suite and told him he had ordered dinner served right here in their quarters. "Whatever celebrating I'm going to do, I'm going to have to do tonight. Because tomorrow I'm not even allowed to drink coffee. I gotta go—I mean, Singer, I gotta *not* go on Thursday, for about nine hours. Two hours' pre-pressurization, before the plane takes off, but all suited up; and then the duration of the flight. If I had to travel all the way to Pakistan, I'd probably have to start drying out tonight to effect that much continence. But I don't. Go to bed. I'll pummel you awake at seven."

And it required that Blackford do exactly that. Singer was doggedly asleep, even six hours after diving into bed. But following his shower and a drag on his beloved cigarette, Singer was relaxed, speaking in those long, rounded sentences Blackford had remarked when he first met him in London. Singer had been married ten years and was now divorced. He was very sentimental in his occasional references to Ruth, whose alcoholism had proved beyond the capacity of Singer either to cure or to endure. There were no children; Singer, at fifty-five, was happy in his work and entirely serious about it. His avocation was the study of Russian history, and he had taught himself the language, achieving—or so Blackford had been told by a Russian defector who had worked with both of them—an extraordinary fluency for someone who came so late to the language. Blackford wished he could borrow that facility for the next—what? Five days? Ten days? Ten weeks? Ten years? The question always quietly uppermost in his mind: *how long?* Rufus, at their last meeting, of course sensed this, and there had been a moment when, instead of the routine handclasp, Rufus drew him close and gave him a quick, embarrassed hug. Turning then his back to Blackford, who was on his way out of The Quarters, Rufus said huskily, "I'll see you again, Blackford, you can count on that. I don't know when, but soon." It was characteristic of Rufus (everyone always assumed that he was motivated only by his professionalism) to dispatch Singer all the way to Tokyo, to see Blackford off, so to speak. Blackford could think of no other reason, really, why Singer was seven thousand miles from home.

"We begin with this." From the refrigerator Blackford brought out a carefully selected bottle of Riesling, which he uncorked. "At eight, a Japanese girl will come around with something or other. It will taste good."

"Hmm." Singer, dressed in khaki pants and a light sweater, leaned back in an armchair. "This *is* good! Ugh, what a flight. The things I do for you, Black. And I mean, all *you* have to do is fly a few thousand miles over Central Asia!— Did I tell you I figured out an easy way to navigate? Well, you make sure that on your left, there are five Communists for every Communist on your right. That way, you'll fly right between Khrushchev's Russia and Mao's China, without missing a thing! Here's to you, boy." Singer raised his glass and gave Blackford a fatherly wink.

Blackford was anxious for news of Tango. The arrests had taken place the Saturday of his departure. The English-language press in Tokyo had carried a fairly full account, together with a statement by Hans Steiner's lawyer.

"I see he got himself old J. Daniel Umin."

"Yup. Umin is having a ball. He has told the press that the injustice already done to Hans Steiner—he always refers to him as 'the internationally renowned artist'—is the greatest injustice since Dred Scott."

Blackford's laughter was the closest he had come to release since Michael's death. The days with Sally in Bermuda were days that had brought him nourishment of an entirely different order. This was the laughter of the trade. The kind of amusement professional students of Soviet behavior derive from reading a bald lie in the Communist press, inevitably introduced by the phrase, "As everyone knows . . ." Intraoffice jokes. They are the most satisfying. Inside jokes. Yes, gallows humor, even. "I caught him on television, Black. I'll tell you, that character is the meanest, funniest son of a bitch I ever saw. I got to confess I'd give one nut to stick J. Daniel Umin in a Soviet courtroom for just one hour."

"Is he doing Steiner any good?"

"I don't think Seneca could spring Steiner."

"Is there a trial date?"

"Hell, no. Umin has introduced enough motions to delay a trial till fall at the earliest. Which, as you know my dear Blackford, doesn't bother Rufus one bit."

"Yeah, right. But tell me, did they find the mole?"

"Yup."

Blackford waited. "Are you going to tell me who it was?"

"Under the circumstances, I can. The mole is Amanda Gaither."

Blackford put his glass down. He stared at Singer, his lips parted. Singer could hear the exhalation of breath.

"What the hell," Singer said, struggling at once to console and dismiss. "You can make out a solid case for the inconceivability of most of them. Look at the social background of Lawrence Duggan, Alger Hiss, Donald Maclean. . . . She was recruited while at Vassar."

"Who by? The President, I suppose you're now going to tell me."

"No. It was done out of New York."

Again Blackford paused, his wineglass forgotten, his eyes glazed.

". . . How did she . . . bring it off?"

Singer poured another glass of wine.

"Well, my boy, it happens that your old friend Singer Callaway was in the very room when J. Edgar Hoover's technician explained it—or tried to—to Rufus. He even brought in the piece."

"The piece of what?"

"The piece of hardware, I'd guess you'd call it. Maybe 'electronic hardware' would be more accurate. But before I explain how it worked, let me tell you what happened, okay?"

"Yeah."

"As you know, Amanda" (It crossed Singer's mind to amuse himself by characterizing her "your every-now-and-then-girl-friend Amanda," but he pulled away from jocularity in reaction to the gravity of the expression he looked up at. Singer resolved to cant the analysis of what happened on the technical, rather than the human end, at which level he was in any case better prepared to cope, having very little original to say to explain why Amanda Gaither would choose to work for the people who operated Gulag, rather than for the people who wanted to confine Gulag's boundaries.) "Amanda worked—I'll tell you, in a minute, why I'm using the past tense (she doesn't work for him any longer)—in the office of the Director himself. Among other things, she was in charge of the beautiful new Xerox 914. Seven copies per minute . . . neat, dry stuff—you're familiar with it.

"Anyway, that was one of her jobs, to run the thing, keep up the paper supply, teach authorized assistants how to work it— that kind of thing. How she brought it off was by a thing the FBI have called the 'diverter.'"

"The what?"

"The diverter. First let me tell you what she did, then I'll tell you how it worked. Or do you care?"

"I care," Blackford said. He leaned almost unnoticeably forward on his chair, running his finger around the undrained wineglass.

"Okay. Well, under the rig was—is—a foot switch. If activated, which our Amanda could do by a slight movement of her toe as she bent over the machine to put down the documents, the diverter stayed activated till she nudged the switch again."

"Come on, Singer."

"Easy. So, she would push the switch. Then put the document, as usual, face down on the glass plate on top of the machine, positioned for the scanner. Then she'd press the Run button, and the machine would begin to crank, delivering whatever number of copies she had designated on the counter. The magic of it was simple: the diverter would make an extra copy."

Blackford intruded. "Couldn't people see the extra copy being made?"

"No, no, you don't understand. The diverter didn't extrude an extra copy on the tray. If the orders were for, say, two copies of a document, she'd set the exposed counter button at 'two.' And two copies would pop out of the machine. But, ho ho ho, a third copy had been made. In sequence, it was actually the first copy. But instead of ejecting into the delivery tray, it was kicked down into the bottom of the machine, where it sat under the internal mechanism. Sat there until Amanda retrieved it. Retrieved them."

"Retrieved it—them—when?"

"We filmed her. Toward the end of the day, usually, Tidy-up time. She'd open up the big panels on the 914, normal practice: check the feed mechanisms, take out mangled sheets of Xerox paper, that sort of thing. While at it, she would pick up copies of the national treasures. Take them, casually, and put them on one of the file baskets where papers are habitually collected for USIA. One of her jobs was to address them. Simple. She addressed the *un*classified papers to USIA, at their post office box number, and the *classified* papers to a Soviet drop, using an official-type post office box address . . . Benni's box." Singer looked up cautiously. It was not his assignment to come to Tokyo to upset the principal field executive of the Marco Polo operation. He could tell that Blackford had absorbed the Michael-Benni shock.

"How did the diverter actually work?"

"Remarkably simply. Even I understood it, though maybe

only because Hoover made his guy repeat it about five hundred times.

"To begin with, our friends in the KGB tracked the new Xerox 914 machines coming off production. We still haven't picked up the cutie-pie at *that* end of the business. That was last July.

"Anyway, next thing we know, a unit is at a Washington distributor, more or less ready for delivery, and some guy shows up after hours and corners the technician who's supposed to check out the machines pre-delivery. He Has a Secret. It's worth a couple of grand to him if the technician will make a few adjustments in the machine. 'Cause the guy's principal competitor in the real estate business is going to get delivery of the machine, and our guy would like to know who his clients are he's sending prospectuses of real estate property to . . . and, you know, we live in a competitive society, got to make a buck. The Xerox technician bites, and says, 'Well, what you got in mind?' Our guy says, 'Well, it happens when I was at M.I.T., my roommate was an engineering nut, and now works in the research center in Rochester, and he showed me how easy it would be to install a 'diverter.' Amazing. A solenoid-driven—"

"What's 'solenoid-driven'?"

"Beats the shit out of me. A 'solenoid-driven' metal blade intercepts the Xeroxed copies of the secret documents, sliding them into the bottom of the machine. There's a spring-loaded unit operated by a black box of some kind, with wires to the foot switch, power supply, and wire leads into the control box where the 'number' gauge is. The black box is nicely hidden, behind where anyone would look except at overhaul time, and if that was scheduled, our Amanda, otherwise Tovarich X23-Z, could remove the black box and its fittings, in like maybe three minutes.

"Anyway, when Amanda had that foot switch kicked over, a metal blade would intercept the first copy of any run, directing it into the cavity at the bottom of the machine. Amanda's role was *that* simple. With the kick switch on, she'd push the Run button. The machine goes into motion and comes up with the designated number of copies. *But*—before it ejects the first of those copies, it has made an extra copy, diverted to the bottom of the machine. A complete one-document cycle (the Xerox boys are real proud of this) takes exactly 9.1 seconds. But a non-expert has no idea how long the warm-up period takes. In the case of Amanda's machine the warm-up period, sounding in with a gentle purr—you guessed it—took 9.1 seconds before the visible copies would start going through. The purr period was making copies for the Kremlin."

Singer was clearly caught up with the mechanical excitement of it all, which he had mastered at such pains, thanks to Mr. Hoover's corresponding incapacity to grasp technical detail easily.

"See, Black, just when the first copy starts to climb up out of the bottom of the machine to arrive at the delivery tray, the diverter goes to work. A metal blade—the FBI people call it the 'guillotine'—comes down. Catches the leading edge of the paper and drives it down through the gap. One of these, and the black box cuts off the current to the solenoids, the springs snap the blade back up out of the way, and the machine operates in a conventional way. But put in another first copy of paper, and the pressure reactivates the black box for a return performance. Neat?"

"Neat. The technician did it for two grand?"

"Claims it took him only two nights' work, period. His 'client' came up with the black box, 'anniversary present' from his old roommate at M.I.T. Needless to say, we have no lead to the 'client.' It was all cash."

"I'll be damned."

"Hoover's reaction exactly. The Xerox mechanic says he had every reason to believe the unit was going out on a purchase order to the Drexel Real Estate firm."

Blackford laughed. "Maybe that was the cover name our leader Mr. Dulles was giving the Agency last summer." His voice sobered. "But tell me about Amanda."

"Well, of course, Rufus had instructed that there should be no difference whatever in procedures on the Monday after the arrests, *nothing* to make Amanda suspicious. On the other hand, Benni had no one to take secret papers to, at least not until the KGB reinstructed him, which would take time; so we were set to just, well, let things ride. Let Amanda go on using the diverter without knowing who'd pick the stuff up from Benni. She saved us the trouble."

"How so?"

"We had her under continuous observation, of course, from the moment we found out. We watched her when Klaus was arrested. She stayed home. On Sunday she called a professional delivery service and gave the messenger boy a letter to deliver to Benni."

"Did you intercept?"

"Uh-huh. And consummated delivery to Benni within a half hour."

"Saying?"

"Saying that she was not going to sit around Washington waiting to be picked up. She was leaving that afternoon for Mexico, where she would tuck in with the Mexican consul she had one of her flings with last year. She told Benni maybe she'd marry him, maybe she wouldn't, but in any case she could be reached in care of her loverboy, and she gave his address."

"So much for that problem?"

"Wait. So Benni gets this communication. Apparently it gives *him* the shakes, because the next thing he does is board a plane for Rome. We establish that he has called Maria and told her that his first cousin is dying, and Benni wants to be with her. . . . Blackford, have you ever seen a truly *sad* man? I mean, a truly *wretchedly* sad man?"

"Well, yeah, I guess so."

"No, you haven't. I'd have said I had. But I hadn't. Not till I saw J. Edgar Hoover at The Quarters on Sunday afternoon, when we sat there with information that a Central Intelligence mole was en route to the airport to fly unmolested to Mexico, and her superior was en route to the airport to fly unmolested to Rome. He began by saying that of course he would not permit it. Rufus said, 'Mr. Hoover, you have got to *understand*. Tango is over and out; now all that matters is the success of Marco Polo.' It was obvious, but the sheer agony of Hoover, letting two prime spies who'd have faced life sentences sashay out of the country . . . He made Dulles promise that at the earliest opportunity the CIA would release a statement saying that the FBI had permitted the spies to go out for overriding reasons of national importance."

"What did Dulles say?"

"He said if Marco Polo works, it's going to be a long time from now before we'll reveal that we were ever onto the Amanda-Benni operation."

"I must say, rather neat for our team, if you leave out the punishment angle."

"Right. Especially since when Benni gets to Rome he'll establish contact there, and give them Amanda's address in Mexico so the KGB won't think she's ducking out on them."

"What about the diverter?"

"We're going to leave it in the machine for a couple of months. Just in case there's another mole anywhere in the building who might have a reason to check whether we're onto it. All he'd have to do is reach with his foot and see if the stud pin's still sticking out. If it is, the diverter is still presumably in place. A couple of months from now, a Xerox inspector can stumble onto it, remove it, and file some sort of confused report on it, which we can ignore."

Blackford was summoned to the door. He opened it and a lissome Japanese girl followed by a male assistant came in, followed by a trolley with a half-dozen covered trays of hot food. Blackford went for another bottle of wine.

"How do you feel, Singer?"

"I'm beginning to feel good. How do you feel, Black?"

"I'm beginning to feel lousy."

Singer laughed. The laugh was not entirely wholesome. It was sound psychology at once to make light of the danger of a mission, while staying safely on the short side of trivializing it. It was a blend Singer could effect, and Blackford was soon smiling and together they enjoyed the long evening, during which at regular intervals Singer would do his imitation of J. Daniel Umin affirming the chastity of his client. Blackford, in bed, thought about the passionate Amanda and struggled to recall whether she had ever betrayed her extralibidinal preoccupations, but he could recall only, every now and then, her enthusiasm for the prospects of some stallion or other. He doubted she ever could interest herself in a gelding. So it was Amanda, in whose arms he had

lain on the eve of his departure for Berlin to work his labyrin-
thine way from No. 48 Mittelstrasse . . . back to the beautiful,
saucy, dangerous girl who loved—to make love, and probably
understood herself, manipulating the Xerox machine, as involved
in making love to all of mankind.

# CHAPTER 22

At midnight Thursday April 7, Tokyo time (2 P.M. Greenwich time), the meteorologist gave what he called his "90 percent go" signal. Blackford had been on a carefully supervised diet during the entire day, and at nine he was given a tranquilizer intended to induce sleep. When he was awakened at 4 A.M. he couldn't quite remember whether it had worked or not. He had hardly slumbered, yet he could not remember tossing and turning. In any event, the laxative he had been given was effective, and he took his light meal, washed down with a little skimmed milk. Coffee, a diuretic, was proscribed. At five, in the hangar, he would submit to the pre-breathing discipline for two hours before takeoff. He had always found it the single most tedious aspect of the whole U-2 exercise, but the denitrogenization, during which he was given pure oxygen to breathe, protected him against any possibility of bends when at high altitudes. During the two hours, one had to make the conscious effort to reverse the normal process by which one breathes. Ordinarily, inhaling requires a slight expenditure of energy, while exhaling is entirely automatic. Under pressurization, the process is reversed. Conversation would be excluded, so that he and Singer spoke their goodbyes before the helmet was put on. Blackford knew that although Singer departed the hangar, making it possible for Blackford to hasten the passage of the time by reading a paperback novel, Singer would be there when Blackford was summoned by Colonel Sharples to board his aircraft: as indeed, at 6:50 A.M., he was.

He set off in that lumbering gait appropriate when wearing a skintight pressure suit, walking a few yards to the black lady, whose extraordinary wingspan of eighty feet always startled him, the more so as the dawn light exaggerated its huge wingspread. He was helped into the cockpit and, strapping himself in, he began his checklist. He had virtually committed to memory his flight plan, but he reviewed, with exactitude, everything. Among the items to be checked was the destruct mechanism. In order to activate it, you needed first to flip the switch marked ARM. This switch energized the second switch, marked DESTRUCT. Seventy seconds after flipping the Destruct switch, an explosion would take place in the camera section of the aircraft, designed to destroy all the photographic evidence but not to damage the pilot, in the event he had not yet pushed his ejection button. But procedure stipulated that before each flight the pilot should check the timing mechanism, because the seventy seconds were inexact. Accordingly, Blackford triggered it while observing his watch. The timer went off at sixty-five seconds. He had established what he needed to know exactly.

There was no communication with the tower, but Colonel Sharples, standing to one side with Singer and two mechanics, looked up from his watch and, with his thumb stretched up, motioned to Blackford that he was cleared to go.

Taxiing in the U-2 was awkward, though not nearly so much so as landing. In order to save weight, the designer hadn't equipped the aircraft with the conventional tricycle landing gear. Instead it had four wheels. Two, permanently a part of the plane itself, were arranged bicycle-like along the bottom centerline of the fuselage. The larger of these was situated just forward of the wing's leading edge, ahead of the engine's weight. It bore the main load. The second wheel was very small and located well aft, just ahead of the tail structure. At each wing tip, on a rod extending toward the ground, was a small wheel called a "pogo." The U-2 kept itself level by means of these while taxiing and preparing to take off. Once airborne, both pogo wheels and their rods simply dropped away, while the two permanent wheels pulled up into their internal compartments, streamlining doors closing over them. The permanent wheels took care of landing— until air speed was lost, whereupon the heavier wing, as with a glider, grazed the ground, but with no damage done to the wing. Once down, of course, the U-2 couldn't get back into the air without fresh pogo wheels.

The aircraft needed a mere one thousand feet of runway. A spectacular feature—Blackford had told Singer to watch for it— was the speed and verticality of its launching trajectory. It would climb at nearly two miles per minute. Instantly on takeoff, it would raise at an angle better than forty-five degrees. "In three minutes," Blackford said, "you won't be able to see me —you watch."

He brought the aircraft into the wind at the runway's end and looked out one final time at Singer, to whom he raised his hand. He gunned the motor, and twenty-two seconds later he was airborne. He brought the plane around to an azimuth of 320 degrees and headed toward Harbin, in Manchuria. Reaching cruising altitude, he could discern the shape of the entire Korean archipelago. In a matter of minutes, he could see the concrete congestion of Vladivostok. . . . The sky was cloudless. The sun, now low to his right, would duck behind him when, reaching Harbin, he began to veer westward. And on reaching Manchouli, where his instructions told him to begin filming, he would turn west, and would look away from the sun for the balance of the trip.

No extraordinary winds were predicted, and prevailing winds had been factored into his flight plan.

The U-2 traveled at Mach .7, which is to say seven-tenths the speed of sound, or 537 miles per hour. These were statute miles. The nautical mile being fifteen percent longer, Blackford would travel at 456 knots, reaching Harbin 109 minutes after takeoff,

which had been at 0702. At Harbin he would slip into the next
time zone west of Tokyo. On reaching Manchouli, at latitude
117 east, he would still be in the —8 zone. That section of the
flight was calculated at 59 minutes, so that the two legs com-
bined, at 168 minutes, meant that the sun would be only a
little higher off the eastern horizon than it had been at takeoff
time.

Kyakhta would mark the halfway point in his flight over the
frontier of Mongolia. He had a radio signal for Kyakhta, which
in any event would be easy to spot, lying as it does south of the
midpoint of the enormous Lake of Baikal. To Kyakhta would
take 56 minutes, and indeed the local time would be a few min-
utes before 10 A.M. On that leg he would gain over the sun.
From there he would head to Zyranovsk, though he would stay
south of it, closer to the Chinese frontier. At Zyranovsk, in the
heart of Soviet Kazakhstan, the time would be approximately
twenty minutes before ten: yet a little more headway on the sun.
From Zyranovsk he would need to change his heading from west
to southwest—specifically, to 223 degrees—in order to reach
Alma-Ata and effect his rendezvous with the Russians. That
flight would take him 52 minutes in addition to the time con-
sumed in his planned series of flameouts. By the time he was on
the ground—at approximately ten o'clock local time, Alma-Ata
—he would be at 76 degrees 55 minutes east longitude, lying
squarely in the middle of —5 time zone. Approximately as far
from Greenwich, England, on this side as New York City is on
the other, and, Blackford ruminated, only about a hundred miles
farther north. What was the weather like in, oh, Great Barring-
ton, Massachusetts, in early April? Well, about the same as at
Alma-Ata, if you allow for about a thousand feet extra elevation,
over in these parts.

Although he could not take sustained time from navigation
and the constant checking of the instruments, he thought back in
patches on the weekend in Bermuda. The plane—it had proved
convenient to fly from New York, as Sally was lecturing at
Columbia—had been jammed with Ivy Leaguers. The rugby
teams from Yale, Princeton, Harvard, and M.I.T., together with
assorted inamorata, were bound for Bermuda for the spring holi-
day, featuring a rugby tournament, seven days at the Elbow

Beach Hotel (for the girls), a thousand hours of exposure to sun and salt, and an appreciable depletion of the island's reserves of beer, Shetland sweaters, and prophylactics. Blackford felt a generation removed from an expedition in which he had participated as recently as ten years earlier. He had looked up and down the aisle at the girls—chatty, self-confident, cheerful, pleasure-bent, handsome—and at Sally, lovelier at age thirty than anyone else in the aircraft, with that distinctive air of authority, a kind of blonde gentle intelligence, with her sense of participating in two worlds, only one of them available to Blackford.

He thought back, then, to entering their cottage, the porter carrying the two heavy bags. They were registered as Mr. and Mrs. Partridge, "Blackford Partridge" having received a guest card courtesy of his mother Lady Sharkey, in London. It had never before been exactly that open with Sally. They had shared bedrooms together for ten years, but this time, under these auspices, there was a certain disquiet, he remembered, and at first she hadn't spoken, fussing instead with the unpacking. He left to go to rent motorbikes, and when he returned, his bag had also been unpacked, and she was dressed in tennis shorts, sitting in the little living room, reading.

That night they dined in the candlelit room overlooking the ocean, and lingered over the buffet and the wine. Sally talked, and he replied, and he talked, and she replied, and everything either said led to something else. Blackford was tan from the days in Nevada, Sally red from the day's bicycling. He stared in utter appreciation of her distinctive beauty, once again remarking that little aloofness that made her so desirable; and she stared at the beautifully shaped man she loved, who was also her closest companion, with whom, for reasons they could never quite articulate, the ultimate consummation of marriage somehow did not materialize. Always there was a reason. The convention was that the burden was his, the professional preoccupations. In the year with the architects, that glibness wouldn't any longer serve. He wondered whether, tonight, or tomorrow, the subject would arise. He could not bring himself to broach it, not today, three days before his departure for Tokyo. A warm air came on them as they sipped their liqueurs. She wished to go down the long staircase to the beach below, and he followed her. They doffed their shoes on reaching the beach, and, hand in hand, walked southwest, silent now. Blackford found himself measuring the frequency of the light on Gibbs Hill, which, had it existed with that intensity over the past centuries, might have saved one hundred ships from destruction on the legendary reefs. She had stopped, suddenly, and drawn him to her. His hands began to move, and her body was more than pliant. They moved into the shade of the moon, up against the steep embankment. Blackford closed his eyes. And opened them to check the speed gauge, and make a minor adjustment on the trim tab. The mountains below were sending up thermal currents that reminded him he was flying, essentially, a glider.

The following day, on the north end, they took, together, a lesson in scuba diving. It was, of course, wretchedly easy for Blackford. So much was, had been, easy for him. He was impatient with the instructor's repetitions—why did he have to be told more than once that when he felt pressure on his eardrums, he should hold his nostrils together and blow out until the pressure dissipated? Sally had been a little apprehensive. She did not take naturally to the water, and once asked the instructor—a grizzled, wiry man with hair bleached by the sun, whose beefy face and solid paunch suggested a continuing attachment to the liquid way of life—about sharks, and Henry had said that everybody asked about sharks but more people get killed in Bermuda riding bikes than get bitten by sharks in the whole Atlantic. That approach was the wrong one to use on Sally, whose mind was obstinately logical, because of course she replied to Henry that all he had succeeded in coming up with was the reminder that riding motorbikes in Bermuda was dangerous, that she knew this intuitively; what she was interested in was, why wouldn't sharks attack *her?* Blackford had managed to change the subject, and an hour or so later they were in thirty feet of water, and he began to feel the exhilaration of the underwater experience, and looked anxiously to see whether Sally shared the experience, but she seemed preoccupied with the gauges, and he could tell from the bubbles coming from her tank that she was breathing less than naturally. But with her light hair trailing in the current, even with the face mask that gave her a proboscis and the tank and harness that made her, viewed from one particular perspec-

tive, look like a diesel truck, she was, Blackford thought, some-
how distinctive. Like no one else. Would she attract the
sharks? . . . Would he attract the MIGs? Surely no MIG would
interfere with Rufus's carefully plotted Marco Polo? He raised
his sextant and looked at the chronometer. The radio triangula-
tion was correct, or nearly so.

The next evening they spent on a rented sloop. The wind was
an obliging northerly, so Blackford had undertaken to go out
Hamilton Harbor and pursue the tortuous channel, to duck into
the harbor at St. George's, which they reached three hours later
as the sun went down. He eased into the shallow water on the
left side of the channel and threw out the hook, and the little 36-
footer nosed whinnyingly up into the wind as he dropped the
mainsail. The air was both cool and balmy, and Sally had set out
to light the charcoal fire on the grate suspended over the aft pul-
pit. He watched her, so competent in so many matters, using two
or three books of matches, dousing the charcoal with one of
those squirt cans guaranteed to turn a block of ice into a roaring
fire. The radio was on and the musical beat seemed to grow
more exotic as the sky grew hot with color. Blackford had stood
in the cockpit, a rum drink in hand, saying not a word, tapping
his foot to the beat of the music. Waiting. It paid off. She had
suddenly looked up at him. He remembered that expression:
only twice before had she permitted herself the look of a
supplicant. He smiled, whisked the roll of paper towels from the
dispenser, walked aft and with it picked up two pieces of char-
coal. He took them below where he lit the stove, situating the
charcoal in a slotted ladle. In four or five minutes the charcoal
was red hot, and he brought the ladle carefully back to the cock-
pit and poured the burning coals into the recalcitrant mound.
Ten minutes later the coal fire was burning, and ten minutes
after that she put the steaks on, and ten minutes after that, the
sun having now left only the embers of twilight, she was in his
arms as, episodically, they watched the progress of the steak,
their passion burning elsewhere. . . . He could now see the
western end of Lake Baikal.

He would need to come down quickly, but not too quickly.
There had been considerable discussion on the point with Rufus
and area specialists. To descend very slowly would be to run the

risk of the aircraft's being shot down. A U-2 had been dispatched over Alma-Ata from Peshawar to examine the antiaircraft facilities. At one point Rufus considered a night landing, to lessen the possibility of the plane's obliteration. "If the plane is shot down," Rufus had said, in his normal analytical mode, "we run the risk that precisely the evidence we want them to find will be destroyed—if they make a direct hit; or if the plane nose-dives to the ground. You would have bailed out, of course. But if you arrive down with complete documentary evidence of your flight, they'll wonder why you didn't destroy it.

"No, I think you'd better come down together, fast, and far enough away from Alma-Ata to lessen the likelihood that any of their SAMs would reach you going down. The granger on the plane should give you pretty good protection against the possibility that long-range radar would guide fighter pilots to you . . ."

Then he stopped. One of his legendary pauses. Finally: ". . . though what would be absolutely ideal from our point of view," Rufus's face brightened—"would be for a couple of MIGs to *guide* you down. Take you prisoner from the air. Force you to come down at their airfield." Rufus had become quite excited by the possibility, which he then honed. "You could come down, climb out of the plane, and set off the destruct unit."

"That sounds really exciting, Rufus. I climb down off the plane, and seventy seconds later the tail section with the camera blows off killing one general, three colonels, and four Heroes of the Soviet Union, though perhaps the general is merely blinded for life. That's what I call a really soft landing, all right."

"You have a point." Rufus made a note. The following day after telephone discussions with a demolitions expert, Rufus said, as he, Blackford, and Singer were driving to the Aberdeen Proving Grounds:

"They've set up a facsimile, rough but reliable, of the structure of the tail end of the plane. We've reduced the explosive from the regular three pounds to one pound. Let's see what happens."

What happened was a very orderly explosion indeed, rather like a pistol shot through a silencer. The camera within which the explosive was lodged was destroyed, but even the light-skinned carapace of the aircraft was not penetrated. It was that quantity of explosive that Blackford now had on board. In such circumstances there would be no opportunity to destroy the abundant evidence of his log, his charts, the radio signals, all of which would readily betray his itinerary.

"At ten A.M. the Russian MIGs would have good visual contact with you, and wouldn't panic about having to fly into the sun. They would probably try to talk to you from the tower over the emergency channel. You would at that point merely indicate that you were prepared to follow instructions."

"And if the MIGs don't materialize?"

"There's every reason to suppose they will. Remember, they're hot and bothered in that whole area, and north of it, about the U-2s, which are driving Khrushchev crazy, and he's hungry to get his hands on one. The activity out of Peshawar has been intense. If they know that you're down at an altitude where they can tell you what to do, I don't think it likely they'd shoot you down."

Blackford agreed. Still, there was the contingency that no MIGs would show up. In that event, it was decided, Blackford would land the airplane on suitable terrain, destroy the camera, and use his time methodically to destroy his log and charts. But a duplicate set, so to speak a carbon copy, marked "Cmdr. Detachment 10-10, Peshawar" would be lodged in the flap pocket of the cockpit. "These," Rufus said, "you would simply have forgotten to remove and destroy."

Blackford and Singer and Rufus spent four sessions on the variables. Blackford approved the plan, but insisted that in the event he came down unescorted, a defect-on-command must be contrived—to account for the failure of the engine to reignite on reaching lower altitudes.

Aberdeen came up with one. When an aircraft suffers a flameout, it noses down for richer air, on contact with which the pilot flips on the Air Ignition switch. That switch, behind the instrument panel, leads to an "AN" (Army–Navy) connecting plug. If that critical connection is incomplete, the firing mechanism becomes inoperative. The engineers at Aberdeen drilled a small hole on the U-2 instrument panel of the plane Blackford would fly, and threaded a fishing line through it and around the connector. Blackford, when resolved finally to descend, would pull both ends of the line, attached to a ballpoint pen for leverage, long enough to effect permanent disconnection—which disconnection would later be assumed, by the autopsists, to have been the result of sloppy maintenance procedures. Having pulled on the double line until the disconnection was effected, Blackford would need, as a housekeeping chore, merely to pull one end of the fishing line, which would snake the whole of it back through the cable into his hands. The little screw hole in the instrument panel, through which the line had been inserted, would be topped by a conventional snap-in plug. If the hole were subsequently explored, its true purpose would not likely be imagined. Blackford would be left with two or three feet of fishing line, which he could quickly wrap around his navigation pencil as though to give him a better finger grip.

Blackford studied the plan and was satisfied that, on the way down, he could simulate repeated failures to refire the engine.

He made the radio and sextant checks while approaching Manchouli. There was a minor westward course correction to make. Although he felt that the three hours had passed quickly and that he had had time for serene reflection, in fact he was constantly occupied. He had to check the instruments continuously—the rpm, the exhaust gas temperature, the fire warning lights, the compass, the artificial horizon, the radio signals from which he was taking navigational guidance. He would semiautomatically compensate for drift; and now he would be flipping on the camera switches.

At this altitude, topographical differences were exclusively a matter of color shadings. His route over Mongolia took him over high ground, about the altitude of the area surrounding Denver, Colorado, and the color of the ground was not noticeably different. The blues from the lakes, rivers, and oceans were interchangeable with the waters in the far west of the United States. The little traces of white were demure and skittish by contrast with the solid white patches of the Rockies. He knew that someday very soon we'd have a man in space. He'd be orbiting the globe at an altitude three times higher than his own. Whereas he could see several hundred miles, the astronaut would see a few thousand miles. At the nether end, he felt as unrelated to what went on below as if he had been flying over the United States. The spell would break, he knew, when the moment came to put an end to his synthetic security; but for the moment he felt completely estranged from the herdsmen and peasants below, and their harsh rulers, and all those paradoxes—men and women working by day assembling SAM missiles, and returning at night to ancient dwellings without indoor toilets or sources of water closer than communal wells.

Suddenly he experienced a fierce, unaccountable joy. He had maneuvered his aircraft west, beginning the long stretch across the Mongolian border, and the sun was now outside his peripheral vision. Flying in the same direction, he felt somehow that the sun was a personal satellite, moving behind him at the appropriate speed in order to expedite his mission. The aircraft was behaving with exemplary smoothness, and the air about him, at a temperature of minus sixty degrees Fahrenheit, was tranquil in its insubstantiality. But behind his serenity, he knew, was the fusion of two emotions. The first was that he was staking his life, and so requiting the sacrifice of Michael. The second was that, in Bermuda, Sally had indicated that, finally, she . . . understood. The two days had gone by with inexplicable, almost indecipherable synchronization of emotional and psychic concerns. They were truly as one, as much so when separated by a hundred yards on their bicycles as when they lay fused in bed, and he studied the moon's irradiations on her lowered eyelids and lambent hair. She sensed that this next mission was distinctively dangerous, but her energies were for the first time given to convincing him that if in his judgment it was right to go forward, in her judgment, derivatively, it was right to go forward. That certification, which he had never had before, above all things lightened his burden, though, at a complementary level, it heightened his concern; because he cared now, more deeply than ever before, that he should return—to be with her, always.

The more he reflected on what lay ahead, the likelier he thought it that indeed he would be greeted by MIGs. He would contrive his flameout at 72,000 feet, two hundred miles east of Alma-Ata. He would descend to 45,000 feet—a most seductive height for the MIGs. There he would linger for ten minutes. He hoped that notwithstanding the strangeness of the tongue, he would be able to detect from the tempo of the language, over the radio, whether the instructions going out to MIGs were to intercept him. He would drift down slowly from 45,000 feet, hoping to spot the enemy aircraft. Without his engine, there would be no contrail. Perhaps he would ignite it for a minute or two, giving out that cloud trail, helping the enemy pilots to establish visual identification. As if he had succeeded in achieving ignition—only to suffer a successor flameout. He would continue fitfully in his descent. If at 25,000 feet he saw no MIGs, he would proceed down, looking simultaneously for terrain smooth enough to land on, and preferably close to farmers, or men driving automobiles, who would rush out to inspect the mysterious black intruder.

Making now his final southwesterly turn, he found himself gratifyingly on schedule. He had set his watch on Greenwich Mean Time, and his calculations showed him twelve minutes off schedule. Ahead of schedule, actually. He could, if he wished, adjust to the pre-indicated time of arrival. But not by reducing the rpm—the U-2 did not permit you to elect to fly more slowly. Either he would need to drift off course—to tack, so to speak, a little bit en route to the objective—or he would have to reduce his altitude. He decided to do neither, to proceed a few minutes ahead of schedule. If the radars and the MIGs were going to fetch him, they'd as likely do so if he landed at 9:50 as at 10:10.

He was coming now to the Dzhungarsky Alatau mountain range. Two hundred and forty miles to go. Local time, 0930. From his cockpit in the U-2 he could not view the sky behind him, so he indulged himself in a leisurely turn and took a sextant reading on the sun. Reassuringly, he found it doing its duty: it was exactly where it should be, at 44 degrees 15 minutes.

"Ready to go?" he asked himself at 0943. "All set, Blackford. Er . . . good luck, old boy."

He flicked the Air Starter switch. In a few seconds the engine coughed and went dead. He put the nose down, keeping a careful eye on the air speed. "Steady at .7," he said to himself, observing his rate of descent at five hundred feet per minute. He had the radio set at the Alma-Ata tower number, but now switched to see if he could hear anything on the emergency channel. He was still 175 miles from the air base. He heard traffic, but came to no conclusions as to its meaning. He switched back to the Alma-Ata frequency.

At 9:48 he was at 50,000 feet. He found himself subconsciously, and quite unreasonably at that altitude, already looking about for a forced landing site.

At 45,000 feet he saw the contrails. Coming his way. Three of them.

He decided to simulate now an effort to fire the engine. He turned on the Air Starter, caused the engine to spurt a couple of times, then switched it again, choking off the engine and resuming his descent. He figured the rate of closure, given their speed of approach to him and his to them, at very nearly Mach 1.5, so it wouldn't be long. Probably three to four minutes, at which point he would be down to between 42,000 and 43,000 feet. The MIGs were separating now, clearly in response to the squadron leader's orders, which Blackford intercepted on the emergency channel easily identifying, by his tone of voice, the leader. One MIG was headed toward him, another to his right, the third to his left. The first would be on top of him by the time their paths crossed. Blackford decided to wait until 25,000 feet, just before the MIGs were at hand, to cough up the engine.

He estimated they were sixty seconds distant when he turned on the Air Starter switch and ignited the engine. He made a motion to climb, without, however, heading up as steeply as the aircraft could actually manage. He didn't want to have them think that they had better get on with it and shoot him down lest he escape by climbing out of their range. The first plane now climbed directly over him. The other two had swung out and begun their U turns. On the emergency channel he heard in guttural English: "AIRPLANE DOWN AIRPLANE DOWN PURSUE THREE ZERO FIVE PURSUE THREE ZERO FIVE." The first plane was now ahead of him, flying in the same direction, and he could see the tail marking, "ZNS 305." The second and third were respectively a hundred yards on his left, a hundred yards on his right, parallel. Both pilots pointed to the lead plane. The lead plane descended—but at an angle unacceptable to a U-2. Blackford could not follow him down so steeply without structural risk—the "coffin" factor. He therefore

maintained his own maximum permissible descent speed of five
hundred feet per minute, and motioned to the pilot on the right
by running his thumb graphically across his throat. On the radio
he said: "AM DESCENDING AM DESCENDING AT MAXI-
MUM SPEED MAXIMUM SPEED." There were rapid ex-
changes on the radio in Russian. When the plane on the right
then veered away, in a maneuver Blackford knew to be consis-
tent with positioning itself to shoot down the U-2, Blackford
lowered his two landing wheels, the international signal of
submission. The import of the message was apparently received
and accepted, because the lead plane promptly reduced the angle
of descent, adopting the U-2's glide pattern. They were at 15,000
feet when Blackford spotted the field. The lead plane began an
approach turn, designated to bring them to the windward end of
the strip at approximately 2,000 feet. They were headed toward
the landing strip, at 1,500 feet, when the pilot on Blackford's
right pointed to the field, thrusting his finger down to instruct
Blackford to land. At this point Blackford severed the AN con-
nector, retrieving the fishing line. His airplane was now a glider.
The lead plane zoomed up, to get out of Blackford's way. He
headed down to the runway, while his escort planes executed
360-degree turns to place themselves in parade formation behind
Blackford. He focused on the landing. A U-2 could not land ex-
cept by stalling. Any power would lift it off the ground. Obvi-
ously the stall would need to come at an appropriate distance
above the runway. By the time he was fifteen feet over the
ground, there were two escort jeeps carrying men with machine
guns racing on either side of the runway to keep pace. He hoped
he would not ground-loop. His escort detachment obviously
didn't know that the U-2 had no tricycle landing facilities, and
that therefore the possibilities were high that when the heavier
wing touched the runway, the plane would veer sharply. Black-
ford stalled the plane and the wing touched down, lazily. Black-
ford applied brake pressure, allowing the plane gradually to
swing to the left, off the runway onto the grass. It came, finally,
to rest.

"Well," he thought, "here we go."

He flipped the Arm switch. He opened the cockpit cover,
put his foot over the side, and then reached over and flipped the

destruct switch. He was on the ground and surrounded by
armed men when, sixty-five seconds later, the explosion oc-
curred. There was no shrapnel. But a barked order into a walkie-
talkie brought a fire truck, sirens raging. A hose was trained on
the tail section of the aircraft until the smoke was gone. The
MIGs roared down, at intervals of about a minute.

Blackford calmly devoted himself to detaching first his face
plate, then his helmet. He looked up at the fifteen or eighteen
men surrounding him, several with automatic weapons. One man
was obviously in charge. Blackford smiled, executed a salute in-
tended rather as a greeting than an obeisance, and said cheer-
fully:

"Could I please use your telephone?"

# CHAPTER 23

On April 14, addressing the Supreme Soviet in Moscow, Nikita Khrushchev announced that an American spy plane had been brought down by Soviet fighters, that the evidence was conclusive that the pilot was an "important agent" of the Central Intelligence Agency, and that the trial of the American spy by a military court, pursuant to Soviet law, would proceed in a fortnight. He said that such an "unprecedented aggressive act" against the sovereignty of the Soviet state revealed the true intentions of the United States to reject coexistence, and that this aggression by the United States would deeply influence the attitude of the Soviet Union at the forthcoming summit conference in Paris. As for the spy, the Soviet Union would not divulge his name, lest any knowledge of his anti-Soviet activities during the preceding decade influence the court. Soviet law, Khrushchev finished darkly, authorizes the death penalty for such behavior as the prosecution would allege the American had engaged in; "but the verdict, of course, will be that of the court."

The U. S. State Department press officer in Washington issued a message to a press chamber swollen with bodies from every news agency, to the effect that flights undertaken in the area to which Chairman Khrushchev alluded were motivated by a desire to collect high-altitude meteorological information, that the aircraft was under the control of NASA, and that it was incorrect to assume that the United States policies sought anything other than coexistence and peaceful solutions to such outstanding problems as the future of Berlin. State Department and White House spokesmen refused to give further details other than that our ambassador in Moscow had been instructed to demand access to the pilot, whose name the State Department declined to disclose.

On April 29, Tass announced that the verdict against the American spy was execution. The Military Division of the Soviet Supreme Court had granted him a week's period during which his court-appointed attorney, the distinguished Dr. Valerian Ryleyev, would have leave to appeal to the Soviet Supreme Court for a reduced sentence. Rufus put in for a White House meeting, which was set for 1:45 at the Oval Office, with the Secretary of State and the Director of the CIA also in attendance.

The President looked grave. "We can't let them shoot that kid."

Rufus replied that he didn't think it likely they would do so, but that the time was certainly appropriate to initiate the suggestion of an exchange. The publicity that had been given to Hans Steiner and his spy ring was incessant. Great public curiosity had been aroused as to his activities, and there was intense interest in what would be revealed at the trial. "It might be useful," Dulles said, "at a certain moment to leak the suggestion that the 'crimes' attributed to our pilot, who was after all tried in the customary Soviet manner—no outside observers—might have been staged in order to distract attention from the activities of Hans Steiner."

"We won't have to leak it," Ike said. "The columnists will jump for it, you watch."

Rufus turned to Secretary Herter. "Mr. Secretary, I wonder whether you'd agree it might make sense to have someone from

outside the Administration approach the Soviets? Things have
got pretty heated, and what we intend might work faster
through a third party."

"Who did you have in mind?" Herter asked.

"Dean Acheson."

The President winced. "Just so *I* don't have to talk to him.
Thinks he's so goddam smart. No, I didn't read his book and I
don't intend to. Who was in charge at Yalta? Who was around
when the Soviets established their eastern empire? When they
got the atom bomb? I think you got a point, Rufus."

The Director intervened. "On the other hand, Rufus, if our
calculations are correct, they're going to want to go quickly
with this."

"I think they do. But if they're talking to Mr. Herter, or to
one of our ambassadors, they'll feel that they're talking with
people in a position to negotiate, and maybe they can make some
public points. If Mr. Acheson goes in, he can say that he has one
offer to make, and he can even say something about how he's not
associated with the administration Khrushchev is so hot and
bothered about."

Eisenhower tapped on the table. "Okay. We'll go with that.
Rufus, you and Herter approach him. Now, let's get onto the
question of our immediate response to the capital sentence."

Herter pulled a sheet of paper out of his briefcase. "I have a
draft statement, Mr. President. It could be issued from my office
or from the White House."

Eisenhower put on his glasses and started to read.

"Hmm. The usual things. . . . It won't do too well under
scrutiny by the press. I think on this one we'll just have to
freeze. Say that our concern is exclusively with the safety of our
'pilot' and that we can't talk about him or anything involving
him until we have passed our position through to the Soviet au-
thorities via our ambassador . . . I like that." He grunted. "I *like*
that: 'The U. S. Attorney General does not intend to ask the jury
for a death sentence against Hans Steiner.' Nice. Let those bas-
tards have it. And by the way"—he took off his glasses and
looked up—"if anybody wants to propose nationalizing the tele-
vision networks, pass the goddam bill and I'll sign it. I like to
watch the news. I mean, it's important. But if I have to listen to

that bastard Umin *one* more time, I'm going to be carted back to
Walter Reed. Did you hear what he said about me—when was it,
night before last? 'If we didn't have a full-time golfer in the
White House, maybe the United States could search for peace
instead of inventing Soviet spies.' Son of a bitch. Hey—don't like
to brag, Allen, but I shot a seventy-four yesterday. Full-time
golfer! If I were a full-time golfer I wouldn't be playing with a
handicap of twelve. Yeah"—he handed the statement back to
Herter—"we'd better issue it out of here, otherwise they'll just
come over and give Hagerty eternal hell anyway. You'll have to
pass around the word: everybody is to clam up on this one."

"Fortunately, Mr. President, there are very few people who
are in a position to throw any light on it," Dulles said.

"That's right." He looked up: "Rufus, I've got to hand it to
you. *If it works.* All right?" He stood up, and simultaneously
pushed the button on his desk. The President's men filed out.

Mikhail Menshikov had been around a long time. Smiling Mike,
he was called, not to his face. He'd have smiled at a hanging. An
old Bolshevik, Menshikov was skilled in the art of survival. It
was known that his addiction to vodka and women would keep
him from ultimate power. This was one reason for his strength.
He knew everyone in the Kremlin, and they knew that he
expected to climb no higher rung on the ladder than the one on
which he now so comfortably reposed, though there had been
hair-raising moments the preceding fall during Khrushchev's
hectic visit, when Menshikov was in charge of all Washington
arrangements, even though the volcanic Chairman slept at
Blair House. He had known Dean Acheson—

". . . well, is it fair to say we have known each other more or
less forever, Dean?"

"It is certainly fair to say that it seems forever since we first
met, Mikhail."

"Ah, Dean, you are always making the jokes at our expense,
but we have a good relationship, you and I. We are friends, is
that correct?"

"No, Mikhail, that isn't correct. We are professionals, and as
professionals we know that when there is no audience whose re-
sponse we seek to stimulate, it saves a great deal of time and

effort merely to say to each other what we have to say to each other."

"Of course, Dean, of course." Menshikov smiled and reached over to fill Acheson's teacup. "You have on your mind?"

"You give us Oakes, we give you Steiner."

"Ah," the muscles in Menshikov's face tightened. "But Oakes is under sentence of death. Steiner has not been proved guilty."

"Mikhail, my comments on that, as a lawyer, are very simple: Anybody condemned of anything in the Soviet Union may, or may not, be guilty. If there is a correspondence between conviction and guilt, it is purely coincidental. My other observation is that Hans Steiner is guilty as hell and the probability is overwhelming that you personally know all about it. As a matter of fact, you probably sat here giving him instructions."

"Oh, Dean, you are making this *so very* difficult."

"No, Mikhail—but why don't we agree that we just won't talk about 'guilt' or 'innocence'? We'll talk about a human being you're in a position to deliver to us, and a human being we're in a position to deliver to you."

"Well of course, Dean, I will certainly relay your message. I don't know how long it will take. . . ."

Acheson had been carefully briefed. "We don't care how long it takes. It can take six months, for all we care. But—and I mean this, Mikhail—no execution."

"My dear Dean, I am hardly in a position to dictate to the Soviet courts what to do."

"No, you're not. But Khrushchev is."

Menshikov permitted himself a fraternal laugh. Acheson left the Embassy at 3:30, having declined an invitation to sample a new vodka. He could not reasonably have predicted that he would be there again—same room, same host, same hour—at 3:30 the following day, pursuant to an imperative telephone call.

"The response from Moscow," Menshikov said, once again pouring tea, "has come to me with quite unprecedented speed. It is the consensus of the Presidium that the matter of the two spies— I mean, your spy and our alleged spy—has proved a major distraction, coming as it has on the eve of the Paris summit. The authorities are prepared to make the exchange on two conditions."

Acheson groaned. "What?"

"The first is that the exchange be effected immediately."

Acheson said nothing.

"The second is that your Justice Department issue a public statement to the effect that the evidence against Steiner was insufficient to proceed to trial."

"As to one: Agreed. As to two: No."

Menshikov raised his hands in an attitude of despair. "What a pity! It might have been so clean."

"No no no, Mikhail. It would be the opposite of 'clean' the way you propose. Because the United States Government is *not* in a mood to compromise American justice in order to repatriate one American."

"But Dean, why do you *care?*"

"Because," Acheson spoke with exaggerated deliberation, "in our country our institutions depend on the integrity of their operations." He had no sooner said this than, as a lawyer, he regretted having done so. But, of course, too late. Menshikov pounced:

"Oh? Like the integrity of the CIA? Like sending airplanes over the Soviet Union to watch the little clouds fly?"

Acheson attempted a recovery. "How you aim your intercontinental ballistic missiles is a legitimate matter of interest to the United States—and certainly indispensable to the survival of our institutions."

"Ah, Dean. Dean, no wonder you are such an expensive lawyer. *I* would hire you in one *minute* to defend me!"

"You'd be a lot better off with me than with the 'distinguished' Dr. Valerian Ryleyev. Really, Mikhail, you should know that it does *not* impress the American public to learn that the Soviet's renowned thirst for justice caused them to go to the length of recruiting, in order properly to defend Blackford Oakes, the same brilliant advocate who defended the Nazi war criminals. . . . You know, Mikhail, I live out the evening of my life with the nightmare that the Soviet Union will one day discover the art of public relations."

"You are very funny, Dean."

"Where do we go from here?"

"I am authorized to proceed."

"On what terms?"

"Condition one."

"Granted. Do you have a plan in mind?"

"I do."

"This is Thursday. I propose that at eight-thirty A.M. next Wednesday, May eleventh, you arrange to deliver Hans Steiner to the western end of the Glienicker Bridge in Berlin. At the same time we will deliver Blackford Oakes to the eastern end. Both parties will then advance to the international border in the center of the bridge. A representative of our government will satisfy himself as to the identity of Steiner. A representative of your government will identify Oakes. The prisoners will be exchanged."

Acheson paused for a moment. "That's pretty fast, but I suppose we can arrange it. A couple of details, Mikhail. We would furnish Steiner with a *nolle prosequi*, but together with a court order to which he would consent. Under that order he is forever barred from coming into the United States. Should he ever do so, the prosecution can recommence."

"Agreed. We would want a similar signature from Oakes. If he is caught in the Soviet Union, his death sentence is immediately reinstated."

Acheson ruminated that this would severely limit Mr. Oakes's professional flexibility. "Agreed, but we attach a further corollary condition, namely that you continue to decline to disclose the identity of the prisoner." Menshikov began to question the condition, but Acheson interrupted. "Any failure to do so would mean that he would be hounded to death by the press in the United States. If that were to happen, the existing rhetorical hostilities would continue, defeating your purpose in expediting the transfer."

Menshikov paused. "I was not given instructions on that point."

"It is a requirement," Acheson said.

"I shall relay your request."

"How long will it take?"

"You will know by the time you reach your home. Now we have a requirement. As you will have assumed, we have communicated directly with Steiner through his lawyer to ask him if he consents to the proposed arrangement. He has agreed, but there are two conditions."

"What are they?"

"He wishes, first, to liquidate his savings account and to carry the proceeds with him in Swiss currency."

"Agreed."

"And he wishes at least an hour or two in his old residence in order to collect his personal effects. For instance, he has a very extensive library on the history and technology of the camera."

Acheson affected to give this request serious consideration. He had decided on the approach of innocent candor.

"Hm. I suppose there's probably a negative or two floating around there he didn't get around to sending you."

"Come on, Dean, we agreed we would not waste time on matters of guilt or innocence."

"All right," said Acheson. "Now here's another one for you."

"Yes?"

"That mouthpiece you retain. Mr. J. Daniel Umin. He is to absent himself from the scene. He is to be discharged by Steiner before that prison door opens. With a *nolle* in his hand, technically Steiner doesn't need a lawyer. If he wants a formal discharge, get him one. We do not want Umin to striptease his way to the airport for the benefit of the press."

"I shall have to persuade Steiner. He has become very attached to Umin."

"Fine. We'll sweeten the deal. You take Umin to East Berlin and promise to keep him there."

"All right, all right. I shall have to discuss the matter directly with Steiner. This means that you must instruct the people at the Federal Detention Center to let me get through to him."

"When?"

"Tomorrow morning at eight."

Acheson rose. "Here's my home telephone number. Let me know tonight if we have a deal. Don't be late. There are a lot of logistics to take care of if we're going to meet your deadline."

Menshikov shrugged his shoulders. "How can I guarantee? It is midnight in Moscow. I will do the best I can."

"I'll settle for that," said Acheson rising. "Talk to you later, Mikhail."

They shook hands and, picking up his black derby, Acheson went to the door.

# CHAPTER 24

On May 5, at noon—or he supposed it to be noon, because the guard had slid the tray through the slot at the bottom of the door moments before—Blackford pounded on the door of his cell. He did so using the aluminum tray, the slurpy contents of which he had emptied into the open toilet. He would need to make a great deal of noise at his end in order for just a little bit of noise to come out at the other end of the soundproofed door. He beat the tray regularly, over the windowed rectangle of the door. He did this for five minutes, until he was wet with perspiration. Then he heard the lock turning and drew back, hoping to catch his breath. By the time the heavy door was opened he was seated on his bunk. The guard, apparently on orders, had summoned the major who spoke English and had given Blackford the copy of *Time* magazine at the trial—could it have been only a week ago?

"Major, I demand to see Ryleyev. My mathematics is rusty,

but if I can still count to seven, I am supposed to be executed to-
morrow morning at dawn. Now, we won't turn this into a semi-
nar on Soviet justice, but my attorney hasn't been here for five
days, when I signed the appeal, and I haven't heard a single word
from him. I haven't heard a single word from the American Em-
bassy, and I'm not going to put up with this crap any longer."

"What do you propose to do about it. . . . McKINLEY?"

"I . . . I wish to write out a personal testament."

"I think we can provide you with writing utensils."

"I may have something to say that would interest Soviet au-
thorities."

The major's face brightened. "I think we can arrange to take
you back to the conference room. But we would expect you to
be more cooperative than during that first week."

"What's the trouble? Shortage of electricity in the 'confer-
ence' room? Prods not working?"

"I can see that your attitude has not changed."

"My attitude has—evolved. I wish, as I say, to make a few
declarations. But before doing that, I would have to speak to Dr.
Ryleyev."

The major looked hard at Blackford. He had not shaved his
face since the trial, and it was now bearded, his facial hair
blonder than the hair on his head. His voice, though it had some-
thing of the old spring, was that of someone near to desperation.
The major knew the changing timbre of men's voices. He had
himself led—how many? two hundred? five hundred?—down
that last staircase in the cellar, to the corner section. No one who
had ever been led there returned. And the executioners and
guards were not talkative. Still, somehow all the prisoners had an
exact and highly accurate idea not only of the staircase and the
cavernous room to which it led, but an exact picture of the
equipment—the coffin at the end of the room, the crematorium
opposite, the drain on the floor, the spigot and big black hose to
wash away the counterrevolutionary blood, and the eyehook
through which the prisoner's manacles were strung, to save the
guards the need to hold down the prisoner while staying clear of
the bullet's trajectory. Overhead was a crossbeam. During the
twenties the prisoners were hanged, but that took too long.
Socialist efficiency required more expeditious executions, and it

was said, in the gallows humor that made its way about, that any executioner who consumed more than three minutes from the time the cavern was entered to the time the coffin was wheeled out to the crematorium would himself be executed. The major reasoned there was little to lose in forwarding McKINLEY's request to Shelepin.

"You will hear from us."

"I will hear from you within one half hour, or you can forget the whole thing. And another thing, major, I don't merely want something to read, which is how I usually put it to you. I *require* something to read. I don't care if it's a Sears and Roebuck catalogue, though I suppose that would be counterrevolutionary in these parts. Bring me something in English. I know there's a library exactly two floors from here. How do I know? I'm a convicted spy, right? That's how I know. Bring me . . . a novel by Jane Austen . . . some Shakespeare . . . the Bible . . . *Gone With the Wind.* I never read *Gone With the Wind,* and how can anybody die without reading *Gone With the Wind?* Bring me *The Brothers Karamazov.* See how you've broadened my tastes? Bring me Lenin's Last Will and Testament—" But the door had quietly shut, and Blackford was talking to himself.

He lay on his bed and thought furiously. Then he got down on the floor and did fifty more push-ups. How many did that total, that day? Five hundred? Somehow they helped. Then he brushed his teeth, for the fifth time. Then he knelt beside his bed, and prayed. How clamorous, he thought, must have been the prayers from this building, over the years. Did God shroud the Lubyanka with a silencer, so that nothing could reach His ears from this encephalophonic misery hole? He declined to believe this. He prayed: What, Lord, was *happening?* What should he do? How could he put them off? If only for another week. Perhaps till the summit. That would be just ten days down the line. He knew Rufus wouldn't let Ike just forget the whole thing. And they did have Klaus. Old Klaus had to be worth *something* to these guys? But, Lord, I'll leave the details to you. Please let me out of here. I'll do what I can to stall. But *I* don't have a plan—

He heard the door opening, rose, and assumed his regular position on the bunk. It was Dr. Ryleyev. He sat down on the stool by the toilet.

"Goddammit, Ryleyev, where in the hell have you been?"

"I have been attending to your appeal, McKINLEY."

"What's the word?"

"The Supreme Court has not granted a commutation."

"Does that mean . . . tomorrow?"

"If the Supreme Court, or Chairman Khrushchev, does not act."

"What are their—office hours?"

"A commutation could come down right up until the moment of—"

"Like, five fifty-nine A.M.?"

"That is correct. There is instant telephone communication with the commandant."

"Now listen, Ryleyev. I've said I'd go to the conference room and talk a little. If I do, will that get me a commutation?"

"That depends on what you tell them."

"What specifically do they want to know?"

"Everything."

"I don't know everything."

"You know more than you have told us."

"So now it's 'us.' I thought you were supposed to be on *my* side."

"I am an officer of the court. And a Soviet patriot."

Blackford elected not to take up the invitation to a polemical exchange.

"Well, I'm going to strike some terms. I'll tell you a lot about the U-2 you don't know. My terms are: commutation to . . . ten years."

"I will relay your offer, and return."

An hour later, the door opened and the major, two guards, and Ryleyev accompanied Blackford out of his cell. The major stared at the prisoner. He had shaved his beard. His hair was brushed. His stride and manner had something of the old jaunt. He sighed. Well, they would soon know.

At the end of the table, as before, sat the squat, bald colonel with the decorations. No new one, Blackford observed. Hadn't tortured enough extra people since a month ago, he guessed. The major indicated the chair Blackford was to occupy.

Blackford had decided to take the initiative. Somewhat to the colonel's surprise, Blackford began the conversation. "Well, Dr. Ryleyev, do you have my commutation?"

Ryleyev looked up at the colonel, requesting, by that gesture, permission to reply directly. The colonel nodded.

"The representative of the Supreme Court instructs me that a commutation would be given only after receiving your full confession and evaluating it."

"Then take me back to the cell."

There was conversation in Russian, including a telephone call by the colonel.

Ryleyev spoke again. "The authorities are willing to defer your execution by one week, pending their evaluation of your confession. At the end of the week, if your confession proves useful you will receive your commutation. Otherwise, the sentence will be carried out."

One week. Blackford thought. One precious week. Might make all the difference. That would take us to the eve of the summit. Unlikely they'd execute him the weekend before. . . .

"All right, let's see the one-week commutation."

Ryleyev spoke to the colonel. Blackford repressed a smile. Of what use was a piece of paper promising anything? But it must have a psychic leverage of some sort. After all, the colonel was now arguing, which showed there was a reluctance to issue it. Again the colonel was on the telephone. His instructions were apparently explicit because he said simply "*Da.* . . . *Da.* . . . *Da.* . . . *Da.* . . ." Then he reached into his briefcase and brought out a form. Filling it out, he handed it to Ryleyev, who read it and then passed it to Blackford at his side. Blackford looked at the form. It was printed, and, below, signed. The colonel had only filled in a couple of blanks.

"Translate it for me, Ryleyev."

Ryleyev adjusted his glasses. "It says," he pointed to the printed portion, " 'By order of the Supreme Court of the Soviet Union, the capital sentence decreed to take place on ["May 6, 1960" had been written in] the convicted prisoner ["McKINLEY"] is deferred until ["May 13, 1960" had been written in].' " There followed the signatures, and the inevitable stamp.

Ryleyev picked up the form. But Blackford snatched it from him, and to the considerable bewilderment of all present he folded it neatly and inserted it into the shirt pocket of his prison garb.

"Proceed," the colonel said in Russian, and now Blackford talked to the interpreter, and to the two stenographers.

He had decided on a strategy. He thanked the good Lord for Rufus, who had told Blackford the direction the "minutes" of the National Security Council would go with respect to U-2 flights.

And so, in halting tones, blurring here and there a detail, Blackford painfully and slowly reconstructed the activities of the U-2 detachments out of Turkey and Pakistan, of the routes they had taken, the pictures they had developed, the extraordinary clarity of their work, the known placement of Soviet missile batteries, the general layout of the Tyura Tam intercontinental ballistic layout . . . He consumed an hour and a half. The colonel and the major could hardly suppress their excitement. Tea and cakes were brought in, and three books in English. Blackford complained of hoarseness and fatigue. But anyway, he said, he had come to the end of the story. The colonel barked into the telephone and then told the stenographers to go, to make their transcripts. The colonel's agitation was understandable. He did not know that he was hearing what his superiors had been reading over the preceding five months from the minutes of the National Security Council executive committee.

Blackford, clutching his books with his right hand, and with the uneaten cake cupped in his left hand, was led courteously back to his cell. On reaching it, he put everything down and stretched out on the couch, his eyes closed, his heart pounding. Suddenly he opened his eyes and, wrestling with the button on his shirt pocket, took out the document. He read just the name and the new date, folded it neatly, and put it back. Again he closed his eyes, and tried to frame his thanks.

# CHAPTER 25

At 1 P.M., Anthony Trust for the CIA, Charles Wilkinson for the FBI, and Assistant U. S. Attorney John Ames for the Justice Department sat in the back seat of the limousine outside the Federal House of Detention at 427 West Street in Manhattan. Five minutes later, the door opened and a guard emerged, handcuffed to the tall, spare photographer. Beside them was J. Daniel Umin, who had insisted that his client would not discharge him until after Steiner was airborne. Ames, acting on Rufus's instructions, wrested from Umin the guarantee that he would not speak to or otherwise communicate with any member of the press between the time his client left the House of Detention and the time he boarded the Constellation at McGuire Air Force Base. To this Umin agreed, attaching the condition that he must be permitted to accompany Steiner everywhere he went, which meant also to the Fulton Street residence.

In the front seat of the limousine, Umin sat alongside the policeman who drove. In the jump seat was Steiner, still handcuffed to the guard. Behind them were Trust, Wilkinson, and Ames, all three carrying handguns. Rufus had warned of the possibility of Steiner's attempting suicide, although the operative conviction of the entire maneuver was that Steiner desired to deliver the Marco Polo Protocols to his patrons.

They drove directly to Fulton Street. The guards had been alerted, and it had been days since the last of the newspapermen covering the little building had abandoned their monitorship. Anthony Trust and John Ames stayed in the car. Umin, his handcuffed client, and—two paces behind them—the FBI's Wilkinson moved to the door. The signal was given, and it was opened from the inside by another agent.

Steiner advised the agent that he desired three large suitcases from the attic floor. When these were brought down, he asked that he be released from the handcuffs so that he could negotiate the packing of the especially delicate camera equipment. To Umin, Steiner said, "Here is the list of books I want to take. Would you pick them up from the library wall? They're all over in that area"—he pointed. Umin, cigar in mouth, began transporting books into one of the open suitcases. Steiner disassembled camera equipment and used sheets and towels to protect them as he placed them in the second bag. Into the third bag went selected shoes and suits from the wardrobe assembled from closets upstairs. In an hour all the bags were shut and locked. Umin insisted they be sealed, and provided tape for this purpose.

They drove then—a police car in front, another behind—over the Brooklyn Bridge, around the Battery, and through the Holland Tunnel. Steiner said nothing. Umin was incapable of saying nothing. He began to complain about things in general, and Anthony took extreme pleasure in causing the automatic partition window in the limousine to rise, cutting Umin off, so to speak, without a cent; though he could be seen complaining to the driver, who did not reply.

At McGuire Air Force Base in New Jersey, the detachment drove directly to a C-118 Constellation. The crew had instructions not to inquire about the cargo. At 5:20, Steiner shook Umin's hand and accepted from him a package of Swiss bank notes, as per arrangement. The plane took off moments later, and

Umin looked over to see the driver of the limousine and the two police cars speeding away, leaving him far out on the tarmac, alone. It had begun to rain, so that by the time Umin reached the pay telephone at the dispatcher's office, he was very wet. And very angry—at being ditched in the downpour. But, withal, still very pleased with himself. He called for a taxi.

The airplane stopped at Wiesbaden for refueling, and arrived at its destination, Tempelhof Airfield in Berlin, just before one in the afternoon of the next day. Steiner was taken to a cell at Andrews Army Base in Berlin, where he was kept under observation. His clothes were taken from him, and he was given cordless pajamas. His three sealed suitcases were stored in the empty cell opposite, which was then locked.

At midnight at the Lubyanka—why do so many things happen at midnight in the Soviet Union? Blackford wondered—his cell door was opened, and the major appeared. More news about the delay? Was the stay of execution still in force—or had they found out? Then Blackford noticed: The major carried a suitcase.

"You are going to Berlin, where you will be released. I am not authorized to say more. It will all be much easier if you do not attempt any conversation."

Blackford could have wept with joy. Conversation? He would dance the rhumba with the major, if he followed his inclinations. These, with overpowering discipline, he managed to restrain. He affected an air of pure fatalism.

"What are my instructions?"

"In the suitcase you will find a suit approximately your size. I will come to fetch you in ten minutes."

Blackford was ready in three. The ten minutes went slowly. One hour later he was airborne. Five hours later he landed, at dawn, in East Berlin. He was given breakfast in the airplane, in which he sat until 7:30. A car then drove up. The major, a guard, and a plainclothesman escorted him, handcuffed, into the waiting car. Wordlessly, they drove toward an unknown destination.

At exactly 8:30, in the early morning fog, the two parties approached each other over the Glienecker Bridge. The American party lugged three suitcases on a trolley. The Russian party brought only the single suitcase, carried by the guard.

Just short of the white line at the center of the bridge the major from the KGB stepped forward, by prearrangement, to identify Steiner. Anthony mused that this procedure would not have been sanctioned by J. Daniel Umin. Steiner, an innocent victim of McCarthyism, could hardly have been identified by a KGB official. The major looked at Steiner, muttered something in a low tone of voice, inaudible to anyone else, and nodded.

Anthony Trust, charged to identify the American, stepped over the white line. "How're you doing, buddy?" he asked softly.

"As of the moment I'm all right, thanks, A. But when I get in I'd like some Pepto-Bismol." This, thought Anthony smiling as he retreated across the white line, was the authentic man.

Ames handed Steiner two documents and indicated where he must sign the instrument giving up his United States citizenship, and the court order consenting never again to enter the United States in any capacity. Steiner signed the two papers, using one of his suitcases as a writing surface. The two documents having been executed, Ames drew from his pocket Attorney General William P. Rogers' release. Wilkinson removed his handcuffs. Without uttering a word, Steiner stepped over the white line, whence his three escorts, characteristically appropriating the West German trolley, wheeled his baggage to the end of the bridge. He got into a car that slipped quickly into the fog.

That was on May 11. On May 13, Chairman Khrushchev summoned the press to the Kremlin and proceeded to make one of the most startling speeches in the annals of diplomacy. He ripped into Eisenhower. "I think that when the President stops being President, the best job we could give him in our country would be as director of a children's home. He would not harm children. But as head of a mighty state, he is more dangerous and might do a lot of harm. I saw the way he behaved at the Geneva conference in 1955, when every time the President had to speak he took another note prepared for him by Secretary of State Dulles. . . . One shuddered at the thought of what a great force is in such hands. Foster Dulles died, but Allen Dulles lives on."

On and on he went. When finally he stopped, there was a most extraordinary uproar, unprecedented in Kremlin press conferences. The question of course was whether, in the light of his verbal offensive against Eisenhower, the Chairman still planned to go on to Paris for the scheduled summit conference the following Monday.

Khrushchev replied that he would go to Paris, but that he would demand from Eisenhower an apology for the U-2 flight and for all other violations of Soviet territory, plus a promise that they would never be repeated, and that those who had authorized the flight that had ended at Alma-Ata—and here Khrushchev paused and added, *"and I mean everybody"*—should be "disavowed and punished."

Khrushchev then announced—and this vaguely perplexed analysts around the world who studied his entire statement—that if the scheduled summit conference did not materialize, and another one was subsequently scheduled, he would "personally insist that it include the Chairman of the People's Republic of China." It had heretofore always been assumed that the head of the Soviet Union spoke for the united Communist world.

The next few days were of course given over to hectic exchanges between a deeply distressed Harold Macmillan, an imperiously distracted President de Gaulle, and an American President whose attentions oscillated from sheer animal rage at Khrushchev's choice of words, to a calm consideration of what next to do.

He had now three objectives. The first to persuade his allies that he would not repay Khrushchev's tirade by pulling out of the summit. "Everybody knows I don't like summits, especially with the Soviets. But if this summit doesn't come off," he snapped at Herter, "it'll be because Khrushchev pulls out." A second objective was to persuade the American public that he was not easily intimidated. Nixon had told the President, immediately on hearing of Khrushchev's tirade, that if President Eisenhower actually went on to apologize to Khrushchev after he, Nixon, had publicly defended the U-2 flights, citing them as necessary responses to the Soviets' refusal to endorse President Eisenhower's earlier Open Skies proposal, then Nixon, facing the Democratic candidate, would be saddled with one hell of a burden: Either he would need to repudiate his own President, or else he would have to swallow his words about the strategic necessity of the U-2 flights—both alternatives politically disastrous. Eisenhower meanwhile sensed that the American people would be appalled by any categorical apology. He disclosed to Herter, Gates, and Dulles that he would propitiate the Soviet Union only to the extent of agreeing, in Paris, that no further flights would be dispatched. Nixon was not informed of this concession, with the embarrassing result that, on television the Sunday night before the summit convened, Nixon affirmed the continuing necessity of U-2 flights to guard against surprise attack.

Eisenhower's third objective—and this he stressed in his personal conversations with Macmillan and de Gaulle over the telephone—would be to interpret cautiously but decisively an aborted summit as effective postponement of the Soviet Union's ultimatum on Berlin. That crisis, after all, was the major one on the international agenda. On the one hand the Soviet Union had said A: a separate peace treaty with East Germany, unilaterally consummated, will deprive you—the United States, Great Britain, France—of any juridical right of access to Berlin. And to this position, the United States had said: Not-A. That meant: Confrontation. What all the world, including presumably the superpowers, wished to avoid. "Notice," Ike had said to Macmillan over the telephone, "that Khrushchev . . . said, you know . . . cut it out . . . to the . . . well, friendly countries that our U-2s come from." (Khrushchev had said, "Rocket forces will destroy the bases from which they take off.") "But in making again the threat to conclude a separate peace treaty with East Germany, he said that he would proceed 'unilaterally' unless a settlement was reached *'in a reasonable time.'*" When Macmillan, over the telephone, questioned Ike as to whether he had any explanation for Khrushchev's violent, aberrational outburst after allowing the whole U-2 episode to die down and going so far as to exchange the American pilot, condemned to death by a Soviet court, Eisenhower was uncomfortable. He did not wish to deceive his old friend. But he knew, as a soldier, the primacy of confidentiality. All he could bring himself to say was that when they met in Paris he, Ike, would perhaps speculate on possible reasons for Khrushchev's behavior.

The American public was up in arms. Influential congressmen, in high oratorical form, urged the President not to go to Paris. Several pundits opined that Khrushchev's volatility validated the thesis that summit conferences were generically hazardous. Go-to-Paris petitions and don't-go-to-Paris petitions were intensively circulated. On Thursday, Eisenhower directed press secretary Hagerty "for godsake" to stop giving out daily reports on the ratio of telegrams pro-con to the White House (they were in fact running about 70–30 against Ike's going to Paris). And when, at 7 P.M. on May 14, he stepped out of his limousine at Andrews to board Air Force One, the President pointedly ignored the microphones that had so hopefully been set up by newsmen against the possibility that he would finally break the stoic silence and say *something* about his reaction to Khrushchev's atavistic blast. But then the President suddenly stopped at the top of his companionway, turned to the cameras, grinned his famous grin, and waved goodbye to the American people. Entering the aircraft, he headed straight for his private quarters.

"Bring me Secretary Herter and a bourbon," he said to his aide.

"As you were. Bring me a bourbon and Secretary Herter."

# CHAPTER 26

Sunday morning he rested. In the afternoon he called on President de Gaulle, who was volubly displeased by the background noise to the summit but which noise, he announced, he proposed to ignore. Returning to the residence of the American ambassador where he was staying, the President had dinner with his son, went early to bed, and the next morning breakfasted with Macmillan who, thankfully, didn't bring up the question of what might have motivated Khrushchev's notorious outburst. Macmillan had in fact evolved a thesis: the Kremlin had decided it was fruitless to negotiate seriously with a lame-duck President. This was hardly a point he wished to make to the lame duck, so he indulged the prerogative of speaking with an accent so exaggeratedly British, and with so many ers and ahs, that he was not certain Eisenhower understood his oblique reference to "the American elections."

The French press that Monday morning gave equal publicity

to the awful tension that would shroud the cabinet room at the Élysée Palace when Eisenhower and Khrushchev encountered each other, and to the five-ton Soviet "spaceship" (with a dummy astronaut aboard) which had been launched, without previous publicity, the preceding day, one of those exquisitely subtle coincidences for which the Bolsheviks are renowned.

To the dismay of French protocol officials, Khrushchev sent word that he desired a one-hour postponement, from 10 A.M. to 11 A.M. The principals had been requested to arrive promptly, at three-minute intervals. They were telephoned to move the schedule back by one hour.

Khrushchev, accompanied by General Malinovsky, Foreign Minister Gromyko, and assorted aides and interpreters, arrived first. President de Gaulle greeted him and escorted the party up the large staircase to the ornate salon which had been a favorite dining room of Madame Pompadour and now was used for meetings of the French Cabinet. The small room was distinguished by four huge French windows, the pale green walls trimmed in beige silk, a crystal and gold chandelier dangling over the round conference table, covered with the traditional green felt cloth. Khrushchev was escorted to the far end. Prime Minister Macmillan was next to arrive, and was seated opposite Khrushchev. He murmured a greeting, but Khrushchev, remaining seated, ignored it.

President Eisenhower was then brought in. He went to his seat between Khrushchev and Macmillan. He and Khrushchev exchanged neither word nor glance. President de Gaulle sat down opposite Eisenhower, his back to the black marble fireplace with the ornate gold-leaf decorations on the mantelpiece.

As host, De Gaulle opened the meeting. He asked whether anyone had a statement to make.

Khrushchev snapped, "Yes."

Eisenhower said he also would make a statement.

Macmillan said he would reserve the right to comment on the two statements after they were made.

De Gaulle then turned to Eisenhower, who as chief of state as well as chief of government outranked both Khrushchev and Macmillan, and asked him to proceed—

At which point Khrushchev began talking.

Though the imagery was substantially subdued, it was a re-iteration of his press performance in Moscow. While he spoke, Eisenhower made notes on his prepared statement. De Gaulle, with Premier Debré on one side and Foreign Minister Couve de Murville on the other, was impassive. Harold Macmillan, on the other hand, soon looked as though he were about to weep. Eisenhower's face became red. Khrushchev finished his diatribe against U.S. aggression with two statements calculated especially to inflame Eisenhower. The first was that if Eisenhower did not apologize and the summit was aborted, the Soviet Union would regretfully conclude that this administration in Washington did not want peaceful coexistence, but perhaps the succeeding one would. "Therefore, we would think that there is no better way out than to postpone the conference of heads of government for approximately six to eight months." Macmillan looked meaningfully at his Foreign Minister. And, finally, Khrushchev said that as to President Eisenhower's projected visit to Moscow during the summer—an invitation agreed to at Camp David the preceding September—"unfortunately" the Soviet people could not receive Eisenhower "with the proper cordiality"; accordingly the visit should be "postponed."

Eisenhower, masking his rage with some difficulty, then read from his statement. He said what everyone expected him to say, that it was the responsibility of the United States to assure the safety of its people and of its allies from surprise attack. "As is well known," he said unintentionally using the most conventional Communist locution for introducing a lie, "not only the United States but other countries are constantly the targets of elaborate and persistent espionage by the Soviet Union." At that point Eisenhower interpolated his intention not to dispatch any further U-2s. De Gaulle meditated on the philosophical incompatibility of the two positions—i.e., that the U-2s were obligatory, and that they would not thenceforward be used.

To be sure, Eisenhower said slowly, his decision would not be binding on his successor.

Khrushchev banged his fist on the table, declaring the President's statement inadmissible in that it conveyed no expression of regret, nor commitment to punish the guilty parties. At this point Macmillan attempted a word, but Eisenhower was also talking, and the interpreters' voices rose in an effort to effect communication. It was a babble interrupted by President de Gaulle's gaveling everyone to silence.

He turned to Khrushchev. As they sat there, observed De Gaulle, a Soviet Sputnik was overflying France at the rate of eighteen times per day. Who had granted the Soviet Union that permission? Perhaps there were cameras on the Sputnik?

"As God is my witness," said Khrushchev, "our hands are clean and our soul is pure." There was not now, he said, nor would there ever be, a camera on a Sputnik. In that case, said De Gaulle, how had the Soviet Union managed to get pictures of the dark side of the moon from a Sputnik?

Well, said Khrushchev, that one was different.

De Gaulle said that, in fact, he had no objection to anyone's taking pictures of France. Khrushchev said De Gaulle obviously meant he had no objection to *his allies;* he, Khrushchev, had no objection to any of his *allies* taking pictures of the Soviet Union. Herter forced himself not to look at Defense Secretary Gates, seated at Eisenhower's left.

Khrushchev seemed now quite out of control. He would not stop even to give the translators an opportunity to relay what he was saying. They were therefore driven to attempting simultaneous translation. Ambassador Bohlen, seated behind Eisenhower and conversant with Russian, attempted to translate for his principal, even as a French official attempted similar service for President de Gaulle. At this point Khrushchev said that the United States was engaged in trying to drive a wedge between the Soviet Union and its allies. Eisenhower blurted out that this was preposterous. Khrushchev, seated only a few feet from him, was now talking directly at Eisenhower. His hands trembling, Khrushchev reached over to General Malinovsky and snapped his fingers. General Malinovsky, face white, drew with visible reluctance a sheaf of papers from his briefcase. Khrushchev snatched them and caused general alarm in the room by standing up. He pounded the papers down in front of Eisenhower. "What," he screamed, "do you call *these?* Look at them," he shrieked. Eisenhower picked them up, scanned them, and tossed them back to Khrushchev.

"Obvious forgeries," he commented.

Khrushchev retrieved the papers and, blanched with fury, thrust them back to Malinovsky and stormed out of the room, down the staircase, into his waiting car.

De Gaulle asked everyone in the room to leave save the principals and Colonel Vernon Walters, who would translate for all.

"Gentlemen," said De Gaulle, "I do not know Khrushchev well enough to make a final determination, but it would appear to me that his agitation is genuine. He is not a stable man."

Harold Macmillan, exhausted after the kind of scene he could not imagine had occurred in Great Britain since the death of Cromwell, looked dejected. He dropped all protocol. "Ike, pray, what *were* those papers?"

"They were headed: 'The Marco Polo Protocols.'"

"How do you know they were forgeries?"

"Because we forged them."

The meeting between the three allies lasted another two hours.

# EPILOGUE

The Christmas tree at the corner of the living room twinkled its sleepy beneficence over the gaily wrapped gifts. The logs in the fireplace popped, and flames warmed the room. On the mantelpiece were Christmas cards Sally had received. On either side, capacious bookcases. Opposite, a large semicircular red couch on which four could sit, with reading lamps at either side, a coffee table in front. Sally poured a second glass of champagne and walked to the Christmas tree.

"While I fuss in the kitchen—it's going to take me a while—you can look at one of your Christmas presents." She handed Blackford, who had taken off his coat and was sitting comfortably on the couch, a large rectangular package. Blackford took it, looked inquisitively at the little note on the card by the red ribbon. "To darling Blacky, who thinks there's only one spy in the (inchoate) family." He looked up at her. She grinned with obvious delight and went off to the kitchen, closing the door.

Blackford removed the wrapping paper.

It was a picture frame, atlas-size. Framed fragments of newspaper clippings from recent months . . .

". . . The Communist Chinese press reported that Khrushchev had spoken but made no mention of his subject."

". . . The Chinese-Soviet ideological rift had become evident with publication of conflicting theses in connection with observances of Lenin's 90th birthday."

"In a direct challenge to Khrushchev's view that nuclear war could mean destruction for both camps, the Chinese article said . . ."

"The President said that the apparent divergence in Soviet and Chinese views . . ."

"Soviet Labor Delegates Denounce Chou En-lai Criticism."

"Khrushchev Denies Dispute with China."

"No Soviet Envoy at Red China Anniversary."

"*Pravda* Denounces Red Chinese 'Dogmatism.' "

And, across the bottom, a headline from that morning's Washington *Post:* "Russian Advisers Reported Exiting China."

And under it all, a composite headline, cannibalized from types of uneven and irregular size, and pasted together. His own name he recognized as clipped from the distinctive typeface of the 1951 Yale Classbook.

BLACKFORD OAKES, Prominent WASHINGTONIAN, APPOINTED Arbitrator in SOVIET-CHINA RIFT By Chairman KHRUSHCHEV, Chairman Mao.

He must, Blackford thought to himself, be sure to have his Christmas present on display next time he invited Rufus or Allen Dulles to dinner.

He got up, walked into the kitchen, and tweaked her behind as she ladled the sauce.

"You're under arrest," he growled.

# ACKNOWLEDGMENTS

I am indebted to *Operation Overflight*, by (the late) Francis Gary Powers with Curt Gentry (Holt, Rinehart and Winston, 1970) and to *The U-2 Affair*, by David Wise and Thomas B. Ross (Random House, 1962) for much of the descriptive material. All but the final words in the chapter on the summit conference in Paris were actually spoken by the principals. The news excerpts were taken from *Facts on File*, Volume 20. Once again I am indebted to Alfred Aya, Jr., of San Francisco. I asked him to design a Xerox "diverter," and in due course received from him a multipage document, including charts and diagrams, which could not be improved on by the faculty of M.I.T. Anyone owning a Xerox Model 914 and desiring to install a diverter should apply to Mr. Aya. I learned that when he ate out as a child he would occasionally make a routine pre-dinner "inspection" trip of his hosts' kitchen, whereafter the corn would turn up blue, the cauliflower yellow, and the mashed potatoes pink.

He found this awfully funny, and I can only rejoice that he has dedicated his avocational life to perversity. I am grateful also to friends, professional and personal—and, in fact, no one in the first category is not also in the second—who read the manuscript, making suggestions, some of them positively transmutative. First and foremost, Samuel Vaughan, president of Doubleday and Betty Prashker. And then, in rough chronological order: Alfred Aya, Jr. (of course), Thomas Wendel, Charles P. Wallen, Jr., Hugh Kenner, Sophie Wilkins, Marvin Liebman, Richard Clurman. My wife Patricia, brother Reid, sister Priscilla, son Christopher. And, in the office, Frances Bronson, Dorothy McCartney (whose research was invaluable), and Susan Stark. I am most grateful to Chaucy Bennetts of Doubleday for her highly discerning copy reading. As ever, I am also grateful to Joseph Isola for the copy editing.

Stamford, Connecticut
May 31, 1981
W.F.B.